Date Night in December

Also by Jaqueline Snowe

Snowed in for Christmas

Christmas Sweater Weather

Date Night in December

JAQUELINE SNOWE

FOREVER
New York Boston

This book is a work of fiction. Names, characters, places, and incidents are the product of the author's imagination or are used fictitiously. Any resemblance to actual events, locales, or persons, living or dead, is coincidental.

Copyright © 2025 by Jaqueline Snowe

Cover design and illustration by YY Liak
Cover copyright © 2025 by Hachette Book Group, Inc.

Hachette Book Group supports the right to free expression and the value of copyright. The purpose of copyright is to encourage writers and artists to produce the creative works that enrich our culture.

The scanning, uploading, and distribution of this book without permission is a theft of the author's intellectual property. If you would like permission to use material from the book (other than for review purposes), please contact permissions@hbgusa.com. Thank you for your support of the author's rights.

Forever
Hachette Book Group
1290 Avenue of the Americas, New York, NY 10104
read-forever.com
@readforeverpub

First Edition: October 2025

Forever is an imprint of Grand Central Publishing. The Forever name and logo are registered trademarks of Hachette Book Group, Inc.

The publisher is not responsible for websites (or their content) that are not owned by the publisher.

The Hachette Speakers Bureau provides a wide range of authors for speaking events. To find out more, go to hachettespeakersbureau.com or email HachetteSpeakers@hbgusa.com.

Forever books may be purchased in bulk for business, educational, or promotional use. For information, please contact your local bookseller or the Hachette Book Group Special Markets Department at special.markets@hbgusa.com.

Library of Congress Cataloging-in-Publication Data

Names: Snowe, Jaqueline author
Title: Date night in December / Jaqueline Snowe.
Description: First edition. | New York : Forever, 2025.
Identifiers: LCCN 2025017956 | ISBN 9781538739853 trade paperback | ISBN 9781538739860 ebook
Subjects: LCGFT: Christmas fiction | Romance fiction | Novels
Classification: LCC PS3619.N693 D38 2025 | DDC 813/.6—dc23/eng/20250428
LC record available at https://lccn.loc.gov/2025017956

ISBN: 9781538739853 (trade paperback), 9781538739860 (ebook)

Printed in the United States of America

LSC-C

Printing 1, 2025

To anyone who's ever felt adrift—this is your reminder that life's best moments come when you find your way back to yourself and the people who feel like home.

CHAPTER ONE

LANEY

"Good morning, honey." My mom ran her hand over my shoulder, squeezing it for a second before beelining toward the coffee maker. "Did you sleep alright? Do you want to use our down comforter?"

I breathed in the smells of home. My dad had woken up early to make my mom and me breakfast, sneaking in his famous fudge on the side. He was a firm believer in the "breakfast dessert" camp, and I loved it. It had been years since I had dessert for breakfast, and I should adopt that way of life again. My new, single life.

"I slept okay, considering…" I waved my bare left hand in the air. My voice cracked when my mom met my gaze, her comforting smile causing my eyes to water. "Don't look at me like that. Stop it."

"Honey, I just want to hug you." She scrunched her face and pointed to the green storage boxes lining the edge of the living room. It was officially the *garland-ing* in our household. It was an annual day for my parents, and they had had decades of collecting the gaudiest colorful garland. "Your grandfather made me clean the house during my first heartbreak, and it was therapeutic. So can you help me hang these in the welcome foyer?"

"I want to sit here and mope though."

She clicked her tongue. "Sorry, girly, that's a no. It's December first. It's our favorite time of year, and yes, I want to hold you like you're eight and watch a Disney movie, but we have work to do."

I had remained close with my parents over the last decade, but I was rarely home for more than a long weekend, often with my husband. It was comforting to be home with them and see nothing had changed. They still had dinner right at 5:30. My dad would pour a glass of red wine for each of them, and they'd watch their shows right at 7:00. The routine made me feel safe. I knew where they'd be and what they were doing, without question. After living with unknowns and broken promises, I was comfortable being home where I knew expectations.

My mom arched her infamous left brow and put a hand on her hip, and I knew I had no choice. "I won't be cheery about it, but I can help."

"Good. We can put on sad acoustic Christmas music if you prefer."

I snorted. "When did you become sassier?"

"Being alone with your father the last fifteen years." She took the lid off the first storage bin and handed me blue, gold, silver, and dark green garland. They were all made of tinsel, and the familiar dusty smell brought back years of memories.

I didn't even have to ask how she wanted them arranged. My mother, a free spirit at heart, liked her garland organized by how she felt about the colors. Dark green was her favorite, followed by silver, and then gold and then blue. As I stepped on the small ladder to place some dark green garland at the intersection of the living room and foyer, right next to the window, I laughed. "I'm surrounded by Christmas fanatics. You and Dad, and Sophia."

"It's good for you. Remember, let them loop a good six inches between placing the tacks."

"Oh, I remember, Mother." I smiled to myself. The heartbreak was less painful with specific tasks to complete. We worked in silence with Bing Crosby playing in the background, and gratitude overwhelmed me. I was so glad I was home.

"Oh! I forgot to ask you yesterday," my mom said a good thirty minutes into our garland-ing. "Two questions, honestly. The first: Do you wanna help me and your dad set up the tree tonight? If you want to avoid more festive cheer, that's fine. But we're gonna put on *Christmas with the Kranks* and get tipsy."

I chuckled. "That sounds great, actually."

She smiled. "It's so nice having you home, even if it's under not-ideal circumstances."

I sighed. "You can just say it. I'm leaving my husband."

She winced and twisted her lips in displeasure, pausing as she held on to a purple garland we bought in Vegas one year. "It breaks my heart, hon, 'cause that man loves you, but you need to trust your gut."

"Am I foolish? Am I being too selfish?" There, I had asked the questions that had plagued me last night. Was I putting my needs first to the detriment of Connor's? Sure, but at what point can I stand up for myself and my needs? It was a horrible cycle of what came first—the chicken or the egg. There wasn't a real winner or loser, but either way, our hearts hurt. It was easier to ask my mother while I faced a window. I didn't want to see any judgment.

I continued, "He's never been cruel or hurt me or cheated or lied. He's never done anything so horrible that people would gasp. I was just sad and lonely. Sick of being an afterthought."

"No. You're not being foolish or selfish. You're choosing yourself, and that's brave and hard. I love Connor; I truly see him as a son. But his work drives him, and I remember you crying that night three years ago when you brought me to an event because he canceled last minute. You tried hiding it from me, but I saw."

My mom's confession caused my eyes to sting as I hung the white-and-red garland in a pattern. "There are twenty examples of that from this year. He also forgot our anniversary. I spent weeks negotiating a price for a vintage typewriter, knowing he'd love it. He scheduled a work dinner instead. It broke the final hope I had."

"You don't owe me anything, dear. Not to me or your father. You're in control of your choices and happiness, and we're going to support you no matter what. We're here if you want to talk or if you want to cry. Hell, your dad will get drunk with you in the basement while he yells at the Bears again. Stay here as long as you need."

"I'm having my stuff packed up today. Is that...crazy?"

"If it's what you need to have peace of mind, then no." She clapped her hands as she stared at the two windows we had decorated. "Every year, they take my breath away."

I stepped off the ladder and admired our work. It wouldn't win any awards, but it was definitely my home.

"Let's sit and admire, drink our coffee for a minute."

We made our way to the couch, and she added peppermint creamer to her coffee. Once she sat next to me, she slapped my thigh with excitement. "Oh, did I tell you Ms. Laneri from next door is running one of those rentals now? She stays in the mother-in-law suite in the back and rents out the house. We had the most interesting person stay there last month. They sold rocks, I think. Like, the guy had a spreadsheet of the types of rocks he sells!"

I tuned my mom out as she continued telling me all about rock guy. I cuddled up next to her, and she put her arm around me. It didn't matter that I was thirty-five. I needed my mom. My assistant, Newt, was taking the photography events for the next two days, letting me mope and get my shit together before I returned for back-to-back weddings. I loved my photography business, but I wasn't done being sad yet.

"Oh! The other question I had. Becky needs an answer soon, but I figured I'd try to get you some work while you stay here. We have our annual festival starting up tomorrow. Twenty-four days of events, parades, dances, the gala—you know the drill."

I sure did know the drill. I grew up going to all the holiday activities, loving the magic and happiness in the air here in Cherrywood. My high school boyfriend Matt and I would hit up every event. There was something romantic about the holiday cheer everywhere. It'd be a challenge to get through it while starting a divorce, but I'd manage.

"What about it?"

"They want an event photographer! The mayor wants to do a documentary or something about the town and needs photos or videos to help get more people here. I honestly don't know the details. I just heard they needed someone, and it was a paid gig."

I chewed my lip. Taking pictures of happy people didn't sound like the best choice, but then again, it's what made me fall in love with photography in the first place—capturing those fleeting moments of utter bliss. The way a snowflake falls on someone's hair. The crinkling of your eyes when you smile at someone you love. Women drinking hot cocoa, bonding over their decades of friendship.

Okay, my brain had woken up a little from sadness due to the potential here.

"Okay, this sounds interesting."

"I knew you'd like it! Okay, hon, I'll pass Becky your number."

We stayed like that for an hour, watching the news and cuddling until my mom had to get ready for a bridge game. She was a retired artist and still had commissions, but she was so religious about her game circle.

"You sure you'll be okay alone?" she asked, putting on her puffy coat and hat.

"Yes, Mom. Plus, I have all this garland with me. Who would feel alone with all these colors?"

She narrowed her eyes at me but smiled. "Smart alek."

"Go bridge. Be wild."

"Love you."

"You too."

She shut the door, leaving me in the quiet. It was strange how I had spent so much time alone living with Connor, yet the silence here was different. I hadn't yet turned my phone on, but it was time to check in with my best friend, Sophia, to see how the packing was going.

I powered it on, and a text from her popped up immediately.

Soph: Have you seen the news? Check this link.

I hit it and gasped. Connor's company had had a data breach. Oh shit. I scanned the article, reading a few quotes from him, while my stomach ached. This was one of his greatest worries. Cyberattacks were terrifying and on the rise, and he always said it wasn't *if*, but *when* it would happen to them. He must be so stressed. She felt the same intense urge to help him. I could send him his favorite meal and his lucky shirt. He loved that stupid thing whenever he had a stressful day.

The ideas flowed through me, my mind and body almost going on autopilot.

The need to support him might never go away, but I debated whether to text him. He forgot our dang anniversary a week ago. What would I even say? My chest tightened as I scanned the news again, hoping to find an update from today.

Someone knocked on the front door, so I set my phone down and sighed. Only here, in my hometown, would people actually knock. In our condo, people would leave stuff on the front step and assume we'd check the camera. I missed the personal touch of interactions.

I mentally prepared to see one of my mom's friends stopping by to say hi or bringing a casserole because she'd told her friends I was here. Honestly, a casserole sounded pretty tasty. Smiling, I twisted the faded gold handle to see a large figure standing there. My smile fell off my face.

Connor.

My heart leaped to my throat, my pulse spiking as his beautiful—and sad—gray eyes met mine. "What..."

"Hey, Laney, can I come in?" He shoved his hands in his pockets, his jaw flexing as he studied my face.

Shadows had formed under his eyes, and his shoulders slumped. There was no evidence of my confident, sexy husband. The man who walked into a boardroom and dominated. The man who never shied away from anything.

A blast of wind danced over my neck, causing me to shiver. "Yeah, sure."

I swallowed hard as I walked inside my parents' house. Connor had been here a hundred times before, yet the formality, the not touching him, was so messed up. He blew into his hands before hanging his coat on the rack and facing me.

I couldn't take it anymore. He hadn't explained his appearance, and I had to know.

"What are you doing here? Why come here?"

His eyes warmed. "To see you, to talk to you."

My breath caught in my throat at his admission, but it was too late. Too damn late.

I dug my nails into my palm, needing the sting to ground me. "Why are you doing this? I told you what I want, and you're disrespecting it," I snapped, unable to steady my own voice.

"I don't consider this disrespect," he said, his tone low. "This is me fighting for you because, baby, I haven't gone this long without holding you, and it's killing me. I know it has to be hurting you too."

He wasn't wrong.

"I'm not happy about any of this, Connor, but just because

it hurts doesn't mean it's not the right choice." I wrapped my arms around myself, needing the barrier. He stepped toward me and placed his large hands on my shoulders, the familiar warmth settling over me like my favorite sweatshirt. My muscles tensed once my brain caught up to the physical touch.

He winced and quickly lifted his hands. "Can I touch you?"

Instead of answering, I moved toward the kitchen. "Can I get you a coffee or something? I think it's still fresh for Dad. I'm sure you haven't been sleeping."

He sighed. It almost sounded like relief.

"I'd love a coffee. Thanks, Laney."

Ugh. Hearing him say my name shouldn't cause an avalanche of feelings in my gut, but it did.

"My parents don't have oat milk, I'm sorry."

"Hon—Laney, that's okay. I'll take it black."

"We might have regular milk or cinnamon. I know you like that when it gets cold outside." Oh my God. My nerves had gotten the best of me, and I was rambling. "I didn't know you were coming. Obviously. I didn't prepare for you. But why would I? Why are you here? Wait, the cyber event!" I spun and leaned against the counter, finding him staring at me with a small smile.

That barely there grin paired with his dimples was a wildly dangerous combination. No. Don't look at him. Focus on the coffee.

"You're so fucking cute when you ramble like that. I love your stream of consciousness."

"No, you don't," I blurted out. My face heated as a very clear memory came to the surface. The previous me wouldn't have said anything because work mattered so much to Connor. Now though? It didn't matter.

"When we were at the party last spring, you excused us after I went on a rambling story about my trip to Texas. You said, 'She gets so chatty when she has a drink. Excuse us,' to the board member. Then you pulled me away and blocked me from talking to any other board member the entire night, like I'm embarrassing to you."

My chest ached like someone had squeezed all the air out of my lungs. I couldn't catch my breath as I stared at my future ex-husband. His mouth fell open, and I swore he paled, matching the eggshell walls in the kitchen. I knew every expression of his, but this one was new.

Shock, maybe?

"Laney," he rasped, shaking his head and placing his palms flat on the table. He stood, his tortured gaze zeroing in on me. "That's...that's not what happened. Is that what you thought?"

My throat dried up. My palms sweated.

Buzz. Buzz.

Thank goodness. Glancing at my smartwatch, I saw my mom's name pop up, saving me from answering this confusing question. I needed a break. I quickly picked up my phone. "Hi, Mom, what's up?"

"Laney." She used her serious voice. "I wanted to give you a heads-up. We have someone renting the house next to us."

"Okay." I bit my lip, avoiding Connor's piercing stare. "Why are you telling me?"

"It's Connor. He rented the house for December."

CHAPTER TWO

CONNOR

Laney gasped and covered her mouth with her hand, her attention moving toward me. Her gorgeous eyes lacked their usual warmth or joy, and seeing her sad gutted me, leaving me without any rational thought except wanting to know how to fix it.

A flash of anger danced behind her eyes, and my chest ached. I loved feisty Laney. It wasn't a side she showed often. I just wasn't familiar with being on this end of it.

"What is it?"

"You rented the house next door?" She slammed the coffee down in front of me and spilled it on the table. "You can't stay there."

"Why?" I figured it was the perfect place to stay to win her back.

Her face reddened as she spat, "You just can't."

"Not sure that's the rule, babe. I paid, and it's happening."

She gritted her teeth. "Are you hoping to torture me?"

"The opposite." I smiled briefly. "I'm here to fight for you."

"What about... your job? The cyber breach? You can't take off work."

"I'm the boss. Of course I can." I shrugged. I needed her to truly understand that this wasn't an off-the-cuff choice.

My dad hadn't heard about the event yet, which would lead to me getting an earful, but this was my wife we were talking about. My other half. It still didn't make sense that no one in my life thought that her leaving was a big deal.

Laney sniffed, and I knew I'd said the wrong thing. Her face crumpled, and her shoulders slumped. A gnawing ache formed in my gut, and I stood there, helpless, as she let out a humorless laugh.

"If you can take off work whenever, then how am I supposed to feel about when I asked you to come to a photography show? Or the weekend trip to see my college friends? Or the anniversary dinner you forgot about? Your words and actions don't align, Connor, and it's exhausting and devastating to think you'll never change."

Before I could respond, she pointed to the door. Her chin wobbled, and I hated more than anything that I put that tremble there. The way she swiped under her eye with her finger, not able to hide her tears... that was my fault.

She was right. I hadn't prioritized those nights. One of our employees had been involved in a sexual assault case that involved another colleague, and then Petra—my executive assistant—learned her mom passed, and she'd needed help. Both reasons seemed solid at the time, but hearing them from Laney now...

What if I can't save this?

"Please, leave. I can't make you go back to our...your condo, but please, leave me be. I know you care for me and hate seeing me cry, but every time we talk, that's all I want to do, okay?" She ran her hands over her face before opening the front door. "I don't know why you're making this so much harder on us."

There was one thing I had learned from being the CEO of a multimillion-dollar business for the last decade: it was when to argue, when to be quiet, and when to be patient. Laney wasn't in the place to talk this out and figure out solutions. Her pain was too loud and fresh. It'd just hurt us if I spoke up, so I sighed and stopped right in front of her.

"I'll be next door. We'll talk soon."

Then, without kissing my wife, I walked out of her parents' house with my heart beating in my throat. The brisk Illinois air hit my face, the sting welcome as it distracted me from the growing pressure in my chest. This was just unacceptable. Our marriage wasn't ending.

I'd convince her. Hell, I'd won over executives ten times more terrifying than my wife. But was that even the same thing?

I entered the rental and slammed the door shut. That didn't go as planned. I foolishly thought seeing me would help... When did things get so bad?

It was barely 10:00 in the morning, and I needed a damn drink. The house wasn't stocked at all. In my rush to get here, I had shoved three outfits into a suitcase. I'd need more if I was going to stay here.

Like clockwork, my emails pinged with media requests. *Where is the CEO during a breach? Is it worse than we think?*

I dove in, welcoming the distraction while I figured out what to do about my marriage.

* * * *

I knew peace wouldn't last long. My dad would find out about me leaving, and sure enough, a few hours later, he called. I shoved the late lunch I had ordered to the side and answered the call, steeling myself for a berating.

"Father."

"Why are you not in the office? Dennis told me you're dealing with an emergency? You better be in the hospital right now. I didn't convince my friends to invest in this company to have my son bail when shit gets hard."

My stomach sank. He would never understand my reasons.

"I'll be back after the holidays. The team can handle everything. Hell, they are the ones that do the work. I just smile for the press."

"Don't try to be cute with me. You belong there, not in some suburb."

"So you do know where I am."

"Petra informed me that your wife left you. You seem to be under the impression you can save the marriage, yet many believe that's a waste of your time. If Laney isn't happy receiving your generous salary, the condo you provide for her, and her luxury lifestyle, then who cares? Let her go."

"Do not speak about her like that. What the fuck, Dad?" In less than twelve hours, both my assistant Petra and my dad had insulted my wife. "I'm trying to save my marriage because it matters to me. She matters to me."

He scoffed. "The company matters more. She's fine, but she's not worth losing the company. I always knew her artsy values would be an issue. I think you understand what's at stake here, son."

"You're threatening me with your influence over the board. You're explicitly saying that I should give up on my wife, my marriage of nine years, because you'll remove me as CEO. I'm correct, right?" A sliver of cold seeped into my spine, making me sit up straighter. I had never spoken up against him. He could ruin me, despite the good job I'd been doing and the increase in profit I'd been making every year. The constant game of politics had slowly sucked the life out of me, and I was fucking tired. "Am I right, Dad?" I asked again.

He cleared his throat. "You're being dramatic, which must be because your wife is messing with your head. You should be better disciplined and not let your emotions distract you like this. That means you're weak, and I know I raised you better than this. I expect you at the office in a week or you, Dennis, and I will meet to talk about expectations and job duties."

Then my dad hung up.

Pounding formed at the base of my skull, a scalding migraine from pure anger. If I were home, I'd use a massive ice pack that goes over my face and eases the stress instantly. Laney bought it for me after my third year in the job, and it became our routine. She'd put on a playlist, let me lay my head in her lap, and we'd relax until the headache faded.

Knowing I didn't have that comfort—and might not ever again—broke me. The feelings I had refused to feel bubbled up, and I tossed my phone on the table and rushed outside. Condensation covered my face from the chill, and I inhaled, staring up at the star-covered sky. There were no clouds here or pollution like the city. The blinking lights twinkled, almost mocking me with their beauty. People were happy here, not constantly hustling and working fourteen-hour days. They enjoyed life—something I seemed to have forgotten how to do. I had had what I wanted and lost it.

I wasn't sure how long I stood out there, my hands turning to ice and my face numb, but laughter from next door distracted me. Light spilled out of the open garage door, and Laney's familiar chuckle drifted toward me. God, I had missed that sound.

"There's no way it'll fit! You need to saw it!"

"I will not saw it. This is the tree I picked, damn it, and it'll work."

"Dad, I'm telling you—" She broke off into a fit of laughter. "This is like a movie scene. You're being unreasonable."

"I'll tell you what's unreasonable—it's this stupid doorframe. I'm gonna take it off."

"Don't you dare touch my doorframe, Steven, or you'll be sleeping on the porch tonight," Laney's mom said.

My lips curved up, despite not feeling joy. Laney's parents were the epitome of warmth and love. They laughed loudly, showed emotion with ease, and focused more on loving flaws than pointing them out. When I first met them, I was jealous of Laney. I wanted parents like hers.

Hers would never tell her to end a marriage because work mattered more.

"Hon, take a breather. Can you throw this out on the curb? Walk it off."

"Fine. But do not mess with my tree. I cut it down myself, and I love it."

Footsteps thudded on the concrete as Steve carried a box of trash toward the curb. He grumbled something under his breath, but then his attention landed on me.

"Connor, why the hell are you standing outside like a creepo?"

I almost laughed. "I needed fresh air."

Steve frowned and glanced at the garage, then back at me, and then back.

"Hmm, okay. Now, Laney might be upset if I do this, but a man's gotta do what a man's gotta do."

"Meaning…?"

"Can you help me get this tree inside our house? The ladies are tough, obviously, but they aren't trying hard enough. This is one of those battles I refuse to give up on because the whole damn time they yapped about it being too big for the house. Man-to-man, you see my point?"

Regardless of my thoughts, I nodded. I wanted to be around their joy, around my wife, and if that meant helping Steve with this task, then I'd do it. "Sure."

"Good man." He nodded but then reached out and squeezed my shoulder. "I know this is a hard season. I'm not sure what the future will bring, but I support a guy trying, and I know that's what you're doing here. My daughter is stubborn and brilliant, and I'm on her side no matter what, but we love you too, Connor, so don't give up too quickly."

My throat prickled from the kindness of his words. "I won't."

"Good. If you tell either of them I said that, I will find a way to hurt you. Now come on."

He marched back into the garage, and sure enough, a huge-ass evergreen tree sat halfway shoved into their house. There was honestly no way it'd fit through the doorway, but I couldn't miss the chance to help.

"Hey, can we use your back entrance? It has double doors that open."

"Smart man. Yup." He clicked his tongue. "Let's drag her out. Honey! Open the back door. We're coming in that way!"

"What?"

"Unlock the back door, please!"

"Unlock what?"

Oh my God. If Laney were here, we'd make eye contact and laugh our asses off. These two were like characters in a sitcom.

"Sherry Marie, I swear on Laney's life, you can damn well hear me. Now, I'm marching around and breaking the door down myself!"

My lips twitched as we yanked the tree over and over. It was stuck in the door, and my muscles tensed as I changed my grip. The wood cut into my skin, and the smells of evergreen and sap filled the air.

"Steve, it's pretty tight."

"No. Don't bail on me." He grunted and pulled hard. So hard that he stumbled backward and landed on his ass. He howled. It wasn't a quiet one either. It was like a coyote, and Laney ran into the garage, eyes wide.

"What happened?"

"Your dad busted his butt."

"Dad, are you... Wait, Connor, why are you—"

"You foolish man." Laney's mom walked in with a smile on her lips. "You are such a moron, but I love you."

"My ass needs ice." Steve pushed up with a groan. "You win. I'll saw the tree down."

"Laney and I can move it," I piped up. She stared at me with her eyes hooded, her teeth on her full bottom lip.

"We've moved trees larger than this, haven't we?"

She nodded, but her frown grew. "Why are you here?"

"I asked him for help, but it was no use. I pretty much broke my tailbone, and the tree is still in the doorway." Her dad ran a hand over his butt.

"Come on. I'll get you ice and put on a rom-com."

"The kissing ones?"

"Yes. Your favorite." Her mom chuckled as she rolled her eyes. "Never boring with you, Steven. That's for sure."

Laney's mom and dad walked inside. The front door closed with a thud, leaving Laney alone with me in the garage. She wore an oversized sweater and jeans that I loved. Her hair was up, she had no makeup on, and she looked beautiful. Her bare left hand pissed me off, and I could tell she wanted to tell me to leave. So I used a trick I had up my sleeve: her competitiveness.

"So, you think you can help me move this thing, or no?"

CHAPTER THREE

LANEY

Before I could answer, Connor held up his hands and smiled. "Your dad legit asked me for help. He saw me standing outside, and I couldn't turn him down."

Connor wore jeans and a nice sweater. No gloves, no hat, no coat.

"Why were you outside?"

"Fair question." He flashed a tight smile at me. "My dad called, and I needed air after that conversation. You know how he is."

I sure did. His dad was emotionally abusive, but every time I brought it up, Connor would deflect or defend him out of loyalty. After a while, Connor stopped mentioning his father altogether because it would lead to an argument. Yet another example of why we didn't belong together anymore. Despite my initial shock of seeing him here, and the burst of joy from being in his presence, the familiar dread filled me. "Let's get this tree inside."

"I'm thinking we cut off one of the branches." He pointed

to the right, where a three-inch branch was stuck against the frame. "Does he have a saw? I can do it fast, so he can't stop me."

"Do you know how to use a saw, Connor?" I rummaged through my dad's pseudo-shop area and pulled out the handheld. He owned the local hardware store and always had a large stockpile at home. My parents made me trim our trees and rosebushes growing up. I even learned enough basic woodworking that I sometimes built my own sets for photography events. My backgrounds for photo booths were one of my cool selling points.

"I know how to saw a branch off, Laney." His tone bit, his usual arrogance leaking out. He was confident and used to being good at everything, yet I couldn't recall a single time he'd used a saw.

"I don't mind." I walked up to the trunk, but he stilled me with his hand on my waist. The warmth of his palm caused my breath to hitch.

"What?"

"You have an event this weekend. I don't want you to hurt your hands, even though I know you know how. This isn't about your skills, but me trying to protect you." He held my stare, enunciating every word as his gaze heated. "Let me do this one thing, please."

"Fine." I handed him the saw and stepped back. I didn't need to be this close to him. His cologne lingered in the air, and his unshaven look was my weakness. I loved the scruff and lumberjack look when his beard grew out. It paired so well with his thick hair. His broad shoulders filled out the beige sweater, and I fisted my hands to prevent myself from rubbing them over his pecs.

In another world, where we went back to the old versions of ourselves, I'd tease the hell out of him with small touches all night. Then, once we were alone, he'd unleash and spend hours touching me. It had been weeks since we had sex, and while sex was never our issue, it wasn't enough.

"There." Connor tossed the branch on the floor, and then we easily pushed the tree through the frame.

"We can get this monstrosity set up for your dad, then I'll head out. I promise."

Everything felt so familiar, and different, as we hoisted the tree into the stand in my parents' living room. It made me remember our first holiday as husband and wife as if it were yesterday.

> *"I feel like I got the better end of the deal." Connor held my hips, a huge smile on his face as he swirled me around in my parents' living room. "Your family is so welcoming. Your parents are ... they've just taken to me like I'm one of theirs."*
>
> *"They love you." I beamed. "It's so easy to, husband."*
>
> *"God, I love hearing you call me that. Say it again, wife." His eyes heated, and that always made my knees weak. I was completely smitten and in love and delirious with happiness. I fell forward, and he caught me.*
>
> *"Breathe, baby."*
>
> *"Sometimes I forget around you." I blushed and ran my hands over his pecs and stomach, loving that we were married. From the moment I met Connor, I fell hard and knew he was special. Our connection and chemistry were magnetic, and it only deepened the more we talked. Marrying him was the easiest decision in the world.*

"You know what?" I asked, smiling at the joy on his face. He loved my ideas, even if they were silly. He'd be on board just because it made me happy. "We should start our own holiday tradition. Something random. Wild. Weird. Something just for us that we can do every year."

"Oh, like... a naked tradition?"

I rolled my eyes. "Stop it. No, like maybe we make a holiday ornament for each other? Or we do an adventure calendar? Or we visit every pancake place within an hour?"

"Oh, okay, I like this." He rubbed his thumbs over my hips, right to left, the mere contact on my skin making me squirm.

"We could vow to find a different coffee shop every year and visit it. There have to be a hundred of them in the city. We'll never run out."

"Yes! And we can buy a mug from each one!"

"I love you so fucking much." He yanked me against him and kissed me hard. "Merry Christmas, Laney. Here's to forever."

I stared at the upright tree, my eyes prickling as the memory blurred into the present.

"What should we do with the mugs?"

He tilted his head to the side, giving him the puppy-dog look I adored. "The mugs?"

"Our holiday tradition. Do you want to split the mugs, or do you want to get rid of them?"

"Christ." He pinched his nose. "We're not getting rid of our mugs, Laney. They stay together. They were meant to stay together."

Was he talking about us or the actual mugs? I wasn't sure. I yawned. It was emotionally exhausting to be near him.

"We can talk about the mugs later. You need to get some rest. Your event is on Friday, right? Do you want a ride there?" he asked.

A part of me loved this attention. When we first got married, he loved driving me to events. He was my biggest cheerleader and would create a playlist based on the theme of the event. That stopped four years ago when work became too busy, and while I understood life changed, I missed his consideration. Right now his offering didn't change a thing.

"I should be able to drive myself."

"Right." He swallowed hard. "I'll head to the rental. Have a good night."

I nodded, my stomach twisting into a pretzel. This was painful. Neither one of us wanted him to leave, but he had to. It was too little too late. The silence grew, each second causing the ache in my chest to double. Connor stared at me, the indecision on his face matching mine. His chest heaved, and he kept cracking his knuckles.

I had to be strong. Sophia told me he'd be hard to resist, that he'd try to fix this. Boy, was she right.

"Good—"

"I'm not going away. I just...need you to know that. I'll leave and go sleep alone, wishing I was next to you, but I'm not leaving. We're not getting rid of our fucking mugs. You are my wife." He exhaled and marched toward the door. "I love you, Laney, and I'm so sorry you felt like the only option was to walk away. I'll fix it. Just wait."

He didn't look back before walking out the front door, leaving me to sit with his parting words.

You are my wife.

I loved hearing that. I loved the fierceness, the protectiveness, the desire in those words, but words were just that. I plopped down face-first on the couch, moaning into the pillow. I came here to avoid him.

"Not you too." My mom joined me in the living room, her tone amused. "You and your dad are whining, and I'm too old to deal with whiny children."

"I broke my ass, woman!" My dad's voice carried from upstairs, making me laugh.

"Your father is a handful. Did Connor leave?"

"Yes, Mom. Why else would I be whining face down on the couch? My husband keeps showing up when I'm trying to leave him. It's quite annoying."

"He looked miserable."

"Whose side are you on?"

"Always yours." She patted my back and ran her fingers through my hair. "Decorating this green beast is canceled. Do you want to put on a sad movie and cry it out? We can bust out the futon and watch it in our spare bedroom?"

My heart ached from nostalgia. We used to have movie nights in their bedroom with the biggest TV in the house. Feeling so accepted by my parents, I was content. I was never the kid who rebelled against her parents in her teens. They have always been such a source of comfort that I didn't realize how much I missed them while living in the city. I never felt alone here.

"Yeah, I kinda do. But what about Dad's rom-coms?"

"He can cry with us. He's the one who invited Connor here, so he doesn't get to pick the movie."

"Bullshit!" my dad yelled.

My mom and I chuckled before she patted my knee. "Grab your blanket and join us."

And that's how I ended my night, curled up on my parents' spare mattress, bawling my eyes out to a holiday movie. I ugly cried, but for the first time since leaving the city, I didn't think about Connor or my marriage. I just lived inside the story of the movie, and it felt good.

* * * *

The next morning, I stood in front of the town hall, where tables lined either side of the walkway. It was the annual gingerbread house decorating competition, and they had hired me to photograph it. Marla, my mom's best friend and the town's lead gossiper, ran the event. She waved me over. "Laney, it's so good to see you!"

"Hi, Marla," I said, hoping she wouldn't bring up Connor. My mom promised she wouldn't but, let's be real, Marla loves drama. "Great turnout this year."

"I had to rush order more materials since we had a few last-minute sign-ups." Marla placed her hands on her hips with a wide smile on her face. "I'd love you to get a shot of every pair decorating, action shots, then a posed photo at the end. Is that doable?"

"Absolutely." I held up my camera and forced a smile. "I'll get started now."

"Thanks, doll. And hey," she said, her smile faltering. "You look good. Glad you're home."

Those words seemed to hold more weight than a casual greeting, and my eyes prickled as she gave me a half hug. Marla didn't say more though. She took off toward the welcome tent, which was all green and red and decked out with twinkle lights. I adjusted my scarf because the chill was getting to me, and I walked the grounds.

There were at least fifty tables of people working on gingerbread houses. I'd participated in the competition quite a few times with my mom, my dad, and my friends. Never with Connor though. We never came back to Cherrywood this early in the month because he was always too busy with work.

I still couldn't believe he was staying next door to my parents' house.

I snapped a few photos of a group of young kids running around a large candy cane sculpture, their laughter wild and free. *Click.* The photo was perfect. If I had to create a postcard of this town, I'd use this shot. A tall Christmas tree in the back, kids smiling, town square off to the right... It showcased how special and happy this place was.

I continued to capture the contestants, grinning at an older couple who were bickering about what color gumdrops to use, when a familiar voice said my name.

"Laney Whitfield, is that you?"

No way. I turned to find my high school sweetheart standing before me in a bright green coat and yellow pants. "Matt, are you dressed like Buddy the Elf?"

"Laney, you shouldn't have to ask that. Yes, of course I am."

He rolled his eyes and moved closer. "Get in here. It's been too long."

Matt pulled me into a bear hug, his specialty back in the day, and I returned the gesture. Age had been kind to him. He still had the mischievous look that was always on his face back in high school, and it was clear he was happy. His face had so many laugh lines.

"You look amazing. Damn, and you smell the same."

I chuckled. "I was gonna say the same thing. Lacoste cologne still?"

"You know it." He smiled so wide that it stretched across his face, then adjusted the green elf hat. He looked ridiculous, so I stepped back, snapping a photo of him.

"Uh, what was that? What are you doing?"

"I'm in town for the month and staying with my parents. Figured I'd get some work in and photograph Cherrywood events. The better question is why are you dressed like that?"

"Right. Fair question. You'll never believe where I ended up." He smiled and pointed to two tables that had a bunch of teenagers. "I'm teaching algebra at our high school and in charge of student council. Every year, we send students to this event. I lost a bet with the class so I had to dress up as Buddy. Wish I looked cooler if I knew I would run into you."

Despite dating for three years, we had parted on good terms. I'd wanted to head to Illinois State for college, while he went to Iowa. We cried and hugged but mutually agreed to break up.

He looked adorable. "Matt, this is amazing. Good for you," I said, a genuine happiness taking over. "I can totally see you as a teacher."

He beamed with pride. "Do I know my shit? Yes. Do I know

teenagers? Absolutely the heck not. Their buzzwords change all the time, and *rizz* now means charisma? If you're dripping with rizz, then it's a good thing. We should totally grab a drink and catch up. I promise I won't wear this."

He was still so much the same. I laughed, for real, and it was like my muscles relaxed for the first time in days. Matt was carefree, kind, no drama.

"It'd be great to grab a drink with you."

"My number hasn't changed. Not saying you still have it—don't wanna assume or be weird. You got married, yeah?" His gaze dropped to my empty left hand, and he raised his brows. "Or maybe not?"

"That is a story to share over a drink. Maybe even two."

"Deal. So is your number the same or..."

"Are you asking for my number, Matt Heathen?" I swore I needed this distraction. Seeing Matt brought me back to high school, back to memories and laughter. I loved my time in high school in this town. Cherrywood was special.

"You can do better than that."

"Laney, what's your number so I can take you out for a drink? Was that better?"

"Much." I handed him my phone just as the hair on the back of my neck stood on end. Almost like someone was watching me. I scanned the tables around us, but no one stood out. I shook it off and blamed residual guilt. I'd grab drinks with Matt even if Connor and I were together. I would've told him about it, and he wouldn't have cared. Yet it felt weird to let Matt call me by my maiden name.

Damn. All my business stuff was set up in my married name. I'd have to change that and go back to Whitfield.

"It was so good seeing you." He pulled me in for another hug, squeezing me for an extra beat. "I want to hear about everything cool, and I can fill you in on how nothing has changed at Beaumont High School."

"I have a photography event tomorrow but am free after that."

"Any night, I'll cancel plans. You tell me."

I snorted as he waved and walked the other way. Then that prickly feeling returned. I had no reason to feel guilty, and I forced the worry away. Instead, I focused on my assignment, taking photos of the couples. Another Cherrywood special was requiring everyone to dress in red or green. As a photographer, I loved the cohesion. It made the photos instantly more cheerful, and a pang formed in my chest. I'd missed this place so much.

"Laney, who was that guy?"

I stilled. *Connor.* Swallowing the tightness in my throat, I kept my eye on the camera. "Why are you here? Were you following me?"

"What? No. I didn't have food and walked to the grocery store and happened to recognize your coat..." He trailed off and cleared his throat. "And saw a guy hugging you and making you laugh."

It was the slight crack of his voice on the last word that made my guilt grow. Connor once told me that my laugh was his favorite part of me, and that every time he heard it, he wanted to keep it. He never cared about my guy friends but felt a pang whenever my laughter was directed at anyone other than him.

I let the camera hang around my neck and finally met Connor's gaze. Despite not owing him an explanation, I wanted to provide one. Ease any worry. "It was just Matt. We went to high school together and haven't seen each other in years."

"High school boyfriend Matt?" he asked. His nostrils flared as he stared at my left hand. "Please say no."

"We dated a decade ago. That has nothing to do with this. He's a great guy, and we ended on good terms. You know this. I'm not sure what this"—I gestured to him—"is, but me hugging Matt is not a big deal at all."

"Laney, you are gorgeous, and now he thinks you're single. It is a big deal because any man that knows you and dated you will do anything to get back with you. Trust me." He exhaled and ran a hand over his face, his wedding ring very much visible. "Tell me, did he ask you if you were married?"

I nodded because I was a terrible liar.

"And what did you say? The truth, I hope."

"Connor, I'm at a job I'm getting paid for. I need to photograph everyone." I didn't want to have this chat here, where my neighbors could hear us. Everyone knew everyone, and I didn't want to be a part of the gossip.

"So you told him you're leaving me." A muscle twitched in his cheek. "He thinks he has a shot now."

"Would you stop?" I whispered and approached him. "I didn't say anything like that. I said it's complicated, okay? Now I need to go."

"Do you need any help?"

"No. You haven't helped me at an event in years. Don't start now." I pushed away from him, my temper and emotions getting the best of me.

What the hell was that display of jealousy?

It was confusing. When all Connor's attention was on work,

anything he gave me was extra. He never showed jealousy when a bartender winked at me or someone's eyes lingered on me. I didn't understand why it was happening now. It was just another difficult thing to sort through.

I walked away, forcing myself not to look back when I got a text.

> **Matt:** Hi Laney, it's Matt. Matthew Heathen. It was so nice running into you. Is Monday too soon for a drink?

My instant smile surprised me. Matt represented a simpler time in my life, yet the expression on Connor's face and the anger there stopped me from responding. This wasn't cheating. Even if we weren't separated yet, I wanted to remain faithful. This was grabbing drinks with a friend.

Hell, how many times had Connor and his assistant grabbed a drink after a stressful day? The uneasy feeling of worry returned just thinking about the nights he came home late with whiskey on his breath. Yeah, I could grab a damn drink with Matt.

Connor had had nine years to be jealous and put me first. I wasn't stopping myself from things I enjoyed because he was upset. This new era was about *me*.

CHAPTER FOUR

CONNOR

The next day, the annoyance of seeing Laney with Matt had dulled by only one degree. The image of them hugging, a smile on her face, her ringless finger right there, played over and over in my mind. Was he a better choice for her? Would he make her happier? When she'd told me about him when we first started dating, she spoke fondly of him. Exes were supposed to be that—exes. Ones you didn't think about or see ever again.

No. I couldn't picture them together without losing my mind.

I was better for Laney, but did I show it? She'd taken care of all the groceries and meals for our entire marriage. Did she hate that? I don't think we discussed it. She just started doing it at the start because I was busting my ass to earn a promotion, and then we never brought it up again. I should've asked her. I should've made sure to touch base with her, see what changes were needed in our marriage.

That's also why I was watching YouTube videos on how to make something besides mac and cheese or grilled cheese.

Laney had spoiled me with her cooking, and I totally took it for granted.

Just add that to the list. I rubbed my palms into my eyes, the headache a constant at this point, as my phone rang. A stupid burst of hope had me thinking it was Laney, but no. Petra, my executive assistant.

"Petra," I answered, my tone sharp. Although we had emailed since our last chat, I hadn't spoken with her since she learned my wife left me. "What's going on?"

"Hope you're enjoying the small-town life, boss."

I sighed. "Not exactly. Did you find out more about the cyberattack?"

The timing couldn't have been worse. Not only did my wife leave me on the night we were breached, but the attack also happened right in the middle of intense negotiations with a new business. While I didn't need to be physically in the office as we investigated who, how, and when someone broke into our network, I had to be involved every second as the CEO. It was fucking exhausting. *Why* did I do this? The challenge of succeeding drove me at first, then money. But now? I scrubbed a hand over my face as frustration and a deep bone-tired exhaustion hit me.

"Jen is with me. We're pretty sure we found the compromised account, which wouldn't be a big deal, but—"

"We believe, possibly, that someone took a bribe to let the hackers in," Jen, my CTO, chimed in. "I'm running a script compiling all outbound emails on company devices to see if they were stupid enough to leave evidence. Whatever I find, I'll send a report to you, but when we went to talk to Nate, he seemed...too relaxed. No concern. It was weird."

Nate Remington was on the development team.

"He'd have the skills to leave a door open for someone to get in. He wrote most of our fucking automations."

"Yeah, I know." Jen sighed. "I'm having Jeremy monitor our network, and we augmented our team with a twenty-four-seven service. We're okay now, Connor, but I want to nail his ass."

My adrenaline spiked. "Get our lawyer on the line. Let's see what our options are."

We moved from the phone to a Zoom call while the company's general counsel, Jeff, explained our options. It was daunting, but if we found the evidence needed, we could not only press charges, but it could also help with the costs of recovery. The call took over two hours, and my stomach growled something fierce. I had never made lunch. Work had distracted me.

I eyed my watch and cringed. How had this much time gone by? Laney's event was in six hours, damn it. I wanted to talk to her before she left. My wife liked arriving early to prep, and I wanted to drive her. There was a snowstorm on the way.

I didn't have time to eat, so I shoved a spoon into the jar of peanut butter, dipped it in jelly, and put it into my mouth. Once Laney was safe and at the event, I'd sneak off and find a snack. I could survive a few hours hungry if it meant time with my wife. After shoving myself into my coat, I grabbed my phone and keys and jogged toward her parents' house. Her car still sat outside, my shoulders sagged in relief. Thank God. She hadn't left yet.

I raised my hand to knock just as Laney opened the door.

"Connor!"

"Hi," I said, a little breathless. She looked stunning. She wore a red dress that dipped low, and her hair was done in curls that surrounded her face. Her lips were bright red and so damn kissable. She loved dressing up and going out for a nice meal. We used to do it once a week and talk for hours, sharing a bottle of wine. We hadn't in a while, and that was my fault too. I scanned her, rubbing a hand over my chest. "You look beautiful, hon."

She chewed her lip, but a pretty blush danced across her face. "Thanks. I have a Christmas charity event tonight back in the city."

"That's what I'm here for." I cleared my throat. "There is a severe weather warning tonight, something about sleet and ice. I know I can't convince you to cancel the event, but can I please drive you? I have my SUV, which is safer, and we don't even have to talk."

Her eye twitched as she blew out a loud breath. She didn't like bad weather.

"The weather does have me nervous."

"I know. I don't want you to have to drive by yourself in that." I fought the urge to push a piece of her hair behind her ear. "I can help with the event or stay in the car, whatever you need."

She nodded, the relief evident on her face. "Thanks, Connor. Yeah, if you're really sure. My stomach has been in knots thinking about the drive back."

"I'm sure." My lips curved up. The thought of being in the car with her had my stomach somersaulting like it did when I first met her. She was giving me a chance.

"Here, I'll carry that." I took the bag off her shoulder and hoisted it onto mine.

"Do you need anything else?"

"No, I don't think so." She rubbed her lips together, her eyes moving over my face.

"What's... you have something on your face."

"I do?" I wiped the left side, but she shook her head.

"Right here." She smiled as she reached forward with her thumb and swiped to the right of my mouth. I almost shuddered at having her touch me.

"Is this jelly?"

My face flushed. "Yes." I didn't want to admit that I couldn't cook and had resorted to a peanut butter and jelly sandwich. Hell, I didn't even make that because work got in the way.

"I'll put this in the back. You get in the front."

She remained quiet as I loaded her equipment into the trunk. This was a good sign. She was letting me drive her. Sure, it was because she was terrified of driving in bad weather, but I'd take whatever I could get. She wasn't shoving me away or worse—having Matt drive her.

After we buckled in, I plugged the event location into GPS.

"Okay, what music are you feeling?"

"How did you know where the event is?"

"I always know where you are." I met her gaze. "I know you might not believe this, but I check your schedule every day. Even if I never shared that with you, my morning routine is always to see your calendar if there was any opening where we could grab lunch."

"We haven't grabbed lunch in months," she whispered, her attention moving to the window. "We used to."

Sadness pierced me at her resigned tone. It was her giving-up tone.

"I know we did, hon, and I'm so sorry I stopped prioritizing that time together. Life got away from me the last few years."

She hummed in response, not confirming whether she believed me. She crossed one leg over the other, her dress revealing her very toned leg, and heat coursed through me. My wife was ridiculously hot. I was obsessed with every part of her. We'd been intimate weeks ago, and if I had known that it could've been the last time with her, I would've slowed down. I would've spent an hour on every part of her, savoring her sounds and the way she felt.

"Thanks for letting me drive you. I like being around you." There, that was genuine and tested the waters. If she shut me down, I'd be quiet and drive in silence. I gripped the wheel as she played with a button on her coat, her nervous energy quite palpable.

"I loved when we drove around in the summer with the windows down and seeing who could sing the loudest." She grinned, the expression so surprising that my breath caught in my throat. "Do you remember that car of teens who saw us and laughed their asses off?"

"I sure do." I chuckled. "You really brought your best Celine Dion that day."

"And you and your Freddie Mercury."

The pang behind my heart relaxed. This was good.

"Are you up for another singing challenge?"

"Right now?" Her eyebrows skyrocketed.

"Why the hell not? We have an hour in the car, and I have a feeling taking over me I can't stop." I dialed the radio to the station where there was always a holiday song playing once it hit December. "Christmas edition, obviously."

"Connor, we can't..."

"Why?" I glanced at her, and she stared at me, a half smile, half wince on her face. "Are you afraid you'll lose?"

She wet her bottom lip before laughing. "You know I'll kick your ass, but us singing, having fun...is that weird?"

"Uh, no? Why would it be weird?"

"Because we're divorcing?"

"Right. That."

She snorted. "Yeah, just a little thing called divorce. No biggie."

"Are you joking about the D-word right now, Laney Reynolds? That is highly inappropriate."

She laughed again and leaned her head against the window. "I shouldn't be telling you this..."

I prepared for the worst. "What is it?"

"Being around you like this, how we used to be, definitely makes me question if I'm doing the right thing. I never stopped loving you, Connor. I hope you know that. I probably never will."

Fuck. I swallowed down the emotion and tried to put on my CEO hat. Be strategic. I played people chess all day, every day. I adjusted my plan based on people's needs, and while I didn't want to play my wife, I could be strategic in getting her back. We passed a billboard promising the best New Year's gala around, and an idea struck.

"Laney, hon, I have an idea."

"I'm still divorcing you—"

"Just, stop. Okay? I know you are." Nerves penetrated my spine. I would like more time for the idea to marinate, but my opening was right now, and I couldn't miss it. "I have an idea. You don't have to answer now, consider it. But I've been thinking... Let me try all month to win your heart back. I'm right next door, and I'm not giving up. If I can't prove to you we're worth another shot by New Year's Day, then I'll sign your papers."

Her lips formed a pretty *oh* as she stared at me.

"Connor."

"I'm serious. I'll beat you."

"No, I mean... you'll sign them...?" Her voice trailed off, like she was disappointed to hear me say that.

It took all my courage, but I nodded.

"I want you happy, baby. Your smile lights up every room, and I've seen how sad you've been. So yes. I will sign them after New Year's if that's what you really want. You deserve to have someone who makes you happy. I want to be that person, but I won't prevent you from your happiness because I'm selfish."

She sniffed and wiped her face with the back of her hand. If I wasn't driving, I'd wipe her tears and kiss them away, but maybe it was better that I couldn't.

"Ugh, I was having a good eyelash day. Now it's ruined."

"No, you still look beautiful."

She flipped the visor down and fixed her makeup, but while she did that, she spoke to me. "Thank you."

"For what?"

"Just... I wasn't sure what I imagined when I left, but it wasn't this."

"Me fighting for you? You didn't expect that?" I scoffed. "Then you truly have no idea how I feel about you."

"I figured you'd be upset, but I also assumed you'd be too busy at work to really do anything about it. I mean, how are you not in the office right now? With the cyberattack and your dad?"

"I have a good team back there. They can handle it. I've talked to them every day, and my physical presence isn't mandatory." I ignored the stab of fury I felt knowing that Petra and my dad thought the company mattered more. If they believed that and Laney did too, then I really was a shit husband. I reached across the console and took her hand in mine. She didn't flinch, and I used that to my advantage.

"Laney, I want to be very explicit because it's clear we haven't been on the same page for a while. If I had to choose my job or you, then I'd pick you."

She squeezed my hand, but then she released it.

"Thanks for saying that, and I think you believe those words, but you haven't chosen me. Time and time again. It shouldn't take me leaving you for you to tell me that."

I wanted to snap. To argue. To pull over and yank her onto my lap to kiss her and remind her how good we were together. But I did none of those things. She was right. I had twenty-nine days to prove to her my words were true. If I wanted our marriage to survive, then I had to respect her and earn her trust.

"You're right. I'm also—"

"I could've told you how upset I was instead of brushing it aside. But I never wanted to distract you from your job. You worked so hard to get there, and plus, with your dad always around... I never wanted to burden you with my feelings, so I never communicated them. I'm sorry for that. I could've been better."

"Baby." It was like an entire golf ball had lodged itself in my throat. "You are never a burden to me. I hate that you felt that way."

"If we try to fix our marriage for a month, what does that mean?"

"We date."

"And you'll really sign the papers if I ask?" Her voice was small, hesitant.

"Yes. You date me for December, and if I'm not what you want, then I'll let you go."

CHAPTER FIVE

LANEY

I couldn't get Connor's idea out of my head. Date him for the month, then he'd walk away if I asked him to. He had been so reluctant to sign the divorce papers, and this seemed like an easy possibility. The issue wasn't waiting until New Year's. It was falling for him again. When Connor put his heart into something, he did it well.

But one month wasn't a true test of what someone could be. This was so hard.

Sometimes, on late nights, I'd wear headphones while I worked to pass the time. I wore mine now and hoped no one would notice.

Plus the holiday party was in full swing.

A design firm in the city had hired me months ago to photograph their annual party. They'd gone all out with decorations on the top-floor bar. The place had floor-to-ceiling windows overlooking Chicago, and it was stunning.

Connor helped me unload after I told him I'd give him an answer tomorrow. My focus should be on this event—which, ha! It sure wasn't. He snuck off to grab a snack after his stomach had made some whale sounds in the car.

I needed advice, and that meant calling my best friend. I had her on the line within thirty seconds.

"Are you alive? Are you back?"

I snorted. "Hi, Soph. I'm at my event downtown."

"Girl, come stay with me tonight. The weather is already getting pretty bad. You can't drive back."

Everyone in my life knew I hated driving in winter weather. When I was sixteen and a baby driver, I slid across four lanes of traffic, and it scared the hell out of me. No one had been hurt, but even a hint of ice made me nervous.

"About that...Connor drove me."

"And this is the same man that you're divorcing?" There was a hint of amusement in her voice.

"Yeah, so...he's renting the house next to my parents for the whole month."

"Hmm, that's honestly better than I had assumed. Nice work, Connor."

"Soph." I laughed as I snapped a few pictures of some women, all dressed as elves. They wore cute tights and pointed shoes. The men were dressed as Santas, and it was honestly amusing as hell to see all the outfits. There wasn't one person not in costume. They were all holding glasses of champagne and all smiles. The light was hitting just right, and I knew these would be the best photos I took. I went vertical and got the city lights in the back, and, damn, I loved this job.

"So, Connor, your desperate, hot husband, offered to drive you because he knows you hate this weather. And he left his job in the midst of a huge crisis. You know it has been all over the news. It's been endless, and there are even pieces questioning where the CEO is during this."

"Wait, really?" Unease settled low in my gut. "What are they saying?"

"The usual bullshit. Probably started by his dad."

Soph knew all the drama around Connor and his father. I rarely kept anything from her. We had no secrets, which was why I wanted to ask her about Connor's deal.

"Hey, I don't have long."

"Okay, what's going on?" she asked.

"Connor proposed that I don't mention divorce for the entire month and that I date him until New Year's. Then, if he couldn't prove to me that we belong together, he'd sign the papers."

I wanted a gasp or an *oh no* or a *hell yeah* from her, but she was annoyingly silent.

"Well, Soph, what do you think?"

"The question is more what do you think? How does that offer make you feel?"

"Are you therapist-ing me right now?"

"Laney, if you thought I'd judge or tell you it's a terrible idea, I'm not going to."

"I don't know what to do. A part of me wants it. Even in the car today, it was like things used to be. We laughed and joked, and he was so thoughtful. I forgot that we were divorcing. If I date him for the month, what if I fall hard and he breaks my heart again?"

"I think that's the hard part about love; you gotta take a chance." She cleared her throat. "I'd never tell you what to do, but you gotta follow your gut, and I'll support you and cheer you along the way."

"I sense a *but* coming."

"But...I think you should use this month to really share how you feel. You keep your thoughts to yourself more than you should. Tell him all the horrible nights, the questions, the tears you shed. Don't shy away from anything because it's hard or because you're worried about disrupting his life. It's already disrupted, girl."

"You frighten me." I almost laughed, but tears were right behind the amusement. "In the car, I told him how I actually felt about something. I didn't brush it off."

"And how did he take it?"

"He agreed with me and owned it."

"Hmm. Have you already decided?"

"I told him I'd have an answer tomorrow." The group of elves moved toward the Santas, and they lined up in pairs as the DJ turned up the holiday music. It was a spin on Mariah Carey's classic. I snapped shot after shot, losing myself in the celebration.

A woman holding up her arms, her blond hair going everywhere, winked at me. Wynona was the one who had hired me and knew that one of the Santas was going to propose tonight. That's why she brough me in—to capture the surprise. The music shifted to a slower version of "Santa Baby," which was the cue.

"One sec, Soph."

"Take your time. I'm just nursing a glass of wine before figuring out what romance novel to get lost in."

My favorite part about photography was the way people displayed feelings. They were subtle but so evident to me. One of the Santas got down on one knee and opened a box, and the elf dressed in purple spun and gasped in surprise.

I took a hundred photos of the scene, capturing the small

moments that followed. The way her fiancé kissed her forehead, his lips moving, probably saying how much he loved her. The way the group jumped up and down and cheered.

"I love my job," I said to myself more than Soph.

"You're brilliant at it." Connor joined me, his warm gaze on me. I loved his proud husband look, and it was all over him right now. "Look at what you did, staging this scene to have these memories live on forever."

"Oh, he sounds smitten," Sophia's voice whispered in my ear. "I bet he's staring right at you too, huh?"

"Yeah," I said to both of them. This was too much. "Soph, I gotta go. Bye."

I hung up on her and pointed to my ear. "Sorry, was catching up with her."

"Sorry to intrude. You just had this huge smile on your face, and I couldn't stop myself from joining you." His hands were in his pockets, his tie a little crooked.

"Come here." I slung my camera over my shoulder and smoothed out his tie. "It's not quite right."

"I loved when you knotted my tie for me." His voice was pure gravel and lust. His hand landed on my hip, and he dug his fingers into my skin. "You smell divine, Laney."

Heat spread to my core as I finished adjusting his tie.

"It's the—"

"Dolce I bought you two years ago. I know."

Our eyes locked, and a million memories clashed with the present. I loved this man so much. I loved that he remembered my perfume. His hand moved from my hip to my chin, where he dragged his thumb over my bottom lip. My body froze, goose bumps spreading head to toe at his touch.

"It's taking everything in me not to kiss you, baby. Every ounce of my willpower." His eyes darkened with heat as my tongue wet his thumb.

"Laney! Laney!"

I snapped out of the moment, completely rattled. His touch was magic. "Yes?"

"Get in here! This is the most beautiful setup I've ever seen. I want to tag you in my post!" Wynona waved me over and hugged me. "This is amazing. Thank you, thank you. She's so happy. She had no idea!"

I beamed. This was the best part. The joy. She positioned me to stand in front of the backdrop, and I threw my hands up in the air, smiling. I felt Connor's gaze on me, and when I glanced at him, he wore his infamous smirk. The one that often led to him getting me naked fast.

"Who is that fine man?" Wynona asked, wiggling her brows. "He is hot."

"My husband." The words flew out before I could stop them, and by the way Connor's face lit up, he had heard. "That's Connor."

"Damn, girl. You two fit together well. Connor, your wife is the best!"

"I know." He rocked back on his heels and winked.

Wynona and the group moved toward the bar, where they ordered shots. The party had another hour, and I'd stick around until the end, when things often got silly. Instead of going back to Connor though, I remained near the patio. The freezing air cooled off the feelings overheating me.

Connor staring at me like I was his world. The way he had

touched my lip. The heat in his eyes and the way my body wanted him. Damn it. How could I resist him if we dated?

Was that the point? He knew he'd wear me down if he was around me? But then once January came, he'd be back at work all the time. I leaned against the railing, taking a deep breath as I felt him near me.

"I'm sorry, Laney."

"Sorry? For what?" I snapped my attention toward him. I wasn't expecting an apology.

"I shouldn't have touched you like that." His jaw tightened, and he looked regretful. "Having you fix my tie brought me back to years ago. I can tell it made you uncomfortable."

"I'm not uncomfortable." I bit the inside of my cheek, Soph's advice hitting me hard. I needed to communicate more. Express my needs without worry.

"I'm still struggling with what to do. Attraction was never our issue. I don't want to have my heart broken again, and I'm afraid if I agree to date you for the month, then come January, I'll be devastated."

"That won't happen. I know I need to prove that to you, and I will. Please keep talking to me. Tell me what hurts. What you're afraid of. How we miscommunicated the last few years. Not right now, but this month, can you?"

I nodded. "I'll try."

"Thank you." He grabbed my hand and kissed the inside of my wrist. Flutters exploded over my body as he dropped my hand and I set it on the railing. His chest heaved as he stepped a foot to the side, putting distance between us.

I hated the space. I hated how I needed space between us.

"You're incredible when you work." He cleared his throat. "You wear this smile, and whenever you're taking photos or angling people, you get this look, and it kills me. I want you to have that look on your face every single day."

I swallowed the ball of emotion in my throat. My chest ached because it wasn't Connor who brought me that contented feeling anymore.

Soph's encouragement to be more honest had me blurting out, "I might want to move to my hometown."

"Permanently?" he asked, nothing but curiosity in his voice. "Or for a few months?"

I chewed my lip as I stared at the Chicago skyline. I had enjoyed my time here, but we moved here for Connor's job. I loved the small-town life, the festivals, the friendliness, the silly gossip, and the feeling of comfort. Maybe this was a sign I needed to move back.

"I miss it. I never enjoyed being in the city much, minus..." I took a shaky breath. "I loved you when you used to feel like my home."

"But I don't feel like your home anymore?"

I couldn't even look at him as I shook my head. I'd cry if I spoke. Now home felt like a call with Sophia, a coffee shop with upbeat hipster music, or watching a movie with my parents while we all cried. I hung my head as Connor's warm hand squeezed my shoulder.

"Thank you for sharing that with me. I can't say I like hearing it, but I love how honest you're being. In our goal to be honest, I'll say, if you want to move back to your hometown and want me, I'll go with you."

"Connor," I chided and finally looked at him. His intense

gray eyes stared holes in me. His jaw was flexed, and his nostrils flared. "You can't possibly live outside the city."

"Laney, you are my happy place. So yes. If you want to try again with me and want to move, I move with you."

My eyes shut as more tears welled up. "I don't actually believe you," I whispered, my voice raspy from the hurt. He'd never step down from the role he had worked so hard for. Or if he did, he'd be miserable and resent me.

"I need to finish the party. Excuse me."

He didn't say anything as I forced myself to stay busy. There weren't many more shots to take, and the takedown was always easier than setup. Connor didn't need direction as I packed up and he loaded everything into the back of the SUV, not with how many events he'd helped with at the start of our relationship. We had a comfortable rhythm here.

So why did we lose that same rhythm at home?

I said goodbye to the crew and went to grab my jacket when I saw Connor holding it open for me. Without even thinking, I gave him my back, and he slid the coat on me, his fingers lingering on my neck as he lifted my hair. I shivered from his touch, from the differences between us now.

"Thanks for all the help."

"You're welcome. I wish I did this more often." He waited as I buttoned my coat before he sighed. "I don't know if you'll like this idea, but I'm thinking we stay at our place tonight and drive back in the morning. I've been eyeing the weather, and it's pretty bad."

"Stay at home?" My voice squeaked.

His gaze warmed before he nodded. "It would be safer. We could wake up and drive back to your parents' first thing."

Spending the night in the same place as Connor. My mind spun. Driving on icy roads terrified me, but the thought of being with him did too. Obviously not in the same way, but what the hell should I do?

"Hon, I'll sleep in the living room if you want. Please, I don't want us to get in an accident and have you hurt." He ran a hand over his jawline. "We could get a hotel instead."

"Home is fine." My throat felt like sandpaper. "I'd rather be safe."

His shoulders sagged in obvious relief. "Me too. Come on, then. Let's go before it gets worse." He held out his hand, and I stared at it, nerves almost choking me.

He chuckled. "Baby, you're wearing heels, and it's nothing but ice. This isn't a tactic to win you back. This is about keeping your limbs intact. Promise."

When he said it like that...fine.

And that's how I found myself with our fingers interlaced, walking toward our car to spend the night in our condo. It appeared that, the more I tried to distance myself from him, the closer we got.

I just had to survive this night. Because even if I agreed to date him all December—which I knew I'd say yes to—it wouldn't undo the years of damage.

CHAPTER SIX

CONNOR

Why was I so fucking nervous?

It made zero sense to have my palms sweat and my heart beat so erratically. Each pulse felt like a punch. I knew luck was on my side, that there was the weather and we'd have to stay here. I needed to use this to my advantage since it was damn clear Laney and I wouldn't spend another night together otherwise.

Focus on the road.

Yeah, the streets were all ice and sleet. I'd driven in my fair share of bad weather, but thank fuck Laney had agreed to wait until tomorrow. This was bad. I shuddered, thinking about her trying to navigate this alone. She would have been terrified. I skidded to the right, then left, and then straightened after we hit a patch of black ice.

"Oh God," Laney panted and hugged herself. "That was... Are you okay?"

"I'm fine." My tone was clipped. Ten minutes away from

home. I could do ten minutes. "Distract me. Talk to me about anything."

"Okay, yeah, uh, I'm thinking about redoing my business to focus more on local events near my parents. Two people have told me the town is struggling, and I want to be a part of helping somehow. I like knowing the people I take photos of. Maybe I want to do more weddings than events or festivals. Not sure. I even interviewed a college kid to see if I could hire an intern to help with marketing. Did you know that? I don't think you did. Yeah, you never really asked about my days, so I didn't share. It started because it hurt, and I felt you didn't deserve to hear about my days if you didn't care to ask, but then it became a routine."

We jerked to the right from a gust of wind, and I cursed.

"Sorry! Sorry! My rambling isn't helpful."

"Tell me your favorite memory, something happy," I demanded. If we were going to crash, I wanted to go out on something positive, not my wife reminding me of the ways I was a shitty husband.

"Our Silly Sundays," she practically whispered. "Those days together will always be my favorite thing."

My stomach swooped, not from the black ice but from her comment. Silly Sundays had started as a joke after one ridiculous Sunday where everything went wrong. We referred to that day as the Silliest Sunday and then tried re-creating it every chance we could. We went to the same grocery store where a gallon of milk exploded on us. We visited the bookshop where Laney set off the alarms because her planner's barcode was weird. We'd then grab lunch at the place where the waiter dropped soup all over us. It had been the perfect storm of bad luck, and instead of being mad, we laughed.

"I loved Silly Sundays too," I said, pulling onto our street. "Hey, almost there."

"Good, that's good." She sighed.

Not sure if it was from our chat or the storm, but we were both panting by the time I pulled into our garage. Boxes lined the right wall, and it was a sobering reminder that all her stuff was packed.

"Connor."

"Yes, baby?" I couldn't stop myself.

She rested her hand on my forearm and dug her nails into my arm.

"Thank you for getting us here safely. Thank you for driving me. I-I would've..." She trailed off, closing her eyes as she paled. "I'm not sure what I would've done."

"You're welcome." I wanted to say I'd always do this, every day, but she wouldn't believe me. I had given her no reason to. The answering silence gripped us, and the urge to pull her toward me was so strong I couldn't breathe.

"We should get inside. Start the fireplace."

"Oh! Yes! I love that thing!"

I smiled. I had the fireplace installed in this place for her. She sat in front of it all the time, working on her laptop or reading while I worked or took calls. We even moved our recliner so close to it that it was amazing it never caught fire. I have a lot of good memories in front of that fire, but we hadn't used it this season yet.

We left the car and walked inside. Laney stopped near the kitchen island, staring at the anniversary gift she had given me, and paled. The memory of that night hit me in the gut like someone had tackled me to the ground. The sheer panic of her not being home the night she left me. The wedding ring she left on the table. The note reading *Don't come after me.* My hand was shaking, so I shoved it in my pocket as Laney took a deep breath.

"Uh, my stuff isn't here."

"You can borrow anything of mine." I hung up my coat and then took hers, trying not to let my touch linger. She felt so good. "Do you want an old hoodie?"

She crossed her arms over her chest and nodded, her gaze remaining on the gift. I had no idea if I should comment on it, on how amazing it was, or the fact I had forgotten our anniversary and didn't buy her anything. Guilt clawed at me, an aggressive, painful bastard that physically hurt my insides. How could I forget our anniversary when I damn well knew it was on my calendar?

Work. That was always the answer.

"Want to grab us some drinks while I get you a sweatshirt?" I needed distance from this room, from the sad look in her eyes and from my mistakes.

"Sure."

I bolted up the stairs and yanked my tie off. It was suffocating me. I had avoided our bedroom since Laney left, and the lack of her items messed with me. I couldn't fucking sleep in here. If she left me, forever, I'd move. It was wild how she was downstairs with me because of a blizzard, and I felt alone and terrified.

How do I fix this? How do I convince her I'm not the husband she knew? Was this all a lost cause?

I collapsed onto our bed, covering my face with my hands as I groaned. I had somehow blocked out all the what-ifs, not truly realizing until now that this could really be the end of our marriage. It took seeing our once-vibrant bedroom half empty for reality to take root.

Was it better to give Laney what she wanted and start healing? Hell, there wouldn't be healing for me. There'd be work and no joy. The best parts of my life were whenever I was with her. Being around her for a month—if she agreed—might kill me.

But what choice did I have? I didn't want to lose my wife.

"Connor?" Laney approached our bedroom with a frown.

"Hmm?"

"You've been up here awhile. Are you... okay?" She leaned against the doorframe, her stunning red dress clinging to her curves.

No, I'm not fucking okay.

"This is the first time I've been up here since you left me." My voice was all coarse and heavy. "I wasn't prepared to see... all your stuff gone. It hit me that this is real, that you want to end this."

"I don't know what to say."

"You don't have to say anything." I pushed up from the bed, the moisture in my eyes unshed. "I can't sleep up here though. You can take the bed. I'll stay downstairs."

"Connor, don't be silly. You don't fit on the couch."

"I'm not sleeping in our bed alone," I snapped. I rummaged through one of my drawers, then tossed her an old college hoodie and a pair of boxer shorts.

"Here, sleep in those."

She caught them and chewed the side of her lip as her brows furrowed even more.

"I really think you should—" Laney started.

The power went out.

Awesome.

"Do we have a generator?" she asked, her voice nearing me. "Do you have your phone on you? I can't see."

"No generator." Add it to the list of things I said I'd do and didn't. "Come here."

I reached for her hand and found it in the dark, then gently moved her toward the bed.

"Let me grab clothes and a toothbrush. Then we can head downstairs. We should sleep by the fire without heat running."

She snorted. "That settled our argument pretty easily."

"That wasn't an argument, Laney." I felt my way around the bathroom, grabbing what I needed before shoving sweatpants and a hoodie under my arm. "Hey, hold my hand when we go downstairs."

"I can go down by myself, you know."

"Sure, you're an adult, but humor me."

The answering silence lasted two seconds before she took my hand for the second time that night. The responding butterflies in my stomach would've been laughable if it weren't for the turmoil in my love life. I guided us down the stairs with the light of my phone.

"We can set up a bunch of blankets near the fireplace."

"We'll be okay, right?"

We reached the bottom, and I tossed my stuff onto the counter before placing my hands on both her shoulders and looking at her. The shadows caused by my flashlight only made her worry stick out more. I wanted to remove any inkling of a doubt, make her smile, protect her, kiss her.

"We'll be okay. I'll make sure we're okay, I promise."

"How do you know?" She swallowed so loud her throat clicked.

"Because, baby, we have a gas fireplace, which means we have heat. The pantry is stocked. I have a ton of clothes for additional warmth too. We'll be safe."

Before I could stop myself, I kissed her forehead. Then I moved toward our living room. I could feel the cold seeping in with the absence of heat.

"When I get the fire going, want to grab some sheets and cover the bottom of the doorway?"

"Yeah, I can do that."

We worked together in comfortable silence as she barricaded the two doorways, and I got the fire going. The warmth was immediate.

"Get over here, Laney. Put my clothes on before you freeze."

"G-good call." She shivered as she approached the fire. "I-I'll go change in the bathroom."

"Nonsense." I waved her off. "You're cold. Change here."

She blinked. "This doesn't...but you'll..."

"See you?" I arched a brow. "I've licked every part of you. Bit, teased, sucked all of it too. I can turn around if it makes you more comfortable, but this is silly."

"We're not together though."

"Have you made up your mind, then?" I tensed. I wasn't prepared for her answer, and I didn't mean to blurt out my question. I should be patient. Wait her out. Let her decide, but I couldn't fathom not knowing. She didn't want to put a sweatshirt on in front of me. That fucking hurt.

"Connor..." Her eyes watered. "I'm scared."

My heart broke for her.

"Honey, I am too, okay? I'm barely hanging on right now at the thought of this being our last night in our place. I almost lost it upstairs not seeing your pile of books on the nightstand. I'm fucking terrified."

Tears spilled from her eyes, and I cupped her face, wiping them away with my thumbs.

"I vowed to take care of you for the rest of my life, and I'm the reason you're crying. So trust me when I say, I'm more scared about losing you than anything in my life."

She shivered, her lips trembling as I ran my hands down her arms.

"Let's get you warmed up. We don't have to talk if you don't want to, but I'm still your husband. Let me take care of you a little longer."

She nodded and turned around, lifting her hair and exposing the zipper on the back of her dress. I ran a finger over the seam, wishing like hell I could kiss her. She trusted me to take care of her, and I couldn't blow it. Not when this felt like a win.

"My f-fingers are shaking too badly. Not sure I can undo it," she said.

"That's okay, I can." My own fingers shook as I tried and failed to get the zipper to work. It took three tries before I pulled it down. The fabric fell, exposing her bare back. I clenched my teeth together, fighting the burst of lust at seeing her skin.

"There, it's undone," I barked out.

"Thank you." She let the dress drop, leaving her in only a pair of red panties and a strapless bra that left nothing to the imagination. They were outlined in lace, and my mouth fucking watered. My wife was stunning. Everything about her was lovely, and it physically killed me to have her a foot away and not touch her.

She slid the hoodie on and pulled up the shorts I had given her earlier. My clothes engulfed her, and she looked so cute that I wished I could take a picture. But this moment wasn't mine to steal.

"Thanks for the clothes." She picked up the dress, avoiding my eyes as she set it on the couch. "Do you have socks I could borrow too?"

"Of course. Fuck, sorry." I scolded myself. "Let me—"

"I can get them."

"No, stay here." I jogged toward the stairs, the emotions I had tamped down all evening threatening to burst. Laney always told me I needed a healthy outlet to deal with my emotions, but keeping busy was my outlet. I didn't think I needed more than that. But it was clear this put me at a disadvantage because I was seconds away from screaming.

Laney couldn't even look at me, and it destroyed me.

CHAPTER SEVEN

LANEY

Damn, this was hard. I was home, but not really. I was scared but also felt safe with Connor. I loved him so much, yet still felt like I needed to leave. I couldn't stop shivering, and I had no way to tell if it was the blizzard, the power going out, or being around him.

The delicate way he undid my dress, how he kept wanting to take care of me. Even though he thought he hid his emotions, he was hurting.

"I found a couple pairs of wool socks." He returned to the fireplace, dressed in sweats and a hoodie from a diner we had found on our third anniversary together. "I also brought you some pants because it's cold. We can roll up the bottoms."

My throat clogged. "Thank you."

"Of course." He sniffed as his phone went off. He tensed, his eyes widening at me. "I don't know who'd be calling me right now."

"Probably Petra," I said, not quite able to hide my disdain. She called him at all hours of the night without hesitation, as if it weren't rude or inappropriate. "Take it. I'll find blankets and make a little nest."

"I can talk to her tomorrow."

"It's fine." I waved a hand in the air and picked up his sweats. I slid them on quickly. They were way too baggy, but I rolled the waistband three times, and it made them decent. "Seriously, just see what she wants. You would any other night. Tonight isn't different."

"It is fucking different."

I snapped my gaze to him at his tone. The flames caused dark shadows to dance over his face. He seemed wild, untamed. I loved seeing Connor lose control, where the adventurous soul I loved came out from the hard shell. It was wrong, but I wanted to push him. He'd made me feel all sorts of things tonight, so maybe I wanted to unleash his feelings.

"How so? How is it different, Connor? She calls, you answer. Doesn't matter what we're doing. You always make sure to be there for Petra."

His jaw tightened, and his eyes went wide. "Are you insinuating something, Laney?"

I laughed, but it was untamed. "You tell me."

His nostrils flared as he stepped closer to me. "Say it. Say what you're thinking."

"Have you…" I lost my confidence as his gaze darkened. Frustration rolled off him in waves while a muscle in his cheek twitched. "Connor, it's fine. Just—"

His phone buzzed again.

We both glanced at his phone on the couch and then back at each other. Our chests heaved as Connor ran a hand over his jaw, his gaze a cloudy storm.

"Do you want me to fire her?"

"What?"

"Do you. Want me. To fire. Petra?"

I blinked. That was not anything I had expected.

"Uh, I don't...know."

"I'll do it in a heartbeat. If you think for one goddamn second that I would ever touch, look, or think about another woman, then I don't know if we have anything to save."

My stomach bottomed out, the floor beneath me shifting. I grabbed the side of the recliner for balance as he blinked slowly, and when he opened his eyes, they watered.

"I'm gonna try to sleep."

"Connor—"

"I can't right now, Laney. I can't." He shook his head, his voice rough. He left his phone on the couch and marched toward our storage closet.

"Look through my phone. I don't care. If that's part of your reason for leaving me...There's...I would rather die than do that to you."

His words cut me in the worst way. I yanked a pillow and two blankets off the couch, curling up near the fire as sobs threatened to overtake me. I hated feeling bad about this. I hurt him because I wanted him to lose control.

It wasn't right or fair or mature. I just...I loved pushing him to share his actual feelings, and not be the closed-off man he had to be for everyone else. The world saw the CEO Connor, but not me. I missed my Connor. But the agony in his words bothered me.

He joined me a few minutes later, leaving plenty of distance between us. He had never known how to argue. He never learned. We had to learn it together, and since I had emotionally healthy parents who bickered all the time, I knew how to argue. But tonight I'd done a shitty thing. I'd hurt him on purpose. Hurt people hurt people, my mom always said, and that wasn't me.

"Hey," I whispered.

He didn't move.

"Connor."

He sighed and rolled onto his back, not looking at me but at least opening his eyes and acknowledging me. I took that as my sign to continue.

"I shouldn't have insinuated what I did. I truly never thought you'd betray me that way. It's not funny to even joke about it, and for that, I'm sorry. You chose Petra over me, often, and it hurt, and in a way, that felt like an emotional betrayal. Things you used to talk to me about were replaced by her. I used to help you choose your outfits for events, then she started doing it. I used to go out and celebrate with you when you scored a deal. Now it's you and her. I know you'd never cheat on me, but the resentment that built up with feeling replaced caused me to say that."

He pinched his nose, breathing deeply before he rolled onto his side, propping his head up on his hand. His deep gray eyes looked so sad. "Why didn't you say anything to me sooner?"

"I'd try, but you wouldn't hear me." I swallowed as another wave of tears hit me. "I asked if you wanted to try on outfits with me, and you'd say you already had spares at the office. I once drove to your office—did you know? It was last year. I wanted to surprise you, and Petra told me you were on a critical call and to try later."

Even in the dim light, he paled. "What the fuck?"

"I called you, to tell you what she said, but you didn't even let me talk. You answered the phone with *can't talk, love you.* So I went home."

"Laney. My God." He sat up and wrapped his arms around his knees, letting his head hang. "Why didn't you tell me? Why wait until now?"

"Because I knew it'd upset you. Because I kept hoping it was a fluke. Because... it's hard to tell someone you love that you're hurt. It's easier to not talk about it. I'd find a million excuses, but now I wish I had told you."

"Can I hold you, just for a second? You're breaking my heart right now, and I just need you."

Tears sprung in my eyes as I nodded. He crawled toward me and then pulled me up into his chest. He tucked my head into his shoulder, squeezing so hard I had to tap his side.

"Need to breathe."

"Sorry." He rested his chin on my head as he sighed. "For everything."

"I know, Connor."

We remained like that, cuddled together in front of the fire, all the unsaid words lingering in the air.

I'm sorry.

I love you.

But it wasn't enough.

We drifted off to sleep.

I woke up with my entire body on Connor. For one second, I forgot reality and smiled at how warm and snuggly he was. I loved the sleepy man scent he had from a night of cuddling, and I inhaled, taking in everything. The crackle of the electric fire, the coolness of the air around my face, the way he gripped me even while sleeping. Last night was big.

I had said things that had weighed on my chest for months, and I survived it. Connor's question remained though—why didn't I say anything sooner? It shifted my mindset a little. Was our divide truly all his fault? The thought of me being part of the problem caused my pulse to race, and I squirmed, needing to get some air.

"Hmm, I like your body on me, baby." Connor groaned into my neck, his warm lips pressing the spot beneath my ear. "Fuck, how do you always smell so good?"

"What...what are you—" I whimpered when he took my earlobe between his teeth and tugged. I usually loved when he did that.

"Connor." There was more urgency to my tone.

He froze.

"Fuck, fuck." He almost threw me off him. "Laney, I'm sorry. I was dreaming, I think. I—" He blinked and ran his hands through his hair. "I shouldn't've kissed you there."

My face flushed as heat spread through my core. "Hey, it's okay."

"No, it's not. You asked me not to touch you, and I maul you in my sleep." He stood, and I saw his erection pressed against his gray sweatpants.

My God. My mouth watered at the sight of him. Connor was ridiculously sexy, and even after all these years together, I still loved his body and never grew tired of it. If anything, as we aged, I loved the small differences. The sunlight filtered in through the window, highlighting the slight curl of his hair, his sharp jawline.

"I liked it," I whispered, damn well knowing it could change things. I wasn't sure what I wanted anymore, but I knew I liked being touched by him.

"Laney." He rubbed his lips together, his heated gaze lingering on my mouth. "I need an answer, baby."

"Right now?"

He nodded. "Right now."

This was more nerve-racking than walking down the aisle with him. More unsettling than interviewing for jobs. This choice I made had the possibility of hurting me even more. Visions of his charm yesterday, the way he smiled at me at the event, the way he took my hand and drove me here...the fact I hadn't been forthcoming with all my hurt.

I nodded.

"What's that nod mean?" he almost shouted. "Tell me."

"We can—" I swallowed down the massive ball of nerves. "Date for the month to see if this can work."

He closed his eyes, and his hand shook as he ran it through his hair three times. Then he met my gaze and beamed at me. The joy on his face took my breath away. I couldn't recall the last time he seemed this happy, and something warm and gooey formed in my chest.

"Thank you," he whispered, his smile somehow growing. "This was...I want to...Do you want breakfast?"

My lips curved up. "If you mean you, then yes, I want breakfast."

"Laney." He groaned into his fist and approached me, kneeling down and cupping my face. My skin heated. His touch felt different now. I wasn't at war with myself.

I could enjoy him without worrying about the divorce. That

was at the end of the month, not today. I chewed my lip as the look on my husband's face clouded.

"What is it?"

"I want you. I always want you, but if we're going to do this, really make sure our marriage is what you want, I don't...I can't blur this line. You said it yourself. Attraction wasn't our issue, and I don't want you to do anything you regret. You might say you want me now, but you could hate me in two days, and I really won't survive that."

"I won't hate you." I frowned.

"But you can't say with one hundred percent certainty that you won't regret sleeping with me." He leaned forward and kissed my forehead, lingering for a beat before staring at me affectionately.

Despite the heat coiling in my core from moments before, his words wrapped around me, settling my lust into a comfortable feeling. He was right. One hundred percent correct. A soft laugh escaped me, and I pushed my hair behind my ears.

"Then yes to breakfast. Food is about the only thing that could distract me right now."

His throat bobbed before he nodded. "Thank you for understanding and not being upset with me," Connor said.

"Ba— Connor." My skin flushed as I stumbled over his old nickname. "You're being considerate and rational about this. I can't be upset about that at all. Yeah, my skin feels too tight and I'd really like your hands on me, but it's not the right time."

I stood and adjusted the sweatshirt and sweats. The power must've come back on during the night because there wasn't a chill in the air anymore. I put my hair up in a messy bun and caught Connor staring at me with one dimple popping out.

"What?" I asked, a little nervous. He stared at me, hard.

"You look so fucking pretty in the morning. You're beautiful all the time, but I love the way you look in the morning. You open your eyes, and they can't decide if they are hazel or dark brown, and your face has all these sleepy lines on it. I know I haven't been around when you've woken up lately, but I've missed you in the morning."

I blushed from head to toe. He always had a way of complimenting me and having the words penetrate every protective wall I had and take root in my soul.

"Well, thanks."

"I'll start coffee. Then we can find food."

"Okay, I'll use the restroom."

He winked at me before walking toward the kitchen, his broad back and tight sweatpants causing my eyes to linger. My core still throbbed, but talking and spending time together mattered more than scratching an itch. I quickly used the bathroom and washed my face, taking a minute to breathe.

I thought I'd be upset with myself for agreeing to this month, but a calm sense of right lingered around me. My eyes were brighter. My face had more color.

My parents always preached that your body spoke to you about your happiness. It let you know when you were happy, and when you weren't. I'd thought the idea was a little wild and that my parents were still enjoying their hippie phase, but my body felt happy knowing I'd spend more time with Connor.

With a smile, I left the bathroom and found Connor frowning at the counter. A bag of coffee, a carton of eggs, and bread all sat in a row. His gaze moved to me, and his frown disappeared instantly.

"Hi," he said, appearing so damn cute that my insides swirled.

"Oh, hey." I joined him and nudged his hip with mine. "Is there a reason we're staring at the food?"

"I can't cook at all. I had this wonderful idea to make you breakfast, but I don't know how to make a French press coffee, which is all I have here." He sighed in defeat.

I snorted.

"That's...sad."

"I know, Laney." His expression tightened, and his movements were stiff. "It reminded me that we never talked about how you always took care of us with food. You shopped, you cooked. I never even asked if you liked it or wanted to. You just did it at the start, and I never checked in."

Flashes of frustration hit me. The nights I'd cook for us and his dinner would go cold. The lack of appreciation. I pushed down the urge to avoid the conversation and said, "Sometimes, I was resentful that you always assumed."

He nodded. "Can you teach me?"

"Yes." I smiled. "I'll show you, but I hope you know this is ridiculous. What grown man doesn't know how to make French toast or eggs or French press?"

"One that was selfish and assumed his wife would do it." His jaw tightened. "I need to learn all this because I don't intend to lose you ever again, and that means we take turns cooking."

I don't intend to lose you.

My body hummed, loving that answer. I had no idea if dating for a month would truly solve our problems, but I knew it was the right thing to try. I just had to make sure my heart wouldn't completely shatter by the end of this.

CHAPTER EIGHT

CONNOR

I didn't want to leave our home. I didn't want the storm to clear or the power to come on, but it had. We ate French toast, and I knew we had to return to Laney's hometown, where she would stay with her parents and I'd wake up alone.

She was giving us a chance, and I wanted every second with her.

But Petra wouldn't stop calling or texting, and it was better to deal with that alone. It felt too soon, too raw, to talk work while my wife was finally looking at me with joy instead of devastation.

Laney wore my clothes with her cute, messy hair, and my heart swelled. I wasn't sure we'd ever get to this place, especially after she had insinuated that I had cheated on her. That hurt the most out of all of this—that I led her to believe I'd put Petra and my job first. I had to fix that somehow, but that was a problem to brainstorm later.

Right now was about us talking more.

"Honest thought," I said, waiting for her to face me. She

did, her chin tipped up as she stared at me with her stunning light brown eyes. "I wish the storm had lasted longer, and we were stuck here, just us."

"Honest thought," she whispered, blushing. "I kinda do too."

"Do you want to stay another night?"

She blinked, and I instantly regretted asking. Of course she didn't. She wanted to go back home and have space. I even needed it to regroup, but this was our home. She didn't answer right away, and I winced.

"Sorry, that was a bad idea. I shouldn't have asked and put you in this position. Let's go—"

"Okay." She nodded.

"Okay…what?"

"Let's stay here one more night."

Now it was my turn to blink. She wasn't trying to run away from me. She wasn't in a hurry to get back to her parents. I forgot to breathe.

"We do need to head back tomorrow, and I will stay with my parents this month," she said, her voice soft. "Being here, with you, is confusing. I'm trying to go with my gut instead of overthinking everything, and it's saying to stay here with you in our home."

"Trust that gut, baby," I said, my voice thick with emotion. "I have to kiss you."

"Yeah?" She arched a brow and crouched down. "Then catch me."

She took off from the kitchen and thundered up the stairs. Her action caught me so off guard, it took a good ten seconds to catch up. I laughed. She hadn't done something like this in years, where she'd run off and I'd find her in a closet or something. She thought it was funny as hell to stump me, and my God, my heart grew three damn sizes at hearing her giggle again.

I had to find her. I had to fucking kiss her.

"Where is my wife?" I checked the guest room, the closet, the bathroom. Repeated the process in our third room upstairs that wasn't quite a guest room, not quite an office. She wasn't there. I moved toward our bedroom when a sound alerted me that she was on the stairs.

That little minx.

I bolted down the stairs, catching her in the kitchen. Her eyes lit up and her face was all laughter as she stood between the island and fridge. I almost had her trapped.

"You won't get by me."

"Not so sure about that, big guy."

She darted right, then left, but I was faster. I caught her by the waist and placed her on the counter, caging her there with an arm on either side. Our faces were inches apart and my heart pounded against my rib cage.

Her breath hit my face, her fingers finding my biceps as she clung to me.

My entire body was tuned to hers. The way her pulse at the base of her neck raced, the way her chest heaved, the way her lips parted, and how she leaned forward.

"Laney, sweetheart," I whispered, kissing her jawline. She trembled as I brushed my lips near hers. "I caught you," I teased, then continued down her neck. "So I want my kiss."

"Then kiss me," she demanded, wrapping her legs around my waist and tugging me closer. "I need you to kiss me, Connor."

"Hmm, do you?" I wanted this to last, for us to stay in this moment and live in this bubble forever. I ran my nose along her neck, biting her collarbone lightly.

She let out the sexiest little frustrated groan, and I chuckled against her skin.

"Will you regret it if I kiss you?"

"Not even a little bit. Please, please."

My hands slid under her sweatshirt, gripping her hips as I leaned back and stared down at her.

"You are fucking perfect," I said. Then I finally kissed her.

It was an explosion of feelings. Home. Mine. Joy.

Her full lips met mine with the same desperation, but it wasn't just lust. There was love in the movement. We kissed slowly, taking our time tasting each other. I was in no hurry. I could stay like this for hours, showing her without words how much I loved her. And I would, if she let me.

She nipped at my bottom lip, so I swiped my thumb over her stomach. She rocked her hips against my growing erection, so I pressed into her, deepening the kiss as she tilted her head back. I cradled her neck with one hand, leaving the other on her bare skin, and I slowed the kiss down. I opened my eyes to find her staring right back at me, and my knees weakened at the intensity of her gaze.

Was it possible to fall in love again, twice as strong, from one kiss?

Making out with my wife on the kitchen counter was now a top-ten moment.

She moaned into my mouth, her body squirming as she pleaded. "Connor, I'm burning up. I need...need..."

"Can I touch you?" I loved her sounds, her needy pleas.

"You said—" I sucked the base of her neck. "We shouldn't..."

"I'm not fucking you against a counter, but I can give you what you need with my hand." My body trembled with how much I wanted to give this to her. I wanted to have her fall apart on me, with her eyes on mine.

"Honesty," I rasped out. "I'll help you if you keep your eyes on me."

"Connor." She swallowed. "Yes, touch me, please."

"Okay, baby." I licked my lips as I slid the sweatpants down her legs. She still wore those sexy panties, and I bit my lip as I admired how goddamn good they looked on her. I wanted to get on my knees and taste her, make her scream from my tongue, but that wasn't for today. Not right now.

With my eyes on her, I slid the panties to the side and ran my fingers through her slit.

"So wet for me, Laney. So sexy."

She panted as she stared at me, all trusting and perfect. "You drive me wild, Connor."

"Good." I slid one finger into her, then two. Her eyelids fluttered closed, and I pulled my fingers out.

"No, you keep your eyes on me while I make you feel good. I need your eyes open, sweetheart."

She moaned when I bent down and kissed her slowly again, pumping in and out of her with my fingers before finding her clit with my thumb. She was so wet, so swollen. I pinched the nerves, and she bucked off the counter.

"Connor, this feels so good."

"That's me making my wife feel good," I said, my pulse racing. My cock strained against my pants like a damn rod, but this was about her. I kissed her slowly, and played with her clit just like she liked, and it wasn't long before she trembled. Her thighs tensed, and her eyes widened as she arched her back.

"Eyes on me, baby."

She listened. She rode off the orgasm I gave her, keeping her gaze on mine as she cried out. It was beautiful. Perfect. Maddening.

"Oh my God," she panted, her cheeks a little red as she stared at me. "Connor, that was...intense."

"Mm-hmm." I kissed her mouth, breathing her in before smiling at her. "That was so hot."

She nodded, her gaze never leaving mine. "You've never made me look at you like that before."

"I should've." I swallowed, hard. "I never want to miss a single part of you, or us, together again. Watching your eyes while you came was...amazing."

She ran her fingers through my hair. "I won't regret this. I want you to know that."

"Thank you."

My fingers were still near her pussy, and her thighs clenched. I knew my wife, and I teased her slit again. "Do you want another one?"

She sucked in a breath. "I-I..."

"Honesty, Laney. Do you want me to give you another orgasm?"

She nodded, and I almost wept because I didn't want this to end. I repeated the same process, bringing her to the edge. She grabbed my face, kissing me hard and messily, but she kept her eyes open the whole time as she screamed my name.

"Shit." She leaned back, her chest heaving. "Those were...I can't remember having orgasms like that in a while."

"Good." I kissed her nose and slid out of her, then pulled up her sweats and smiled. "If you need more, let me know."

"Connor, what are you doing?"

I washed my hands, dried them with the towel, and faced her. "What do you want to do today?"

"Connor." She gestured to my erection. "You need release."

"Sure, but I can hop in the shower." I waved her off. "I was thinking—"

"No, you're not going to jack off in the shower." Laney's voice had an angry edge to it. "Let me help you."

"Baby," I said through gritted teeth. I wanted nothing more than to sink into her, but this was about earning her trust and love again. Didn't she get that?

"Those orgasms were to help you feel better. It was not reciprocal. I'm playing for your heart, so I'm okay."

She frowned. "Are you turning me down?"

I nodded and almost laughed. "It's a not right now. When we're ready, we'll know."

"I don't like this."

I chuckled and quickly kissed her. "Let me put you first. Let me choose you first. Now I'm going to shower, but I have an idea for today. Do you trust me?"

* * * *

"Are you sure they'll be open?"

"Yup." I held Laney's hand as we walked a mile in the cold to try a new coffee shop. Walking here after a snowstorm in this weather was probably a terrible idea, but Laney had laughed the entire walk.

Mainly because we kept slipping on the ice. I had fallen on my ass once already, taking her down with me, and yeah, it was pretty damn funny. It had been weeks since I laughed this hard.

"Connor!" she screeched, waving her arms in the air for a solid ten seconds before I caught up to her. Wrapping my arms around her, I steadied her with a huge smile on my face.

"Oh God, thank you."

"Can't have you hurt yourself."

"Speaking of that, how's your ass?"

"Hmm, it's kinda throbbing." I kept an arm around her shoulders as I rubbed my sore glute with the other.

"Worth it though. This place just opened last month and keeps posting about their pastries and drip coffee."

"I can't believe I've never heard of it. I'm online way more than you and always take walks this way."

I kept my mouth closed. She didn't need to know that I'd worked out a deal with the owner to reserve one of the walls to showcase and sell her artwork. I'd thought about it for years but only acted a couple of months ago. They didn't have much of her photography because I wanted to surprise her instead of promising originals she didn't want to sell.

"What's your favorite memory of visiting coffee shops? The best memory?" I asked as we neared the entrance. It was called Espresso SnapShot.

"I loved the one attached to a bed-and-breakfast where they had two cats that lived there. Mittens and Whiskers, and they named those menu items after them. It was precious."

I snorted. "It was a little unsafe to have cats in the café."

"The café was in a house, Connor. They had every right to be there."

I disagreed, but I wanted her in a positive mindset before walking into the café.

"Why is that one your favorite?"

"Because it was just us. We weren't dependent on our phones or our jobs, and we were so wrapped up in each other, I just... fell so hard for you."

I frowned, the math not mathing. "We were already married."

She let out a cute huff, half laugh, half disbelief.

"Sure, but Connor, love is... It goes through seasons and ebbs and flows. There's all sorts of love. Infatuation, lust, friendship, deep love, familiarity, safety. I had all that with you, but that day, that weekend, took us to a deeper place. You told me your biggest fears that day, and I've never once forgotten them."

It took all my power to ask her what she thought of our love.

"I was raised with the very real feeling that sharing insecurities led to loss of love. I felt like, three years in, you'd stick around, and I could share them with you."

"Hey." She stilled, faced me, and touched my cheek. Her attention moved from my eyes to my mouth, then back. Puffs of condensation formed around her lips as she sighed. "Thank you for sharing those with me."

"Thanks for always listening."

She chewed her lip, and I bent down and kissed her quickly before jutting my chin toward the café. So many unsaid words lingered in the air.

Would she still stick around?

Did she still love me that way?

We arrived at the entrance, and I stopped her from going inside.

"Laney—"

"What is it?" Her tone was worried, her eyes wide.

"This was supposed to be a surprise for Christmas, and I know, somehow, I messed it up. It's probably too soon to share this with you."

"Connor." Her gaze softened. "You were going to surprise me at Christmas?" she whispered.

I nodded, but shame clawed up my neck. I had forgotten our fucking anniversary, but at least I had planned this.

"It doesn't make up for anything, and this should've been a conversation instead of me making a choice for you."

A line formed between her brows as she tilted her head. "I'm very confused right now."

"Okay, let's head inside." I swallowed, my stomach an absolute mess. "I hope you... Tell me what you think."

CHAPTER NINE

LANEY

I used to be able to read every expression on Connor's face. The impatience while waiting for someone to answer him was a slight jaw clench. The tightening of his eyes meant he didn't believe you. The nostril flare could be amusement with me or annoyance with others. Right now though? I couldn't read him at all. He stared, face neutral, as he guided me into the coffee shop.

It smelled heavenly the second we walked in. Wonderful scents of cookies and coffee greeted me, and I groaned. "Oh, that smells good."

"Welcome in!" A cheery barista waved. She had bright golden hair in braids and wore a green beanie with the word CAFFEINATED.

I returned the gesture and took in the café. It was decked out with mini Christmas trees, snowflakes, and presents. It was so cozy and homey. Instantly, I could picture myself working at a table here for an afternoon when I needed to get out of the house. Soph and I could plot out her dating schemes. My mom would obsess over all the crafts and art for sale. There was a table with bracelets and key chains.

"Oh, I love this stuff!" I smiled and went over to the table. Connor hated collecting junk. He'd rather have a large or expensive item to display, whereas I loved smaller items. Small key chains with funny phrases, a mini-camera to dangle from a bracelet. Local artists' bookmarks and shirts lined the room. Maybe it was because my mom was an artist and always fought so hard to sell her stuff at places and I wanted to support them, but my eyes welled up, thinking that Connor had known this place had all these items.

"Pick whatever you want. However many you want." He joined me at the table, his posture still stiffer than expected.

"Connor, I love this place. Why are you nervous?" I picked up a blue beaded bracelet that read SNAPSHOT in small gold letters. It was so delicate. "Oh, I love this one."

"I'll buy it." He took it from my hands, but then dropped it with a curse.

Something was wrong. He went from laughing on the walk to this awkward, fumbling man. I bent down with him and waited for him to meet my gaze. A light blush spread across his face, and I melted.

"What's this worry about?"

His gaze flicked over my shoulder, and I followed, craning my neck toward an exposed brick wall that held four photos. They looked familiar. Each scene was at night, the light rays contrasting with the background. My skin prickled. Slowly, I stood, dragging my cold feet across the wooden floor.

I knew those photos. I knew them well. I took them.

"What…" I trailed off as I read a golden plate that hung next to the images.

> LOCAL ARTIST: LANEY REYNOLDS
> Ask barista for prices.
> CapturebyLaney.com

"They're for sale?" I whispered, not quite able to believe I was seeing my photographs here, in a café, with my name. It had always been a secret dream of mine to display my original photos for people to buy. I loved working events, but these stills were for me. I was always too nervous to try to sell them, so they sat hidden from the world. But here they were, for sale, at a coffee shop. My pulse raced as blood rushed to my ears. This was…

"I'm sorry." Connor joined me, his shoulders slumped as he shoved his hands in his pockets. "I should've asked you. I wanted to surprise you, but I know you never explicitly said you wanted this. We can ask them to take them down if you—"

"Absolutely the fuck not." I faced my husband, my heart pounding out of my chest. "This is the best thing…I love it. So much."

He blinked. Then he did his head tilt as he narrowed his eyes.

"You like it?"

"Yes, Connor." I approached him and placed my hands on his chest, my initial shock wearing off as I beamed. "Are you kidding me? My art is on the wall! My photos!"

"You're the famous Laney?" The barista interrupted our moment.

A flicker of irritation danced through me. Didn't she know this was a pivotal moment for us?

"No way. Our owner was telling us about her husband and how romantic it was that he wanted to surprise his wife. Man, can I get a photo of you both?" the barista asked.

Connor kissed my forehead before wrapping me in his arms.

The barista snapped our photo with a wild grin, going on about how the owner, Bea, would be so mad she didn't see the moment I discovered the surprise. Connor handled the conversation, navigating it well without ever taking his hand off me. I couldn't focus. My mind raced with what this meant.

He had planned this weeks ago. Was this after the weekend away? The last time we really connected about five weeks ago? What did it mean? That he did think about me? Did Petra come up with this idea?

It had been her idea to send us on the weekend getaway, so I wouldn't put it past her to suggest this...

"Coffee is on the house. Please, order what you want!"

"Laney, you ready?" Connor's voice was soft, gentle, like he knew this was huge for me and was giving me time to digest it. "Want a cinnamon latte?"

I nodded, not quite in the moment as my thoughts swirled. I had to ask him. I needed to know. I appreciated this so much, so much my stomach ached with longing and regret. How could I leave a man who did this? But then the flip side—how could he do this, plan this surprise, but forget our anniversary?

I felt terrible that I was so unfriendly to the barista, but I at least smiled as Connor bought me the bracelet with SNAPSHOT on it. He slipped it on my wrist, dragging his fingers along my veins in three taps. *I love you.*

He led us to a booth near the front window, overlooking the snowy street. No one was driving and no one dared to walk in the weather, so the city looked peaceful for a rare moment. The pine trees swayed as snow fell off, and it was such a romantic scene.

"You've been speechless. Tell me what's going on in your beautiful brain."

I took a sip of the latte and stared at my bracelet, nerves plucking me. He'd been so nervous about the photographs, worried I'd hate what he'd done, and I wanted to reassure him it was fine. That it was great. But that wasn't honesty, and I had put his feelings first for years.

"I'm amazed." I shrugged and chewed my lip, staring out the window and watching smoke come out the chimney from a house across the street. "Truly, the act of doing this is so thoughtful and wonderful."

He swallowed, nodding, but his brows furrowed. "I sense a *but* coming."

This part was hard. He could recoil or fight back or be insulted. I took a breath. "I have questions."

"Please, ask any of them. I can read your expressions, Laney." He sipped his usual black coffee with oat milk and stared right back at me. He made no moves to look at his phone or outside, just me.

"Was this your idea?"

He frowned. "Yes. Who...else?"

"Did you plan it alone?"

He nodded with a confused look. "Of course, I did."

"So, Petra didn't...She...It wasn't her idea?"

The look in his eyes shuttered, but he masked it fast.

"No. She doesn't know this part of your life. She doesn't know how you wish you could sell your original images to bring people joy and feeling. Those were you-and-me conversations, husband and wife." There was an undercurrent to his tone, but it wasn't anger.

He took my hand in his, tracing my palm with his pointer finger. He might've tried to hide it, but his hand shook.

"This was all me."

My eyes prickled, and I glanced outside again, but he tugged on my hand, drawing my attention.

"Please don't hide from me. Look me in the eye when you ask your next question."

"Why?"

"Because I deserve to see your face. Even if it kills me, I want to see the worry in your eyes. The fact you thought Petra would have anything to do with this fucking hurts, Laney, but let it all out."

"It might hurt, but you forgot our anniversary and told me Petra would reschedule us a dinner somewhere. I don't understand how you can do this, plan this surprise, but forget our anniversary." A tear fell, and I quickly swiped it away. "I-I..."

"Honesty," he urged, his tone soft.

"I know you love me, and this gesture, seeing my photographs for sale, is amazing. It means so much to me. I just... it shows me that, when you care about something, you show up, you prioritize it, but when you don't care or get too busy, you forget. It's the inconsistency that hurts me."

His jaw flexed. "I have nothing else to say besides I messed up on our anniversary. There are no excuses besides me fucking up. If it were my first time not showing up for you, it would've been something we worked through."

"It wasn't the first time," I said softly. "Did you plan this that weekend we went away?"

He nodded. "Is that...bad?"

"No. That makes sense in my timeline."

"Timeline?"

"Yeah. That...weekend we connected. Deeply. It was the old us. It made me forget all about leaving. It makes sense that I was on your mind too."

He swallowed. "Then that following week, I didn't come home for dinner once."

I shook my head. "I researched meals from the hotel to make for you, to surprise you."

He closed his eyes and ran a hand over his face. "Fuck. I had no idea."

"I didn't want to bother you."

"Laney, I need you to bother me. I want all your bothers." He tilted his head and then snorted. "That was a weird sentence."

"It kinda was." I smiled, my shoulders relaxing as the mood shifted. "I'm programmed to never upset you because your job is stressful, and I never wanted to be the nagging wife."

"You expressing yourself to me is not nagging." He squeezed my wrist again, three times. "I'd rather have you yell or cry at me every day than not have you."

He paused and shook his head.

"God, that sounds bad too. I don't want you to cry every day. I never want you sad. How am I making this worse?"

I laughed. "You really are. It's impressive."

He rolled his eyes as the ghost of a smile played on his face.

"I always assumed I'd make things up to you later. I told myself the next trip, the next weekend, next month, next birthday, I'd do something big to make up for it. I realize now that wasn't enough."

"I realized that I'd keep waiting for the next something to keep me hoping. The next weekend away, you'd see how good we were, and we'd go back. That wasn't healthy either."

Connor exhaled, nodding a few times before he leaned over so his elbows were on the table. His face twisted into business mode, no hints of a smile, all serious.

"No matter what you decide at the end of the month, I need you to know you are the best fucking thing that has ever happened to me. That will never change."

"Connor." God, that sounded like a breakup speech. My stomach clenched, and it hit me that, even after all the heartache, I didn't want to leave him. I wanted us to make this work. "What—"

He shook me off. "We have weeks to talk this all out and get to a healthy place where we are both confident and happy. We'll get there." His eyes shuttered as he said those words, like he wasn't sure. "But I am the man I am because of you."

I wanted to believe him so badly. More than breathing. We were in a snow globe right now, cut off from the rest of the world. He could be the version I needed here without the pressures of work, but once Monday hit...that'd be the test.

CHAPTER TEN

CONNOR

"Are you fucking kidding me, Connor? You turn off your phone for an entire day?" Petra blasted me Monday morning. Not only did she show up at the rental house unannounced, but she also looked out of sorts.

Petra was always polished. She cared a lot about making a name for herself and once shared that she'd never let her appearance get in the way of someone's opinion of her. Yet, she stood at the doorway, hair going everywhere and in jeans and a sweatshirt. I didn't even know she owned jeans.

"Uh, come in." I ushered her inside, hating the squish of guilt in my chest. Her car would be visible to Laney and her parents. Despite the progress we had made this weekend, talking and cuddling in front of the fire, her concern that I'd replaced her with Petra cut at me.

"Give me a second, okay? I'm letting Laney know you stopped by."

Her brows rose, the question evident in her eyes. "And why would you need to let her know that?"

"Because, Petra, I'm doing whatever I can to get my wife back." I found my phone on the counter along with the constant buzz of texts and messages that I had avoided all weekend. I hadn't even wanted to check it once we got back to Cherrywood. In my decade of hustling to get to the top, I had never turned my phone off for over twenty-four hours. It was so out of character and stressed me the fuck out, but it had been the right choice.

> ***Connor:*** Hi, good morning. I wanted to let you know Petra showed up unannounced today because I turned my phone off all weekend. I have no idea how long she'll stay.
>
> ***Laney:*** Hi! Okay, thanks for letting me know.
>
> ***Connor:*** Can I take you out for dinner tonight?
>
> ***Laney:*** Would tomorrow work? I have dinner plans tonight, sorry!
>
> ***Connor:*** With who?

I didn't mean to send that so fast, but images of her perfect high school sweetheart came to mind.

> ***Connor:*** Sorry, I wish I could unsend that. Tomorrow would be great!
>
> ***Laney:*** No need to be jealous of Becky. We're

grabbing dinner to talk about the festival that I'll be photographing. It will only take an hour.

Connor: I'm jealous of anyone who spends time with you.

"Connor, Jesus Christ." Petra scoffed. "Are you listening to me at all?"

"Give me a fucking minute." I ignored her and smiled at my phone.

Connor: Let me know when you're done with Becky. I'll pick you up and we can go see an old Christmas movie at the theater.

Laney: !!!!!!

Connor: Those better be YES I WANT TO SEE YOU CONNOR exclamation points.

Laney: Not quite. They are I LOVE POPCORN.

Connor: So, movie date?

Laney: Yes!!!! (those are excited to see you exclamation points)

Laney: Tell Petra hello for me.

"Okay, I'm good now." I pocketed my phone, a grin stretching across my face. This date felt different from anything before. We'd seen movies together, but after living for a few days never knowing if I'd hold her hand again, this was big. She loved movie theater popcorn and black-and-white holiday movies. She'd laugh, cry, and curl up next to me and quote them the whole time.

I'd silence my phone the entire time. I had to.

I snorted as I stared at my assistant of almost ten years. "You look more disheveled than usual, by the way."

Her expression flattened.

"You don't say. My CEO disappeared for a weekend, we had a cyberattack, and you decided to work on your marriage the day it happens. Someone had to keep everything going, and it wasn't you."

"Are things falling apart? Or are we okay?" She had always functioned as more than an executive assistant.

"We're okay, but I'm not. I can't handle you ghosting me like this." She pulled at her hair. "I have this feeling my ex is involved in this. He wants me to suffer, and he knows causing the company issues—causing you pain—would hurt me. It's irrational, but I feel like he had something on Nate to get him to turn on us."

I finally saw what Laney had noticed. Despite Petra and I never crossing a line, it was clear now how Laney assumed that we did. I knew Petra. She was like me—driven, focused, unforgiving, and desperate. I was desperate to prove to myself and my dad that I was cut out to be a CEO. She was desperate to make a name for herself and to help out her family.

But the possessive, almost unhealthy way she spoke about our relationship caused a rock to form in my chest.

"Petra, sit down for a second."

She moved to the kitchen table and sat, her expression open. She was used to taking orders from me, navigating the cutthroat world at a fast pace. This would hurt her. I hated doing it, but if it meant choosing Laney or the company, I'd choose my wife.

"Repeat back what you just said and think about how it would sound to my wife."

She frowned, her fingers tapping the table before she blushed.

"Connor, that's...no, no."

"I agree with you. We've been friends and colleagues for years. Nothing more. But I need to rethink our boundaries, what I depend on you for."

"Connor." She stood up, her blush long gone and replaced with a pale, worried look.

"She can't possibly think..."

"She knows nothing happened. She likes you. We're navigating what our marriage looks like now, what is savable, and it was clear to me that you weren't aware of my priorities. I will pick her over this job. If she gave me the ultimatum, I would pick her."

Petra blinked twice before nodding. "I'm sorry for telling you your marriage wasn't worth saving. That was out of line. I am mortified right now."

I snorted. "Your words woke me up. If you, my friend and colleague, thought I was a bad husband, what the hell would my wife think?"

"No." She stood and scrubbed her face. "I was so focused on revenge, on making Blake pay, that I forgot the human part of living. Oh my God."

"Petra, you're fine."

She paced the kitchen. "I'm not fine. I'm ashamed of myself. All I wanted to do was help my parents out, but my mom is gone, and my dad is living with my brother and nephews. They don't need the money anymore. So why am I hustling so much? Why am I obsessed with proving myself to him?"

"I think that's normal when you had a bad marriage."

"I lost the whole point." She sighed. "I think I quit."

"Yeah, I can't let you do that." I almost laughed. "I think we need to sit down and figure out a way for both of us to be better at work, and in life."

"Laney must hate me. It makes me sick to my stomach. Literally sick." She glanced out the window, a dark expression on her face. "A few years ago, I made sure to check in on your personal life, make sure you had work-life balance. I covered for you when you needed a lunch with her. But I stopped. We had too much work to do to beat Blake. Blake is friends with a board member, and then your dad...It became about winning. Beating them. And I stopped caring about life outside work. I canceled a few of your lunch meetings with Laney, you know? I told myself it was for the business, but what if that is what caused her to...leave?"

I gritted my teeth, thinking about the story Laney shared about Petra turning her away. "I'm not thrilled about the choices you or I made, but my marriage is on me and me alone."

Petra plopped onto the chair again, the wooden legs loudly scratching the floor. "I think I became obsessed with work in a way."

I nodded and sat across from her. "I have a proposition for you."

Asking her to take on a promotion was step one of many to get where I needed to be, and like Petra, I was annoyed I had been so obsessed with being successful that I hadn't thought rationally or strategically when it came to my life.

"I'm surprised you don't want me fired, Connor. I deserve it. I let my personal vendetta against a competitor get in the way of supporting you. Not as a CEO or my boss, but as my friend for ten years."

"I want you to be my COO."

She frowned.

"You'll be my right hand. My number two. You speak for me when I'm not there. You lead our executive team and ensure shit is done and done well. You're already doing it. You have the respect, experience, and my support. It'll be a significant raise, more shares in the company, and provide us both with what we need." I swallowed as my gut settled. I trusted that sixth-sense feeling when it came to work, never questioning it. This was the move. "This will allow me more time at home with my wife. This also gives you more power, more voice. You influence the votes, the board members, the team. We run this place together, instead of you just supporting me."

Her lips trembled.

Fuck.

"If you cry, I will shove you outside. I've never seen you cry, Petra, and today is not the day to start." I pointed a finger at her. "Knock it the fuck off. Do you want the position or not?"

She nodded.

"It'll take me some time to get the board okay with the increase in salary and for you to find your replacement. I already drafted a description and have calls set up with our

CFO and CTO this afternoon. This is going to happen, one way or another."

"Thank you." She stood and held out her hand, her eyes waterier than I liked, but no tears fell.

"I will never let you down again."

"Deal." I shook her hand, smiling until she finally gave me half a smile.

"See, this is good news."

"You're really chipper for a man whose wife might leave him. I don't get it."

"Laney agreed to give me the month to prove to her that we can make this work. This is step one."

Her eyes lit up.

"Okay, we need to brainstorm ideas, ways to—"

"I appreciate you so much. I do, but I have to do this alone." I swallowed the uncomfortable lump in my throat. "If I can't win my wife back on my own merit, then I don't deserve her."

Her eyebrows disappeared into her hairline. "Holy shit, Connor. You're legit."

"You lost yourself the last year or so. Well, I did too. I need to reset."

"Have you considered just powering yourself off and on again?"

"Funny." My lips quirked. "Are you staying in town a bit or did you come just to yell at me this morning?"

Her nostrils flared. "I'm happy you're working on yourself and Laney, but dude, we have so much to fucking do. Are you able to work today?"

"I appreciate you asking instead of demanding. Improvement." I poured another cup of coffee and faced her. "Do you want to find a hotel and stay in town for a bit? We could work here during the day."

"And not go back to the city?" She scrunched her nose. "This is a small town."

"Yeah, and it's charming. It might be good for you. Let me know if you want to get a hotel. I'll reserve one for you since I'm the reason you're here. Now, let's get to work and make sure we both still have jobs."

"I definitely fucking do. It's you who disappeared. Now, here is my theory on how someone influenced our development team..."

* * * *

Cherrywood was beautiful. The sun set hours ago, and holiday lights of every possible color lined the roads and covered the trees. You couldn't walk two steps without someone smiling at you or saying good night or wishing you a good day. It was so different from the city, from the unsmiling faces and dark clothing. The change of pace was startling but not unsettling. If anything, it made me pause. I hadn't paused in years, and I should have. I got why Laney missed this place.

Laney told me she'd meet me right outside the theater, Snowefalls Films, about ten minutes ago, and my pulse raced thinking about seeing her.

I had texted to tell her that Petra was staying in town at a hotel, but that was really all we communicated that day, and I wanted more. Funnily enough, I'd gone days without texting her before, and now a few texts caused me to feel like a teenager.

A part of me wanted to tell Laney everything—the move for Petra, what it meant for us, for my job—but I didn't want to until it was official. If it didn't go through, or if the board fought me, I'd readjust my plan, but I didn't want to give Laney any false hope. Not ever again.

I stood with my hands in my pockets, snow landing on my face as a familiar scent hit me. Laney approached me with a nervous smile. Her lips were red, her hair brushed to the side under an adorable fucking knitted hat. Her red winter coat matched her lips, and she looked perfect.

"Hi," she said, her smile growing. "Small-town Connor looks happy."

"Not the town." I leaned toward her, kissing her neck and breathing her in, and then pulled back. "You."

"Good line." Her eyes danced with amusement. "They're playing *White Christmas*. I'm so excited."

"Your favorite movie." I held out a hand, waiting for her to place hers in mine. I dragged my thumb over her wrist and opened the door with my free hand. "Have you seen it in theaters before?"

"I haven't! I've seen most of them here, but never this one. Prepare for me to ugly cry at the end."

"Oh, I'm prepared." I patted my chest where I had definitely placed a small pack of tissues. "I recall how you get at movies, let alone Christmas movies."

"They are just so magical! I can't help it!"

I laughed and moved my arm around her shoulders, keeping our fingers interlocked as I pulled her closer.

"There is something about the holidays that's special. Even a workaholic Grinch like me can appreciate it."

Laney beamed as I bought the tickets and one large Sprite and popcorn for us to share. *Share* was a loose term because she could destroy a bucket of popcorn on her own, but I was glad to see her smile.

And since it was her hometown, she ran into three people she knew. Her fourth-grade teacher, and then her old neighbor, then one of her friends from high school. She introduced me as her husband even without wearing her ring, which felt like a major win. A massive one. It took a few minutes to get to our seats, but when we did, she didn't jump right into the popcorn. She chewed her lip and stared at me.

"What is it?" I pushed some of her hair behind her ear. Her hat had left it all wild, and while I found it cute, she'd want it in order.

"Thank you for making time for me tonight. This is really special." Her eyes glistened, not quite with tears but with emotion.

My stomach bottomed out. She was being nice, kind, but the words affected me inside. She shouldn't thank me for spending time with her, but that was our reality. Instead of voicing anything, I forced a smile and tilted her chin for a quick kiss.

"There is nowhere else I'd rather be."

Her responding smile was enough to get me through the inner turmoil. I really needed to get the COO position settled, and fast, so Laney would know this was our new forever. That meant finding a way to run to the city without worrying her, because I refused to take any steps backward. My wife was giving me a chance, and I wasn't going to ruin it.

CHAPTER ELEVEN

LANEY

Two days later, I woke up and ran to the bathroom, barely making it to the toilet before throwing up. My eyes stung and my throat burned as I wiped my face and used mouthwash. When it first happened two weeks ago, I figured it was all due to the stress of leaving Connor. But things were okay. They were good right now. He had cooked me dinner last night—it was basic pasta, but the fact that he tried mattered—and he walked me back to my parents' at nine with nothing more than a kiss.

I had wanted to stay longer. I had wanted more, but he insisted we had to continue taking this slow. He was right, but I missed him. I felt a flicker of happiness, and not a fleeting one either.

So the stress sickness shouldn't have come back. Maybe it was the pasta he cooked? Oh God. He'd feel terrible if he knew I got sick from it. The timing was right—food poisoning happened about twelve hours after eating. I almost laughed.

My husband wanted to prove to me he could change and instead made me sick. It was almost funny. I quickly showered, curled my hair, and got ready for the day. My first assignment from Becky for today was to photograph a bunch of high school students at the elementary schools bringing the kids presents and reading to them. I remembered that tradition growing up, and I couldn't think of a better way to spend the afternoon. Capturing all that joy.

I spent extra time on my hair, like the additional hair spray and attention would hide the fact that my stomach swirled with acid. I should probably grab a Sprite before heading to the school.

"Laney! Your man is here."

My dad's voice made me smile. I told my parents the plan for December, and they repeated the same thing they always said—they wanted me happy and would support me no matter what happened. They also encouraged me to listen to Connor, really listen to him, because after forty years of marriage, they said that miscommunication was the root of all evil.

"Okay, he can come in!" I shouted back, eyeing my red dress or dark green one. The evergreen was one of my favorite colors, and I had gold jewelry to wear with it. Yeah, I'd wear this. I slipped it on just as the floor creaked outside my room.

"Thanks for the permission, but I'm already in."

"Connor." I spun, smiling as he leaned against the doorframe to my bedroom. He wore jeans and a dark navy sweater that clung to his chest. My stomach flip-flopped due to how attractive he was.

"Hi."

"That dress looks incredible on you." His gaze heated as he eyed me head to toe slowly returning his eyes to my face. "Damn, Laney."

"Stop," I teased, but I felt my face flush regardless.

"No." He pushed off the frame and met me in front of my dresser, standing behind me so we both stared at the mirror. His eyes burned me in the reflection, so much love and affection there.

"I'm not going to stop telling you how beautiful and amazing you are."

He kissed my collarbone and ran one hand up and down my hip, moving up my arm and tilting my neck back slightly.

"I'm obsessed with your body. Every part of you. I always have been."

I shuddered as he tugged my earlobe between his teeth, and heat pooled between my thighs.

"Connor," I moaned, leaning into his chest until he supported my weight. "What are you—"

"Shh." He kissed my neck, and then turned me around to kiss me on my mouth. He kissed me slowly, taking his time tasting me to the point I was burning up. I moaned against his mouth, causing him to laugh.

"I swear I didn't come here to get you riled up."

"Ugh." I rested my forehead on his chest, my own breath coming out in pants. "Well, I'm riled up, damn it."

He laughed, the deep chuckle as welcome as my favorite playlist. I wrapped my arms around him and squeezed.

He sighed. "Fuck, I've missed your Laney burrito hugs."

"It's been a while, hasn't it?" I smiled against him. "Come be my burrito, baby." I grabbed my blanket and wrapped us up real tight. I used to do this all the time when we started dating. Connor thought it was goofy, but it became an inside joke that died a few years ago.

He remained a statue, minus his hand moving up and down

my spine in taps of three. "I came here to tell you in person that I have to head to the office today."

Just like that, all the joy zapped out.

We were in our snow globe here. The city was not included.

"Baby, I can feel you tensing. I promise I'll come back."

I tried breaking the hug, but he held me tighter. "No, I'm not done with you."

"Connor, you should leave. It's a long drive."

"Sure, but that can wait." He tilted my chin up, his gaze boring into mine. "I don't like how you're stressing. Tell me what you're thinking."

I hesitated, the urge to remain quiet choking me. It would be silly or weak to tell him I was worried he wouldn't come back. Or four days would go by before he remembered me at home.

"I'm not leaving here until we talk this out. This matters. We matter. Now, we promised honesty. Please tell me why you tensed up."

He spoke so softly. How could I deny him?

"This feels familiar. Us being good, then you going to work and... then we go back to what we were before where you forget about me."

He nodded, concern etched on his face.

"I've never forgotten you, but I can see how it felt that way. There's a few things I have to do in person, then I'm coming straight back. I will text you when I get there and when I'm leaving. Can I call on my way back?"

"Sure."

"Baby, your face has your emotions all over it. I'm coming back, okay? I promise."

"Yeah, I know. I'll see you when you get back." I forced a

smile. This was stupid. We couldn't live in this bubble forever. He'd have to go back to work eventually. "Thank you for telling me."

His jaw flexed as he cupped my face, his gaze lingering on my lips. "Send me some photos from today, okay?"

"I will."

He kissed me once, twice, his lips lingering before he sighed. "I don't want to fucking leave you. This is hard for me too, okay? No part of me enjoys this, but it has to be done. So I'll see you tomorrow, okay?"

"Tomorrow it is."

He released me and walked out but paused at the doorway and stared at me. His mouth opened and closed. Then he tapped the door and walked.

"Wait!"

He immediately ran back, hope on his face.

"Drive safe, okay? I'm gonna miss you."

"I will." He smiled—this one genuine. "I love you, Laney."

"You too."

He put a hand on his heart, smiling as he walked backward and right into the hallway wall.

"Damn it!"

"Smooth." I snorted. "So sexy."

"Shut it." He rubbed his side, but the amusement was clear on his face.

"Have an amazing time today. I can't wait to hear about it."

This time, when he walked away, my heart wasn't as heavy. Maybe this time would be different. That bead of hope that I held on to for dear life flared, taunting me. *It's never going to be different. He'll win you over but then disappoint you.*

I pushed the voice away. We were trying for a month. It was only December 6. We had time.

* * * *

"Laney freaking Whitfield! Get your face over here!"

"No way! Laney!"

It was reassuring and strange to see so many high school friends as teachers. These kids had no idea who their teachers used to be, but it was a wonderful cycle of life. These teens wouldn't get away with anything, not with Tessa Farmington and Travis Cornerstone as their teachers. Tessa had been the queen of mischief, Travis second in line. Throw in Matt, and these were my three closest friends growing up.

"You look amazing. It's not even fair." Tessa hugged me hard, putting all her body weight on me. She smelled like a walking snickerdoodle and she passed me to Travis so we all ended up in a weird group hug.

"Look at you all fancy with your camera and shit."

"Stop, Travis! She's a big deal now."

"Guys, I'm not a big deal." I shoved them off me, the strong smell of Travis's cologne making my stomach roll. It wasn't that it smelled bad, it was just too much. "I can't believe you both ended up in the classroom. That is wild."

"If you stayed on social media, you'd know." Tessa arched a brow. "Ms. I'm-going-to-leave-my-hometown-and-disappear," she added.

I blushed.

"Yeah, I'm the worst at staying in touch."

"Don't make her feel bad, T." Travis put his arm around me.

"As someone who also refuses to show my face online, I appreciate the mystery. I just happened to never leave town, and everyone knows everything about me," Tessa said.

"You're right. I'm sorry. I'm just happy to see you. Ah! We need to grab dinner. Tonight. Tomorrow. When?"

"You have zero fucking chill," Travis scoffed, rolling his eyes and squeezing me.

"But for real. Wanna grab food tonight at the pizzeria?"

"Are we talking about pizza?"

My stomach tightened at that voice. Matt Heathen. Travis held out his fist for a bump, which Matt returned, but his eyes were on me.

"Laney, are you still obsessed with pineapple on pizza?"

I scrunched my nose. "I feel like your tone is suggesting that there is a right or wrong answer here."

"There is." He grinned and smoothed his shirt. He wore dark-framed glasses, a black plaid shirt, and khakis. He looked adorable. We hadn't set up our drinks to catch up yet, but a group gathering made more sense. "It's an abomination."

"Disagree. It's perfection."

"Aw, you two are bickering like it's 2008 again. I love it. I need a photo of the four of us!" Tessa handed her phone to one of the students lingering in the hallway, and before we had a moment to protest, I was wedged between Travis and Matt with Tessa on Matt's right.

"Our class will love this." Tessa grinned but snapped her gaze down the hall. "If my seniors are acting up right now, I will lose my mind. Excuse me." She took off where three senior boys were laughing hard. Travis followed, his familiar voice causing the boys to sober up fast.

"I gotta say, it is nice seeing you here back at school." Matt's cheeks turned pink. "So many memories here, you know?"

We both stared at the lockers a few feet away. Mine was there, and we spent a lot of time kissing in front of that locker. My skin heated as my stomach twisted with guilt.

"I do know," I said, unsure if I could look at him. "I should—"

"Laney, hey." He took my hand and immediately dropped it. I faced him, conflicted and unsure what to do.

I had loved him years ago. I cared for him. I wanted him happy, but this in-between with Connor put me in a very weird headspace.

"What is it?"

"The last thing I want to do is make you uncomfortable. I realize I did when I mentioned the memories. Please know that I am not hitting on you. Unless you want me to? Then please, tell me, because I would. But I'm not. I want to hear about your life. That's all, okay?"

Damn. Matt was so freaking sweet, even now. My eyes watered at the gentle genuineness to him. He had always been that way, so in tune with others' feelings. He'd overcommunicate to the point that it was almost annoying. Now? It was so appreciated.

"Thank you. That was... I needed that."

"I had a feeling." He grinned and held out his arms.

"Friends, yeah?"

I hugged him back, relief flooding through me. "Definitely friends."

"Cool." He patted my back and released me. "I gotta wrangle my freshmen into submission. These kids, dude, I swear. The pandemic made them wild animals."

"Charm them with your dad jokes."

"I am in my dad-joke era."

"You kinda always were in that era, Matt."

He laughed.

"It's good to see you, Laney. Pizza is on me tonight. As a friend."

I waved, watching him disappear down the hall. There was a nostalgic magic to being at my high school again with my old friends. I knew my place here. I knew where I fit. I didn't in the city.

I had Sophia. I had Newt, sometimes. But besides them? I didn't have a community. I used to, here. I didn't realize how much I missed it until now. I often felt like an island, waiting for Connor to come visit me. Soph was there and was my rock, but she had an entire community without me.

What if I truly wanted to stay here?

We both knew Connor would never leave his company. I would never ask him to. But did I want to go back to the city, to our condo where I spent all my time alone?

My gut knew the answer, but I pushed it away. It wouldn't do any good to think about it now. My stomach churned, and I cursed the dang pasta from last night. I ran to the bathroom and got sick, found some gum, and put on my game face. I was here to take photos, and I'd take the best damn photos this town has seen. I'd channel all my energy into the event and not the fact I wanted to live here. Connor would never be happy.

CHAPTER TWELVE

CONNOR

Three of the board members loved the idea of bringing Petra up to COO. Dennis and Ryan were the two I had to convince. I could technically take it to a vote, but Dennis had sway over Margaret, who was still new in the role. If Dennis made a ruckus about it, Margaret could fold under pressure.

I hated the fucking politics of this role, but it was my life. The annoying flicker of doubt returned, but I brushed it away. I was too far in to have any regrets.

I knew setting up this meeting with Dennis would have a ripple effect. He'd call my dad, who'd rip into me. I tried to view it from their side, but I couldn't. They had antiquated views of the workplace. They were misogynistic and didn't have the same values about work-life balance.

I eyed my watch. It was 5:00 p.m. and Dennis was an hour late. I wanted to be on the road back to Cherrywood, but no. The prick had told me something came up, and he wouldn't be free again for two weeks, so if I wanted to talk to him, I had to work around his schedule. Instead of working—I desperately needed to catch up on emails—I called Laney.

It rang four times before she answered, a little breathless. "Hello!"

"Hey," I said, grinning at just hearing her voice. "How was the event today?"

"It was amazing." She sighed and covered the phone. She spoke to someone, but I didn't quite hear what she said. "Sorry about that. I stepped out."

"Where are you?" I thought she'd be home with her parents. Not that she couldn't go places, but she didn't have anything on her schedule when I checked it this morning.

"Oh. I reconnected with some friends from high school today. They are all teachers, Connor—it's so funny. They insisted I grab pizza and beer with them. I'm not drinking though, 'cause my stomach feels a little sour, but—"

"Your stomach hurts? Do you need anything?"

"Oh. You're sweet. No, I'm okay."

"So you're grabbing pizza with high school friends," I said slowly, hating the insecurity leaking into my voice. If Matt Heathen was there... "Who are these...friends?"

"Matt is here, if that's what you're wondering. You have nothing to worry about, okay? We talked today, and it was very clear we're friends."

"You talked about us?"

"What? No. Of course not." Her voice quieted. "He made one comment and immediately backtracked, saying he knew I was uncomfortable and that he only wants to be friends."

"What comment?" I barked out. The security camera beeped,

alerting me that Dennis had finally arrived downstairs. What perfect timing.

"You're focusing on the wrong parts. The comment is irrelevant. Matt is not someone you need to worry about whatsoever. I promise." Her voice held no irritation, just patience.

Sometimes I didn't deserve her.

"I'm sorry I'm being an ass. Dennis stood me up and just now waltzed in an hour late. I want to be back with you, and he's delaying it."

"Well, don't stress too much, okay? I'm out tonight, so you can finish up your business without worry."

I could tell she was trying to sound happy but wasn't. It was a façade, and I fucking hated it. Dennis tapped on my office window, his grimy smile peeking through, and I squeezed the pen in my hand until it snapped.

"I gotta go, baby, but I love you. Can I call when I'm done?"

"How about I call when I get back?"

"Perfect. Have fun."

"Bye." She hung up, and that instant disconnection from her made me feel sick. We weren't calibrated at all. In person, we were okay. Distance? Not so much.

"Connor Reynolds. Haven't seen you here in a while." Dennis marched in with his very large beer belly leading the way. He pushed his hair—filled with product—back, and it looked terrible.

"Things came up. Please, have a seat. There's something I'd like to run by you."

I told him the plan about Petra, how it would work financially, and how it fit into the bigger picture of expansion. It would help bring in more revenue and make things more efficient.

I expected a no, yet it still took all my power to not punch him. "What do you mean no?"

"You don't have my support on this. Petra is an executive assistant. She isn't capable of taking on this role, and it's worrying that you're not thinking straight. If you think she'd actually be the one for this—man, it makes me question your position as CEO."

My temple ached. "You're saying that, because she's been an executive assistant, she cannot possibly take on the role."

"Pretty much. She doesn't have the education or experience to handle that responsibility. You need the smartest and most experienced working for you." Dennis shrugged and tapped the top of my desk. "My nephew, for example, graduated from MIT and is wicked smart. Now, I can get behind the position with the caveat that Mick be in the running. You need a man who can handle the tech world."

There it was. The slimy fuckery of this job. I leaned back in my chair, my pulse racing as I contemplated my next steps. Dennis never liked me from the start. It could be because my dad had poisoned him against me. Or the fact he applied for this role ten years ago and he hadn't been chosen.

You'd think there'd be a policy against him running for the board, but nope. He could legally do it and sabotage the company. All with my dad not caring or seeing it.

I steepled my fingers and stared him down.

"You'll approve the position but only if I hire your nephew. That sounds a little...illegal."

"I never said that, Connor. Don't put words in my mouth." His face reddened. "I'm explicitly saying I will never approve Petra getting that role. She is where she belongs, serving you."

My eye twitched, and I tapped my toe in a pattern to prevent myself from exploding.

My wife was out at dinner with her high school boyfriend, one who she had fond memories of and spoke highly of. She had wanted to leave me a week ago. Dennis is sexist, so he's against Petra and wants me to do him a favor. What the fuck was my life anymore? How was this my day-to-day? When was the last time I enjoyed this place?

Speaking of places where we belong...I belonged with my wife.

"Our meeting is over. Thanks for stopping in." I stood and grabbed my jacket off the hook. I put it on, then turned to find Dennis staring at me. I remained quiet. I found that when awful people are left in silence, they fill it with more bullshit that can be used against them later.

"You're leaving me after I busted my ass to have this meeting with you?"

"Yes." I buttoned the coat, eyeing my watch. I'd get caught in traffic, but I could be back in Cherrywood in ninety minutes. I pocketed my phone and signed out of my computer, all while ignoring Dennis's sighs.

"I'm not done talking."

I arched a brow, waiting. He'd fold. He loved hearing himself talk. It took one minute before he stood and sputtered.

"I can't believe you wasted my time like this. Your father will hear about this, and honestly, he's gonna agree that maybe you shouldn't be in this role. You're not cutthroat enough anymore."

"Hmm." I marched toward the door and opened it. "By all means, have the board vote. Now leave my office."

He blinked, his face in utter shock at my audacity. I'd put up with his bullshit for years, catering to him, worried about how he'd mess up my career, but look where that got me. *I* wasn't happy. My wife wasn't happy. What was the point then?

"You have no right to speak—"

"Before you finish that sentence, Dennis, let me remind you that you had me wait three hours for you today. You could've been here at two, and we could've talked about next year's plans or my ideas, but instead, you wanted me to be a pawn in some game of power. I might report to the board, but you are one voice out of five. My work speaks for itself, so please, take a vote. Remove me as CEO if you see fit. Now, I have to get back to my wife. Excuse me."

I left him there, mouth agape, with a new spring in my gait. This would probably hurt my career here, but it was the right choice. Laney had called my ass out. I hadn't put her first in years. I had put this fucking company first, and I refused to believe in a life where this place ruled me. Dennis could call a board meeting and fire me right now. But that could happen at any point. Why live or lead in fear if it could be pulled out from under me at any second?

The ringing of my phone didn't take long, and I knew it wouldn't. My dad's name popped up on my dash as I pulled onto the highway. I wanted to focus on Laney when I got to her, so I answered, preparing myself for a beating.

"Go ahead, let me have it," I answered.

"You are a fucking idiot! How dare you speak to Dennis that way? Are you kidding me? He has done so much for your career, and you treat him like that? And Petra? Please. Connor, she's worthless. You could hire ten of her. I know this separation with Laney is upsetting you, but this isn't you. Get your head out of your ass and go back to the son I know. Get a new wife. Get a new assistant, but be a CEO. You're too emotional right now, and it's disgusting."

"You done?" I gripped the steering wheel, clenching my teeth as my body reacted to his words. They hurt me like he wanted them to. I had catered to Dennis and worried about my father's influence so much that it affected the trajectory of my life. It didn't matter that I was in my thirties; I still wanted my dad's approval, but would that keep me warm at night? Would my dad's approval make me happy? No.

"What the hell did you ask me?"

"If you are done throwing a fit." I barely recognized my voice anymore. "You want me to act like a CEO so damn bad, watch me. I'm running this company the way I want, with or without you and Dennis. Unless you want to ask how my holidays are going, or how Laney is, do not call me."

I hung up.

My skin felt too damn tight, and regret clogged my throat—but it was done and over. It wasn't worth worrying about something I couldn't take back. My father tried calling again, but I ignored it and focused on driving safely to Cherrywood.

An hour and a half later, I made the choice to crash the pizza place. But as I stood outside the doors, I hesitated. I hadn't asked Laney if I could join or if she'd want to see me. She was still inside, sitting in a booth next to some pretty blonde, both of them laughing. They had drank at least two pitchers of beer, and one dude was standing up and acting out a scene from somewhere. The adrenaline from the showdown with Dennis and my dad had worn off, and now, as I watched my wife seem happy without me, I panicked.

I could text her first. See if she'd welcome my presence.

"Uh, what are you doing staring in the window like a weirdo?"

I spun, surprised to see Petra standing near me. "What are you doing here?"

"I'm staying in this tiny-ass town and bored out of my mind. The hotel guy told me this was a cool spot." She pursed her lips. "Not sure how the meetings went today, but my email and phone are blowing up."

"Total disaster." I smiled through my words. "Worth it. I could blow everything up, Petra. I want you to know that if it does get blown up, I'll make sure you land on your feet."

Her nostrils flared. "I appreciate the sentiment. However, I need context."

"Didn't go well with Dennis today." I rocked back on my heels, not wanting to hash this out. "I should—"

"Hey, guys." Laney pushed the door open, her gaze moving from Petra to me and then back.

"Laney, hi." Petra jumped back a foot, her face turning red as she stuttered. "I-I just walked up. I'm not with him."

Laney frowned and stared at me with a what-the-hell-is-going-on look.

"I was debating on walking in to surprise you or not when Petra showed up based on a hotel recommendation. Apparently, this is a hopping spot."

"It is, yeah." Laney sighed and wrapped her arms around her stomach. "You're back."

I nodded, finally smiling. "I wanted to see you."

She gave me a small grin before she met my gaze again.

"I'm heading back to my parents'. My stomach has been weird today, so I'm calling it an early night."

"I'll drive you."

"I should take my car back in case it snows."

I waved my hand in the air. "We'll get it tomorrow. If you don't feel well, I'm driving you back."

"Okay." She shrugged. "Petra, go inside and ask for Tessa, Travis, and Matt. They're a great group and would gladly show you around. I'll text them now."

"Uh, great, thanks." Petra rarely seemed nervous, but my assistant was a mess.

"Laney."

"Yeah?" My wife pushed her hair out of her eyes and stared at Petra without an ounce of dislike or anger.

"Can we...get a coffee this week? Or dessert? Or something?"

Laney didn't even take a second before nodding. "Yeah, that sounds nice."

Petra nodded, and her face returned to her usual mask of not giving a fuck. "Great. If you can find a place, I can arrange a car to pick us up."

Laney chuckled at that. "We're not in the city, Petra. I'll meet you in the café at the hotel. Barb runs it and makes the best cinnamon rolls you've ever had in your life. I'm not sure how long you're in town, but let's try Friday morning?"

"Done. Seven a.m.?"

"Hmm, life is a little slower here. How about eight?

"See you then."

Petra steeled her shoulders and walked into the pizza place, leaving my wife and me standing outside in the cold. All the nerves and worries from the day slipped away as I pulled her toward me.

"Honesty. I feel like I can breathe now that I'm with you again."

"Honesty," she whispered, her face smooshed against my chest. "Me too."

"Let's get you home. Do you want me to stop and get soup anywhere? Or crackers?"

She gave me a gooey smile, the one that had made me fall in love with her ten years ago.

"Maybe we can convince my parents to let you spend the night?"

"Not yet, but soon." I kissed her softly and asked something I should've been asking the last five years. "I want to hear all about your event today. Can you show me some photos?"

CHAPTER THIRTEEN

LANEY

Friday morning arrived fast. Connor had yet to spend the night or do more than kiss me—which was starting to annoy me. He'd work all day and then spend dinner or the evening with me without his phone on him.

Our time together couldn't possibly last, but I was enjoying it. He even somehow found a Polaroid camera and snapped a few photos of us. Then he created a makeshift collage out of them.

He was being too freaking cute. It made my stomach flutter, yet the flutters turned to nerves at the thought of meeting Petra at the hotel. She had never, once, asked me for coffee the whole time she and Connor have been working together. She was always polite to me. She'd sit by me at work events, chatting with me. But never just the two of us. I even tried asking Connor about it, but he shook his head and said he wasn't getting involved. He did share that he'd told Petra I came first, and if that wasn't clear, then that was on him, and everyone in the company should know I was a priority.

"How's the tum?" My dad leaned against the kitchen counter, dressed in his usual uniform of jeans and a dorky T-shirt. It read I HAVE A DIVERSE PORTFOLIO with different photos of tools.

"Better, yeah." I rubbed my gut. "Still a little weird midmorning, but as long as I eat and it's not empty, I'm okay."

"Good. Your mom wants to try this new recipe tonight, and I want to support her, but you gotta nod and tell her it's awesome, even if it's not."

My lips quirked. "Dad."

"Don't give me that look. Sometimes you have to lie a little bit to keep the peace. She thinks I love asparagus, but you wanna know something? I hate it. I hate that food so much, but twice a month she bakes it with bacon and watches me with this smile on her face, so I choke it down." He laughed and wet a towel, then wiped the counter as he glanced over his shoulder at me. "If tonight's recipe has asparagus, I might not survive."

I laughed, definitely picturing meals from childhood that involved that vegetable. "You know she wouldn't care, right?"

He recoiled. "Are you kidding? She'd be devastated and then pissed. Nope. It's a lie I started before we married, and now I have to stick with it. It's the only secret we have." He pointed a finger at me. "So zip it."

"Yes, sir, but, Dad, I don't think I can do dinner."

"Why the hell not?"

"Connor asked me on a date."

He waved his hand in the air. "Bring him too, then. We're supporting your mom's new recipe, so your butt needs to be here."

"Why do I feel fourteen again?"

"Because you're always gonna be our baby, even if you're thirtysomething." He pushed off the counter and kissed the top of my head. "Gotta run to the store for a bit. Can't afford much help now, so it's gonna be me. Be home by five, sharp."

"Yes, Father."

His chat put me in a better mood, giving me something positive to think about on my drive to meet Petra. I loved how much my parents loved each other. Lying about liking a food for that many years... It was weirdly cute. I wasn't sure about Connor's evening plans, but I texted him the update.

> **Laney:** Hey, my dad insisted I be home to try my mom's new recipe tonight. Can we eat with my parents then do the date?
>
> **Connor:** 100%.
>
> **Laney:** Cool, thank you.
>
> **Connor:** I love your parents. Thank you for inviting me.

Frowning, I was suddenly hit by the realization that I hadn't really invited him over to spend time with my family the last week or so. I'd kept us dating separately, and that wasn't right. My parents were a huge part of me, and yeah, having Connor join us for dinner was another great next step.

Now I just had to survive this coffee date.

I pushed open the doors to the hotel, immediately inhaling the mixture of pastries, coffee beans, pine trees, and wood from a fire. The onslaught of smells had me pause. They were so strong. Wow, it smelled like the holidays.

"Laney, good morning." Petra wore black slacks and a white turtleneck. Her hair was pulled up in a high ponytail, and she wore very little makeup. She was a striking woman, and today was no different. "Thank you for meeting me here."

"How are you liking the hotel so far? Barb's family has owned it forever."

She shrugged, a very not-Petra gesture. "It's fine. Pleasant. Everyone is so damn nice."

Smiling, I motioned toward the coffee shop. "Yeah, that's Cherrywood for ya. Did you enjoy the pizza place?"

She didn't answer right away, but a light dusting of blush covered her cheeks. "I did, yes."

That blush was very curious, but I ignored it and focused on the conversation. I was the queen of pretending things were chill while my insides went to war. That was now. "Good, glad you enjoyed it."

We quickly ordered, and our drinks were brought to our small table in the corner. Every table had an ornament hanging from a hook on it. Each ornament had been decorated by a student. Ours was a snowman, but a futuristic one with six lumps and metal teeth. Melody Haines—grade five.

"Now that we have our coffee, there are things I'd like to discuss with you." Petra sat straight and placed her palms on the table.

She reminded me of my husband. All business. Hard to crack. Focused. Too intense. Even now, she stood out like a sore thumb in this happy, cozy place.

I sipped my chai latte and waited.

Petra blinked a few times, her mouth opening and closing before she slunk into her chair, her expression crumbling. "I don't know how to start. I had this whole speech planned, apologizing, probably too many times, but I'm blank. There is nothing."

My gut churned. This was the woman who had replaced me in some ways. I hated the term *work wife*, but she kinda was. She spent all this time with Connor at work, more hours with him a week than I did. She canceled our dinners, made reservations, knew our life. My hand shook around the warm mug, and I slowly exhaled. It was clear she was rattled, and that this mattered to her.

It took a lot of gumption to reach out to me when she must know what was going on in my marriage. Yet I remained quiet. I didn't owe her a thing, and while I did genuinely like her, I didn't have to make it easier on her.

"Look, I want to say sorry to your face." She pressed her lips together, her icy expression softening. "And tell you that... God, this is hard. There has never been, and will never be, anything—" Her voice cracked. "Between Connor and me."

A flash of anger went through me when I realized that Connor freaking told her about my insecurities. An image of the two of them talking, Connor explaining that yeah, *My wife thinks we cheated*, and Petra being like *haha, no way*. But the second I had the thought, I brushed it away. No, that was not what happened.

"I know," I said calmly. "I'm not sure why you're telling me this. I don't know how this came up, but I know there is nothing."

The determined look returned to Petra's face, and she leaned forward. "I assure you, Connor refused to share anything personal with me. I asked, and he said no. This is part of what I want to explain, to apologize for. It's been brutal handling the divorce, and focusing on work, ignoring everything else, became my obsession. It became my life. Because of that, I stopped caring about things that matter." She took a shaky breath and met my eyes head-on. "I want nothing but happiness for Connor, and you, and I forgot. If something got in the way of my mission, then it didn't matter. Lunches with you? No. Dinners? Not if we had to have a meeting. He'd push and say he'd have to leave early, but then I'd pack on so many things, that he'd forget or couldn't."

She pinched her nose, rolling her shoulders before meeting my eyes again. "I hate fucking up, but I did. And Laney, I'm sorry."

"Thank you," I said, taking my time. She had dropped a lot of information on me, and while I appreciated her directness, it didn't change all that much. "It's brave of you to meet with me to say all this. Truly. I appreciate it. I like you, Petra. I think you're good to Connor at work and a solid human. I still remember you brought me, like, ten soups that weekend I was sick."

"Connor said you hadn't eaten in days."

That reminded me of my sore stomach, but I brushed the thought away.

"I'm going to be honest with you."

She bristled. "Please, let me have it."

I snorted. "I'm not angry at you or upset. I really admire your honesty, but Connor is a grown man. He made his choices on his own. I'm sure he told you we're working on our marriage this month—"

"He told me that, and when I offered to help, he told me absolutely not. That he needed to win you back on his own." She half smiled. "Because that man is very much in love with you."

My face heated. "He is. Love isn't always enough, and that's what we're figuring out." I stared around the coffee shop, the weight growing in my core at how badly I wanted to stay in my hometown. I wanted to be happy with Connor and stay here, but I knew those options were not likely to happen.

"He's making changes." Petra lowered her voice, her tone sharp again. "Has he...told you about them?"

I flinched. "No."

She nodded, an *oh shit* expression on her face flashing for a second.

"Then he has his reasons. Probably wants to surprise you, so pretend you didn't hear this, please."

"Sure." I forced a smile, hating that they had another secret together. She was probably right, that he was planning to surprise me, but it didn't make the sting feel any better. I'd tried asking about work three times, and every time he brushed it off, saying we'd talk later. When he was ready.

"I don't have a lot of girlfriends. I'm too brash, too cold, and I never text back. But I'd like to...maybe not be friends, but could we..." Petra trailed off, her cheeks a bright red now. "Grab a drink every month or so?"

My heart clenched. She really was a lot like Connor. He didn't have a lot of friends either. He kept to himself, but I had broken through his walls. It was very clear the two of them had a solid friendship and working relationship because they were carbon copies of each other. I saw that now, even more clearly.

If she truly was like him, then life outside of work had to be tough.

"Yes. We can grab a drink once a month."

Her entire body relaxed as she smiled. This time, her face changed entirely. "Thank you. That means a lot, Laney. Wow. I didn't realize how nervous I was."

I chuckled. I liked seeing her genuine feelings and not the robot she usually was. "I had no idea what today was about, but I like how it's going now."

"You matter to me. Not only as my boss's wife, but as a person, as the person who makes Connor happiest. I should've made more of an effort before, but as I said...I was focused on the wrong things. Next year, my priorities will be different."

"Cheers to that." I held up my tea, and she clinked it. Then she asked me a question that almost had me falling out of my chair.

"Now, can you tell me about this Matt Heathen character? He was very flirty and nice last night. There is no way a human being can be that nice..."

* * * *

The rest of the day, I edited photos from the last two weeks, posted them on my website, created some social media posts, and kept chuckling at the thought of Petra and Matt. They were complete opposites, but it somehow made sense.

Small-town life didn't fit Petra, but if she ever gave it a chance, then Matt would be perfect for her.

"Laney, your man is at the door!" My mom's voice rang up the stairs.

Butterflies exploded inside me. I wore my favorite jeans and an old plaid shirt that Connor had given me. It hung loosely, but I loved the feel of the fabric. My hair was curled, up in a high pony, and I felt cute. I felt good.

Dancing down the stairs, I stopped and wiped my palms on my legs before opening the door. Connor stood there, his wide grin matching my own, and we both moved toward each other at the same time. He picked me up, crushing his mouth against mine in a deep, soul-crushing kiss.

How could I miss him when I had seen him yesterday?

"Hi, baby," he murmured against my lips, without breaking our embrace or our kiss. "Missed you."

Despite our entire history, I blushed. Giggling, I slid down his body, my hands lingering on his shoulders as I found my footing. His eyes danced today; his posture seemed lighter.

Then it hit me. "You seem happy."

"I am." He intertwined our fingers and grinned wide at me. "Feels like a big step to be invited to dinner at your parents'. I'm excited. I love your mom and dad, and I've been thinking about you all day."

"You crossed my mind a few times too." I beamed at him, loving how he rolled his eyes and pulled me toward him.

"You're wearing my old shirt." His nostrils flared, heat in his gaze. "You look really good in it."

A part of me wanted to seduce Connor, entice him to do more than just kiss me. It was driving me wild that he'd kiss me, get me hot, and then leave. He loved seeing me in his shirts, he always had, and a whoosh of anticipation made me feel warm.

He ran his hand down my side, digging his fingers into my waist as his lips parted. "Laney—"

"Hey, Connor! My man! My son-in-law! My neighbor!"

My dad interrupted the moment. My dear father wore an ugly Christmas sweater with my mom's face all over it. He had had it custom-made last year and thought it was the funniest thing ever.

"What can I get you to drink? Beer? Wine?"

"Hi, Mr. Whitfield. Good to see you." Connor held out his hand, and my dad eyed it like a bomb.

"Give me a hug like family, fool." Then my dad wrapped his arms around Connor. My husband's gaze found mine over my dad's shoulder, and he seemed amused. He patted my dad's back, trying to escape the hug while my dad lingered.

We were lingerers. A hug could last two seconds or thirty, depending on the day.

"Okay, leave the poor guy alone," I chimed in.

"I missed him. I wanted a hug." My dad winked at me. "Now, drinks?"

"Beer would be great, thank you." Connor immediately moved next to me, his cologne and body heat soothing me. "Honey, you want something?"

"I'll stick with water."

Connor frowned. "You still not feeling well?"

"This morning was better, but I want to play it safe." I hated throwing up. It was the worst, and I really didn't want to throw up again. "I might even have tea."

"I'll make it for you." Connor's frown deepened, and he kissed the top of my head before disappearing into the kitchen, leaving my dad alone with me in the front hallway.

"You can't divorce him, Laney."

"Wow, what happened to supporting me?"

"Of course, we will, but that man is in love with you. Wild about you. It's easy to see. Are you...feeling better about things with him?"

"I think so, yeah." I chewed my lip, not expecting my dad to ask me this with Connor in the house. "Could we talk about this later, maybe when he's not here?"

"Oh. Right." My dad flinched. "I just like seeing you two happy. That's all. With you both here in town for so long, it's been nice hanging out and spending time with you."

My eyes prickled. I nodded and gave him a quick, two-second hug. "Thanks for being such a good dad."

"I charge by the hour."

I chuckled, relieved from the tension that had been building in my shoulders. While I was mostly secure in my feelings about Connor, we still hadn't discussed work or the fact that I wanted to live here—two hurdles that would be very hard to overcome.

CHAPTER FOURTEEN

CONNOR

Dinner was amazing. I couldn't remember the last time we spent time at Laney's parents' house, enjoying a nice meal, playing cards, and laughing. Her parents were a complete hoot and kind. A stabbing, guilty feeling ached in my gut over my relationship with my dad, but I refused to let anything ruin this moment.

Laney was happy, looking beautiful in my shirt, and kept leaning her head on my shoulder.

Her mom yawned, covering her mouth as she eyed the clock. "Oh my, I'm gonna head upstairs to bed."

"It's only nine, woman." Her dad laughed, but then they did a silent communication thing where her mom glared, he glared back, then she arched a brow, and he stood.

"Yup, I'm tired too."

Laney snorted. "Be more subtle, please."

"Subtle? About what?" Her mom winked and picked up the cards, placing them on a side table. "You two hang out. Talk. It's just really nice seeing you both so happy."

"Thanks, Mom." Laney's voice was soft and genuine, and she somehow snuggled closer to me without sitting on me. Disappointment hit me at the night ending. I wasn't ready to go back to the silent house next door.

"You sure you both can't handle another round?"

"No, dear." Her mom grinned and jutted her head upstairs. "We'll be up there. Hopefully, we'll see you again soon, Connor."

"Absolutely."

Her parents went upstairs, leaving us alone. Her mom's comment had to mean something good. If they wanted to see me again, that meant Laney wasn't saying how awful I had been the last few years.

"That was fun," I said, slowly standing so Laney wouldn't fall down.

"Are you leaving?" Laney frowned and wrapped her arms around herself. Her gaze seemed sad, like she didn't want me to leave.

"The night is wrapping up."

"Yeah, but..." She stared at me a beat before sighing. "You need to go back and work, don't you?"

"No." I frowned. Was I playing this thing wrong? Was leaving after dates, giving her space, the wrong move? "Is that what you think I've been doing all these nights?"

Her eyes flicked to me, questions and doubt swirling in them. "You don't tell me anything about work. Petra hinted at something today, and it hurt to not have any idea what she was talking about. And you always leave after we have a great time."

"Honesty," I whispered, my heart racing at how my plan had backfired. I crouched back down so we were eye to eye.

"I want to surprise you with the changes, and they aren't ready yet. I didn't want to get your hopes up for something in case it didn't happen."

"I appreciate that, sure, but you used to run all those ideas by me at the start. It still feels like you're cutting me out of the conversation. I know you run the business, but I liked when it felt like we were a team."

Fuck.

I plopped onto the chair, gutted. I thought we were doing better. I thought we had made progress, and the worry that she could still ask me to sign the divorce papers was dwindling, but now the doubt fired right back.

"Laney, honey, I'm sorry. I never realized you would feel that way about it."

"Honesty," she said, swallowing. "I should've told you sooner."

I nodded as she moved closer to me, running her fingers through my hair. Her touch felt so good, and I closed my eyes, leaning into her. She used to do this while watching a TV show, and every single time, I'd pass out.

"Why have you been leaving these past few nights after we have such a good time? If it's not to work, then what do you do?"

"Literally replay the night and think of ways to make you smile the next time," I said, keeping my eyes closed as her fingers made circles on my scalp. "I thought I was doing what you wanted, keeping my distance, dating you. Did I...play that wrong?"

Her fingers stilled, and I glanced at her. A blush covered her cheeks, and she cleared her throat. Now I was desperate to know what she was thinking. I knew that look.

"What if I don't want the dates to end?"

The disappointment zapped out of me. "I don't want them to end either. I hope you know I mean it when I say I want to spend every second with you."

She smiled. "So...are you going back to the house alone or..."

She looked at me with those heated, gorgeous eyes. She wet her lips, and while I also wanted to lick her entire body, my mind was working overtime. Laney didn't like the fact that Petra mentioned something that morning—I'd need to talk to her about that. But Laney also didn't like feeling that we weren't a team.

To include her, I could share my plans. At least, part of my plans. I cupped her head softly, holding her as I kissed her.

"I think you should come over with me."

"I think so too, Mr. Reynolds."

"Mr. Reynolds?" I arched a brow. "Hmm, that was kinda hot."

"Stop." She swatted my hand and stood, the rosy blush still on her cheeks. "Let me grab my coat quick."

Within a minute, we were buttoned up and walking toward the house next door. My lust-filled brain knew Laney wanted to be touched. We'd had a very healthy sex life, and I knew she had to be struggling. I was too, but it was different. I didn't want this to be about having sex and then she goes back to her parents and nothing changes.

This has to mean something.

"Still so weird to me that this house is for rent," she said as we walked in. "I grew up coming here for some cookies and cocoa."

"Yeah?"

"I loved the small-town life. It was warm and cozy."

She spoke in the past tense, but I knew what she meant.

"It's great here. I see why you love it so much. We really should visit more often. It's only an hour or so drive."

"Yeah. Visiting more would be... nice."

I knew she wanted to move back here, but I refused to let that ruin the evening.

"Come here."

She sucked in a breath as she walked toward me. I undid her coat and slid it off her shoulders, tossing it on the back of a chair before pulling her toward me by her belt.

"Did you want to tease me by wearing my shirt tonight?"

She nodded, her eyes lighting up with mischief.

"It worked." I kissed her neck, inhaling her perfume. The way the oils mixed with her skin, oof. It drove me wild. My body ached for her.

"You're so fucking pretty, Laney."

"Connor." Her voice was hoarse. She untucked my shirt, her hands landing on my stomach, and I hissed.

"Cold, cold," I teased.

"Oh, stop it." She giggled, and I wanted to eat the sound. I moved my lips from her neck to her mouth, slowing us down a beat.

"Baby," I said between kisses, "I'm going to make you feel good, but I want to show you something first."

She protested, and it was the cutest sound. "Are you sure?"

"Very sure." I kissed her again, then leaned back. "We're teammates, forever, and I need to treat you like one."

Her lips parted, like my comment shocked her, but then she nodded. "I'd like that."

"Then come with me."

I'd never overlook or take for granted the way Laney took my hand and followed me. She trusted me, even after months of heartbreak, and I'd never ruin that again. I brought us toward the kitchen counter where all the papers and plans sat. Petra had printed them all out—the ideas, the job description, and what a typical month would look like in her new role.

I even had a backup plan. If the board voted me out, with my dad's and Dennis's influence, then I'd need to start somewhere else. I'd learned a ton in my CEO role, and starting my own gig wouldn't be too hard. Sure, long hours, but I could control them.

"I don't like that Petra hinted at me keeping something from you."

"No, it wasn't like that." Laney stopped at the edge of the counter, eyeing all the papers. "She actually told me you refused her help to win me back."

I tried to see if there was a tone hidden in there or a worry or concern wedged deep. Scanning her face, I saw no signs of worry. I kissed her wrist, noting the way her lips parted at the gesture.

"You gave me a month to prove to you that I can be the spouse you need, and there was no way I was doing that with anyone's help. If I couldn't earn your trust back on my own, then I don't deserve you."

Laney swallowed as her gaze drifted from me to the papers. My words moved her. I could tell, but her quiet response had me shifting my weight.

"She also asked me to get coffee with her once a month."

Okay, that surprised me. "What did you say?"

"Yes." She laughed, meeting my gaze as her fingers ran over the counter. "She is a lot like you. She apologized for any role she played in our troubles, explained why she is so driven. I like her and can see why she'd be a huge asset. I just didn't like feeling replaced."

"You'd never be replaced." I spun her around, pressing her back into the counter. Her eyes widened as I gripped her waist. "You are my wife, the best part of my life."

"Connor," she whispered, her heart in her eyes, "I know that, truly. I just—"

I kissed her neck, tugging her ear before sliding my hands under the plaid shirt. Her skin was so damn warm.

"I'm not done showing you how you are everything. Let me walk you through something."

"With your mouth on me?"

"Mm-hmm." I slowly dragged my hands over her ribs, cupping the underside of her breasts and groaning. She squirmed on the counter, the movement rubbing against my erection, and I leaned into her.

"Fuck, I've missed your body. You're so sexy," I said.

Her breathing picked up, and I grazed my palms over her hardened nipples, damn well knowing she'd like that. She jumped, and I pushed her bra out of the way and tugged on her pebbled tips. She had the best tits, and I loved to play with them.

"Take off your shirt for me, baby," I murmured, watching the way her chest heaved. She whipped off the plaid shirt and bra and lay on the counter with her breasts bare.

"Goddamn." I licked my lips, the only warning before I sucked one tip into my mouth. Laney arched her back and grabbed my hair, holding me tightly against her.

"Yes, oh yes."

I smiled, flicking her nipple with my tongue before soothing it. I alternated between each breast, hoping she realized she was my queen.

"You are my wife. You come for me with my business plans all around us."

She shuddered as I met her eyes. They were filled with lust. All dilated. Red splotches on her cheeks.

"How are you...talking and doing this?"

"I'm dedicated." I winked before unbuttoning the top of her pants. "Can I make you feel good, baby? Please?"

"When you ask like that..." Her throaty voice went straight to my cock. It swelled, and I wanted nothing more than to sink into her. She stared at me with so much love and want that it threatened my self-control.

"I want you to read the paper to your left." I untied her shoes, setting them to the side, then I slid her pants down. "The one with the dark header at the top."

"W-what?" She frowned.

"You're going to read that while my mouth is on you." I grinned up at her. "Your challenge is to not come until you've read every word."

"Connor!" she scolded, but she had a huge smile on her face. "This is a lot of words."

"Read fast then, baby."

I slid her panties over her thighs, groaning at the sight. My wife was stunning and wet, for me. I inhaled her musky scent, nipping at her inner thighs as she moaned my name. I glanced up at her, finding her watching me.

"Read," I commanded before sliding my tongue between her folds. She bucked, but the paper was at least in her hand.

That paper was the memo I had typed up—hadn't sent—but was going to share with the board Monday morning. It laid out the new structure with Petra, allowing me to have more time at home.

No more than four work dinners a month, max. Board retreats once a quarter, if not a year. If they needed to meet weekly, they could with Petra. If that didn't show Laney I was serious, I wasn't sure what would.

I held both her thighs around my face, finding her swollen nerve with my mouth, and sucked. It had been weeks since my mouth was on her, tasting her and driving her wild. Sweat pooled on her skin, the dampness all around my face as I slid a finger into her. She trembled now. Her thighs shook and tightened around me.

"You're close," I said, flattening my tongue against her. "You finish reading it all yet, baby?"

She made a sound, something like a whine and a moan before she threw the paper on the ground, gripped my hair tight, and screamed my name.

"Yes, Connor, oh my God!"

She came hard. Her legs shook around me, but I never stopped. I stroked and let her ride out the pleasure as long as possible, watching the way her body reacted. She had a mole on her lower stomach that looked like a heart. She had a scar on her inner thigh from a nail on a bench when she was a kid. I knew this woman inside out, and I'd never forget her.

When she stilled, I pressed a soft kiss on her skin before she slid off the counter and wrapped her arms around my shoulders. She trembled, and my stomach clenched.

I cupped the back of her head and held her against me. "What do you need, baby?"

"I can't believe...you're..." She lifted her head and sniffed. "Are you sure?"

"Sure about what?" I scanned her face, totally confused. She was butt naked, face still flushed from an orgasm, and yet tears filled her eyes.

"Stepping away from the CEO role? That's all you've ever wanted."

"I'm not stepping away. I'm adjusting." I pushed her hair behind her ear, smiling softly at her. "I'm pivoting. I still get to do the things I enjoy, bossing others around and making money—"

She rolled her eyes. We both knew I loved the challenge and problem-solving required of the role. I kissed her nose and continued, "We're not where I want to be. There are a lot of hurdles still, I won't lie to you. There's a chance this won't happen. That was the only reason I hadn't told you about it yet, because I didn't want you to get your hopes up."

"You idiot." She grinned so widely that she looked like a cartoon. "The fact you're even thinking about this means so much. I could just...damn it. Come here."

She grabbed my face and kissed me so hard that it knocked me on my back. The air rushed out of my lungs. Her hair hung in waves, her perfect round breasts were almost in my face, and she clung to me.

"I need you. I need you right now. Please. Let me feel your heart."

My chest ached. She used to ask to feel my heart when she felt overwhelmed. She said there was something about the rhythm, when your heartbeat connected with another. It had been too damn long since she asked me that, and my eyes prickled a little.

"Get naked. Right now." She tugged at my shirt, the awkward angle making it get stuck on my shoulder.

"Move faster, Connor."

"Baby," I chuckled, kissing her quickly as I tossed my shirt to the side, "we have all night. We can slow down."

"No. I need to be close to you. I...I fucking love you so much it hurts."

She rarely cussed. She rarely said *fuck*. To hear her exclaim that to me right now? Holy shit. My heart raced, and I held her to me. I didn't realize how much I needed those words. They reassured me that we'd be okay, we could survive this, and relief so strong, so powerful rolled through me that I had to close my eyes and breathe.

Laney kissed me, drawing me back, and I shuddered at the way she stared at me, like she needed me.

Somehow, we removed my clothes. Laney slid onto me while on the kitchen floor of her parents' neighbor's house.

It had been the right choice to show her the plan. I vowed, then and there, to never keep anything from her again.

CHAPTER FIFTEEN

LANEY

"You feel so good," I whispered, my eyes watering on their own. "You feel so right."

"We feel so right." Connor sat up so we were chest to chest, his large arms surrounding me as our foreheads touched. His voice was shaky. I'd never heard this much emotion from him before.

"This is you and me, Laney. We're good together," he whispered, his lips brushing mine as he spoke.

I nodded as a tear trickled down my face, rolling over my lips and down my chin. He wiped it with his thumb, licked it, and in one smooth motion, lifted us up off the floor.

I gasped. "What are you—"

"I'm not fucking my wife on the floor." His muscles rippled as he carried us toward the couch. It was so hot. He had picked me up like I was nothing, still holding tight on to me.

"You ate me out on the counter," I teased, tugging his earlobe with my teeth. He shuddered, and I dragged my tongue down his neck. He smelled like my pleasure, but with sweat mixed in.

"You just told me you fucking love me." He sat on the couch and positioned me on his lap so his cock slid right into me. His gorgeous eyes were filled with lust and love and happiness.

"I need you like this, close to me, where I can see and feel every inch of you."

I gasped when he thrust up, hitting me deep in a wonderful, pleasurable way.

"You're so sexy, Connor." I rocked my hips, taking more of him until he groaned. He gripped my butt and buried his face in my neck, the scruff from his jaw tickling. I couldn't laugh though, not when this felt too good, too important.

He sucked my collarbone as I grinded against him in a perfected rhythm. We'd had sex on the couch before, but never like this. Each kiss felt like ten. The way his hands dragged over my back and ass and then returned to gently cradle my head felt like a declaration.

His throat bobbed when he tilted my chin to stare at me. "Thank you," he whispered. "For giving me—us—another chance."

My eyes prickled, but he didn't give me a second to cry. He kissed me so hard that my soul rearranged itself to fit next to his.

"I love you." He kissed my cheek, my neck, my jaw. "So fucking much."

I trembled and dug my nails into his shoulders. He wasn't close enough. There was too much space, and I had this itch deep in my core, like I needed more of him. I moaned, and he stilled, a fire growing behind his gaze.

"Let me make you feel good," he said.

He flipped us over so I was on my back, and he ground into

me in a slow, deep thrust that had me arching my spine. He took his time fucking me though. He'd pause, suck my breasts until they stung, then kiss them better. He whispered how much he loved me, how much he loved us, before pulling out and spreading my pussy with his tongue.

I'd never seen him like this.

Heat coursed through me. My limbs were on fire, and my throat ached with the need to cry, or orgasm. He brought me to the brink with his mouth before sliding his cock back inside, pinching my clit and causing me to explode. I saw stars, and my ears rang as he watched me, praising me.

"You're so pretty when you come, baby." His eyes lit up. "Nothing better than you like this. Not a fucking thing."

I had barely caught my breath before he lifted one of my legs, kissing my calf and bending my knee so he could thrust deeper. My eyes about rolled to the back of my head when he pinched my nipple.

"No, Laney, you watch us. I want all of you."

Connor had always been demanding in bed, taking charge and always ensuring I was taken care of, but this new version of us was hotter, more intense.

"You're so sexy," I blurted out, my face flushing.

"For you. Only for you."

We didn't speak again after that. Connor took his time with me, kissing or massaging every part of me as he went deeper and deeper. My muscles ached, and my chest heaved, yet the fuzzy feeling of yet another orgasm rooted in my spine.

My thighs tensed, and his eyes widened before he nodded. He repositioned us so we were face-to-face, our hearts beating against each other, and whether it was the intimacy or the way he angled his hips, I fell apart a third time, him with me.

He groaned my name into my mouth, his eyes fluttering as he gripped me so hard it stung. He rested his face on my chest, his heartbeat even more erratic than mine. "Holy shit," he said, his breath dancing along my ribs. He traced my wrist with one of his fingers for a few seconds before he pushed up and crashed onto the couch next to me.

I smiled, the feeling of contentment washing over me like a blanket. Sure, there were things we had to discuss, to figure out, but we were okay. Connor and I were okay. He stared at me, one side of his mouth curving up as I chuckled.

"That was wild."

"I'll say." He pushed his hair out of his face before arching up and leaning toward me. He traced my jaw with his thumb, the most tender expression on his face. "You are exquisite in every way."

Flushing, I glanced away, but he shook his head and made me face him.

"No, this is important. You are my other half, Laney, and I stopped treating you that way. I never stopped loving you, not for a second, but that doesn't excuse the pain I caused you. I am so deeply sorry, but I'm... grateful and excited to learn this new version of us."

I nodded, my stupid eyes welling again.

"I think I am too."

He kissed my lips before standing and offering me his hand. "Come, let's shower."

We used to shower together all the time. Not in a sexy,

let's-have-sex-in-the-shower way, but more in an intimate way where we would talk. He'd wash my hair and tell me about his plans that day, and I'd repeat it on him. I ached for those moments.

"Brilliant idea, husband."

His eyes flashed with heat. "I love it when you call me that, but be careful. That word makes me feel things."

I snorted. "What kind of things, husband?"

He growled and led me to the shower, where, yeah, we washed each other, but we ended up having more fun in there too. My heart burst because it was so happy, despite a small part in the back of my mind that was telling me I had missed something. It was hard to focus on that blip when Connor was all around me. I pushed the worry away and lived in the moment. My husband and I were back together.

* * * *

Morning, baby.

A deep voice woke me up, and I groaned. The bed was too comfy, too warm, too him.

"No."

A soft laugh followed, and then Connor's hand ran down my leg. I'd slept in just one of his large shirts last night, and it was the best sleep I'd gotten in years.

"I forgot how fucking cute and grumpy you are in the morning." He sat on the bed, the smell of coffee drifting around him. He repositioned me so my head was on his lap, and he played with the ends of my hair. "I haven't woken up with you in some time, huh?"

I shook my head. Despite our new connection, there were memories of *before* that lingered, reminding me of the reality of why we had to be here in a rented house.

"Been a while," I said, not opening my eyes. I liked being woken up by him.

He massaged my neck and scalp as he sighed. "New rule—we always wake up together."

"What if you—"

"I know there will be random days you need to leave early, or if one of us has a trip, but overall, I wake up with you. No more meetings before eight."

"Can you even do that?" I yawned and snuggled into him even more. He wore flannel pants that I had bought him three years ago, and the soft cotton felt nice against my face. "I didn't mind waking up alone."

"But you shouldn't have to. And I will do it. It's not about if I can anymore." He stilled and then went back to massaging my head. "What are your plans today? Do you need help taking photos?"

"Shh. Too many questions," I grumbled.

He chuckled and pulled me up so I cuddled against his chest, my legs wrapped around his middle and his hands up the back of my shirt. He smelled like home, and I buried my face into his neck, my stomach flip-flopping.

"You are fucking adorable."

"Have you always been so chatty in the morning?" I nipped his neck, causing him to yelp, and I smiled at him. "Don't recall you talking so damn much."

His eyes widened before he barked out a laugh. "Are you intentionally riling me up? Was last night not enough for you?"

"Hmm, it was fine."

"Laney Reynolds." Connor tugged on my hair until I was forced to look at him. His eyes held that wild, desperate, lusty look again, and I couldn't stop myself. I winked.

"Fuck me, you're perfect."

He kissed me, but I shoved him away. "Dude, morning breath. Come on."

He yanked me back. "You think I give a shit about morning breath?"

"Uh, yes. Normal people do?" I covered my mouth with my hand, suddenly very, very awake. I was still sore, but in the best way ever. "Now that you rudely woke me up, I'm gonna brush my teeth."

He closed his eyes and laughed. "I missed you so much. Never change, baby."

I pinched his side, running to the bathroom before he could retaliate. He wasn't lying when he said he hadn't woken up with me in a long time. These soft moments, the playful barbs... they were what made us *us*, and without all that quality time together we had forgotten what made us work.

Soph had sent me an article about love languages after the first few days at my parents' with the words *I think yours changed, girl*. I hadn't read it, but I knew of the different ways we wanted and expressed love. They were more of a framework to help discuss what you needed, and for a while, I thought mine were acts of service.

Connor bought me flowers. Sent me lunch. Helped at events. They were thoughtful acts, but now I recognized that all I wanted from him was quality time.

Waking up together. Talking over dinner. Complaining

about our jobs over lunch. I didn't want things or acts; I just wanted him.

My cheeks flushed at the realization, and I quickly brushed my teeth. But then a brief bout of dizziness came out of nowhere. I gripped the counter, my heart racing, before it settled. That was weird.

I used the mouthwash and didn't even bother fixing my hair before joining Connor in bed again.

"You look thoughtful." He opened his arms, and I crawled right into them. He felt like my home. That was the damn truth. I might not love living in the city anymore, but I wanted to be where he was. That I knew.

"I can't kiss you when you have your I'm thinking face on."

"What if I'm thinking about kissing you?"

"I'd know." He kissed my forehead. "Your eyes change color when you're turned on. It is by far the hottest part about your body. I can read you so well."

"Huh, I didn't realize that."

"What's on your mind?" he said with a nervous lilt to his tone, and he swallowed with an audible click. Like he was worried.

Even though I was the one who left and needed reassurance, he was still anxious about what I'd say. I wanted to assure my husband that we were okay. I played with his chest, dragging a finger along the smooth skin over his heart, and took a deep breath before saying, "I was thinking about love languages."

"That... was not what I was expecting."

"What were you expecting me to say?"

"That last night was too much. You're sore. You want to leave. Basically, I was drowning in self-doubt for a few minutes there. If you'd put me out of my misery, that'd be great."

"Connor." I sat up and ran a hand through his hair and over his jaw as I smiled. "Last night was amazing, and yes, I am sore, but no, I don't want to leave. That was the best sleep I've had in a damn year. I realized that my love language changed."

A dent formed between his brows, but he was focused, taking in every word with the same determination I saw him use at his office.

"Okay, can you tell me more about what that means?"

"I love all the acts and gifts you've given me, I truly have, but I don't need them. They felt like a way to buy my forgiveness, you know?"

His jaw flexed. "I don't... I'm not sure I understand. Do you not like what I've given you?"

"No, I do. Your gifts are thoughtful." I paused. This was harder than I had imagined in my head.

"I'm trying to explain that all I want or need from you is to spend quality time together. This? This is perfect. Waking up and snuggling with you. No gifts or acts required, just us being together."

He rubbed his lips as he nodded.

"Quality time."

"Yes. We don't have to do anything special either, like no extravagant dates. I just like being with you. Even if we're both sitting in the same room reading different books, that's time we're together. I think... that's what was missing. I'd have these short moments of time with you, but it wouldn't be enough, and I'd be left hurt. So every minute we did spend together, I'd be trying to get over my feelings and not enjoy us."

Connor sighed and ran a hand over my shoulder before cupping my face. "Thank you for explaining that to me. That helps me a lot."

"What's your love language? I know it used to be physical touch, but—"

"You." He smirked. "My love language is you, Laney. Everything."

"That is cheesy, although a little romantic." I blushed at the intense look in his eyes. "You're not kidding?"

"Not in the slightest. I want your touches, your time, your thoughts, your sighs, all of it." His face was serious. "What time do you have to get ready for today's events?"

"Uh, in an hour. Hence, why I wanted to sleep."

"'Hence,'" he mocked, his dimples popping out. "So fucking cute."

My pulse raced as he leaned forward, tugging the shirt up as he said, "Can I have some quality time between your thighs, wife? I promise you'll feel better than if you had slept."

I shuddered as I nodded.

Yeah, I was feeling hopeful about our future. Especially when he made good on his promise.

CHAPTER SIXTEEN

CONNOR

Father: CALL ME OR YOU WILL REGRET IT.

Father: I will do everything in my power to remove you. This behavior is appalling.

Father: You're dead to me.

Never thought my dad would go as far as to be that dramatic, but there was always a first for everything. Seeing him like this made me long for what our family could've been if my mom had survived. Neighbors always told me how she leveled him out to be a little less of a prick. The way he treated me made me want to work twice as hard to not be like him. If I wanted my marriage to last forever, then distancing myself from my father was the right choice.

The past weekend had been a dream come true. I'd been living in my Laney fantasy, spending the last two days laughing, naked, or both, but it was back to reality this Monday morning.

Back to the world where I could either lose my job or fix my life to get what I wanted—more time with my wife.

My insides turned to acid at the thought of my dad actually removing me as CEO. He could. And while the idea of walking away from all this bullshit still felt like a good idea, I wanted to do it on my terms. Not his. And after years of catering to him, I had called him on his bluff.

"It's getting bad, Connor."

I snapped my gaze to Petra. She paled and tilted her laptop toward me.

"The board is demanding a meeting next Wednesday night. You're expected to be there. Two agenda items. The first...my new position, and the second...evaluating the CEO and expectations."

A little more than a week away.

"Love that for us." I sipped the black coffee she had brought to the rental house and stared at the kitchen counter. Thoughts of Laney had me smiling but not enough to fix the dread. I'd hid it from her all weekend, enjoying our quality time together, but I had no idea what to do if the board removed me.

We had good savings, sure, and I could form a new business, but that would be starting over. More late nights. It'd be all-hands-on-deck for whoever joined me. It would mean less time with my wife, which was the whole fucking point of this.

"Petra, what can we do?"

"Your three meetings with the board members in favor of this went well. They were pleased with your vision for growth. Dennis will absolutely try to turn everyone against this idea. Bruce will also go against you. Ryan is the wildcard."

"Three votes get us what we want."

"Correct, but Dennis is vice president and will vote first. He'll blast into you and me."

I ground my teeth together. "You'll be there. I want him to say all this garbage to your face, in front of the entire room."

Petra nodded. "It's nothing I haven't heard before."

"That doesn't make it right." I paced the dining area before gripping the back of a chair. I hated feeling like I had missed something. If they wanted to talk about the CEO role, I could show growth charts and evidence of success. Yet they knew that. This was about Dennis, my father, and some fucked-up feelings I didn't understand. My CFO and CTO were in a group chat, and I immediately added Petra to it.

> *Jen:* Everything has been restored, no data exfiltrated. 100% confirmed. Checked with our ISP to verify.
>
> *CFO:* Business as usual. Nate has been fired and all access has been removed.
>
> *Petra:* Jen, can one of your cyber guys spare half a day on Nate's device?

"What are you thinking?" I asked, appreciating that our CTO and CFO were competent, intelligent people. "You still thinking there's a tie from Nate to your ex?"

She shook her head. "I think it's something bigger."

"Bigger? What does that mean?" My brain spun with a familiar ache that could only be soothed with whiskey, Laney, or sex. Sometimes, all the above. "Nate received payments that we were able to track to your ex—our lawyers are working with law enforcement to see what action we can take."

"Sure, but the way Blake has been acting…"

"Have you been speaking with him, Petra?" My tone was pure ice. "The man who tried to sabotage you, ruin our business, and make you cry?"

"I never cried, asshole." She paced on the other side of the kitchen, her hair all over the place again. "He called me four times. I finally gave in two nights ago."

"Goddamn it, Petra." The urge to say I wish you would've called me was right there, but I didn't say it. I was glad she hadn't. That night with Laney had been precious. It had repaired the foundation I'd destroyed over the last year. "What the hell did he want?"

"He assured me that he had nothing to do with what the feds were saying. He'd never do that to me."

"He stole your idea and used it in his business model. He used you to make his business thrive. He would do that to you." I placed my hands on my hips and fought the compulsion to kick the chair. "Do not let him manipulate you. You are stronger than this."

"I know, Connor. I told him to fuck off and speak to me through our lawyers. I am not an idiot, and I've seen his true colors. He did make one comment though that has me hesitating." She chewed her lip, and a nervous look crossed her face. "He said that, when they heard about our breach, their business doubled down on their protection in case someone went after them next. He made the claim that somehow Nate and Dennis know each other well."

"That's…okay, them knowing each other is not an issue." I

cracked a few knuckles and stared at the checkered wallpaper. I liked Laney's hometown, but the décor in the rental was not my flavor. "That sounds like he wanted to place doubt on him, and it's working. Dennis and Nate knowing each other isn't a big deal."

"I want to ask Jen to look into it." She pursed her lips. "Connor, you've known me for years, and I trust my gut. I have a weird feeling about this. I mean, hell, look at the timeline. The breach happened, then they're questioning the CEO role?"

"He couldn't have planned for me to try and work on my marriage."

"Sure, but a cyberattack could have major setbacks on a business. He probably thought we wouldn't be prepared enough."

"Jen knows her shit."

"Yeah, but how does he feel about women in the workplace, Connor?"

Fuck. She had me there. I pinched the bridge of my nose and nodded.

"As my proposed COO, I expect you to handle this and update me if you find anything of substance. Preferably by next Wednesday."

She was already facing her phone, her fingers flying over the device as she smiled. "Come to think of it, remember that board meeting where Jen spoke about multifactor authentication and Dennis kept rolling his eyes?"

My jaw tensed as I nodded. "What about it?"

"His attitude about the entire thing. He truly thought it wasn't a big deal. I'm right about this, boss. I feel it. I'll get you the evidence to prove it. If I get you that, then during the board meeting next week, you can share it with the rest."

She was so determined, so sure of it, that I smiled.

"Deal, Petra. Find me the shit I need to get Dennis off my back."

* * * *

After working all day, I closed my laptop at six with the hope of convincing my wife to join me for dinner. Instead of calling, I walked over to her parents' house carrying a deep red rose. Our relationship changed after this weekend. It had deepened. Even after all this time together, our connection had shifted into something else. Something with legs and heart and heat. I thought about her all day, wondering if she had eaten lunch or if she was smiling. I was content to let her lead, as long as she didn't mention divorce again.

A car I didn't recognize sat in the driveway. That should've been my first sign.

"Oh, hello, Connor." Sophia answered the door before I knocked, a wineglass in her hands and a smirk on her face. "You look well. I like the small-town scruff on your face. It's hotter than the polished look."

"Have more wine, Soph." I couldn't stop myself from smiling. Laney had to miss her best friend. She was the best friend my wife could have.

"Please, come in. Take your shoes off." She ushered me in, and I elbowed her side.

"What was that for?"

"You're ridiculous. I've been here more than you."

"Sure, but I've never made Laney cry."

I winced, and she immediately paled.

"Oh shit, that was uncalled for. Wow, sorry, dude."

I rubbed my chest, forcing a smile when Laney walked up to me wearing leggings, green fuzzy socks, and an old hoodie of mine. Her hair was in a messy bun, and she had flour on her face, but fuck, she looked beautiful. I scanned her head to toe, my heart fluttering in my chest as she blushed.

"Hi, sweetheart." I walked toward her and kissed her softly, letting my lips linger on hers. She tasted like cookies. "This is for you."

"Oh, thank you." She took the rose and smelled it. "That was nice."

"I saw it at the store this afternoon and thought it'd make you smile. You could take some dramatic pictures of it against the snow. Maybe do some black and whites?"

"That." She beamed. "That is...yes." She hugged me tight and kissed my neck with a whisper. "I love you, thank you."

"I'm gonna butt in here and say you both look great. Coming here for a few weeks was the right choice." Sophia patted my back.

I put my arm around Laney, kissing her cheek. "Why do you taste like cookies?"

"Because we're making some."

"Some? Some is like two dozen," Soph said, following us into the kitchen. "They are making millions."

"It's not millions, Sophia dear. It's ten dozen for a bake sale at the church. Then two dozen for Dad to give away at the shop, then another three for Esmerelda's art fair."

"Okay, fifteen dozen, sorry. Not a million."

The kitchen looked like a cookie factory exploded. Every crevice in the room was covered with pans, cookies, half frosted, half not. Food dye spilled on the counter, and I met her mom's gaze.

"Connor, you here to help too?"

"Do you need it?" I laughed as Laney moved to hand me an apron. She placed it over my head and tied it in the back for me.

"What... what should I do?"

"Frosting. He can be on solids."

"Oh, solids is for amateurs." Sophia winked at me and then went right toward the island and held a container of sprinkles. "This is more advanced."

"Shut up, Soph." Laney grinned as she put on an apron and stood on the other side of the table from me. "We have stations."

"I have more help coming too. I ran into Barb, who saw Kevin, who told Cienna, so it'll be a full house in a bit."

Laney's eyes sparkled. "Oh, I've missed everyone so much."

"They are so happy to see you." Her mom beamed at her, the two of them sharing a smile.

It made my chest ache. Laney had seemed happier here with her parents than she had at our home. At least, the last few years. Was it the house or me? I made a note to ask her, to try to figure out how I could create a world where she was this happy all the time. There had to be a solution somewhere.

Her mom blasted some Christmas tunes and barked out orders like a sergeant. I had no idea she had it in her.

"Mrs. Whitfield, I didn't realize you were so assertive."

"I am around Christmas, good man."

"We were never able to make it back for the annual cookie night, but when I grew up, this was a town tradition." Laney swayed her hips to the music, outlining a cookie that looked like a stocking. "It's like riding a bike! Look, Mom!"

Her mom glanced at the fancy frosting work my wife did. "Nice job, Laney. Sophia, stop eating the decorations!"

"I can't control myself!"

It was a little bit of madness for the next two hours. Laney and Sophia danced around the kitchen, taking turns singing into a spatula while others joined in. Two of the people I saw her with at the pizza place showed up with wine and more batter. They patted my back and went to work. It was a seamless operation, and for the first time in a while, I felt awkward.

"Hey!" Laney nudged my hip with hers, her red lips in a perpetual smile. "You should invite Petra over!"

"Oh, Petra? Yes. I'll invite Matt." The blond girl wiggled her brows. "He wouldn't shut up about her after the pizza place."

Laney's eyes lit up as she stood on her tiptoes and whispered, "Petra and Matt hit it off. Let's play matchmaker!"

"Your Matt and my Petra?" I said, immediately regretting it. It was the wrong thing to say. "Wait, not, you know..."

Her lips pinched together as she narrowed her eyes. "Come with me, now."

My stomach sank. "Laney—"

She shushed me, dragging me by the end of my sweatshirt as we went upstairs. Sophia caught my gaze, winked, and was not helpful. I had no idea how to explain what I had said. Petra was not mine, but thinking about Matt...

"I am so sorry. I shouldn't have—"

She shoved me onto her childhood bed, the lingering scent of her perfume still in the air.

"I am your wife, and you are my husband."

I nodded, very confused. Was she not furious with me? Was she smiling?

"Laney, baby, what's... happening?"

"Reminding you that if you ever again refer to Matt as mine, or Petra as yours, it will be very bad."

Swallowing, I nodded. "Yes, ma'am."

"Good." She leaned down and kissed me, tasting like sugar cookies and frosting. It was a soft kiss, but she moaned and tightened her grip on my shoulders as she slid her tongue into my mouth.

I could get lost in a kiss like this, but her family was downstairs, and I knew how much this decorating night meant to her. I slowed the kiss and rested my forehead on hers. We both were breathing heavily, and I smiled. "That was one hell of a kiss, Laney."

"Yeah, well, I had to remind you that I'm your wife."

"Never once forgot it." I took her hand and kissed the back of it, her eyes softening as I stared at her. "Let's go finish decorating. I made a bet with your dad last week that I'd be better at it, and I can't have him cheat."

"Did you really?" she asked, her smile widening. "What would you win?"

"Five dollars, but it's more about pride."

She giggled and I wanted to bottle up that sound. I followed her back downstairs, wishing like hell that I could figure out a solution where we spent more time here. Because the one thing I learned these last few weeks was that, if given the choice, I'd pick Laney over my job.

I just had to show her that I meant it.

CHAPTER SEVENTEEN

LANEY

Sophia and I walked arm in arm Friday morning, eyeing the shops on Main Street. She wanted to find a few presents for her nieces, and I wanted to hang out with my best friend.

"You're happier here. I wasn't sure if it was the first night, seeing all your old friends, or if it was you and Connor finding your way back to each other. But it's been days now. You're lighter."

I sighed, and my breath formed a puff in front of my face. I tightened my grip on my jacket as a chill went through me. "I know. I miss it. A lot."

"And have you talked to your smitten husband about this?"

"I can never tell whose side you're on."

"Always yours. Even if that means calling you out when you're hiding the truth. You need to tell him how you're feeling. You're both so...Laney." She stopped and grabbed my face with her mittens. "This is the best I've seen both of you. This place is different. I can't explain it. I never thought I'd say I like the small-town life, but damn, it's magical."

"Cherrywood does have that spark to it." I eyed my hometown, a million memories flashing through my mind. The time I stubbed my toe on the curb and Matt gave me a piggyback ride to get ice cream. The night my dad and I danced in the rain, expecting my mom to get mad, but she just joined us and laughed. The day I found out about getting into my dream college.

"I don't think he'll ever leave the city," I said. He had said he'd come with me but that was right after I left and he was desperate.

"You don't speak for him."

"Sophia." I snorted, but then another bout of dizziness hit. It had been a few days since the last one, but I gripped her arm until it passed.

"Dang, is it possible to get vertigo?"

She frowned. "Vertigo? What do you mean?"

"I've been getting dizzy the last week or so. Only for a few seconds, but then it passes."

Sophia clicked her tongue, but then her eyes widened. "Laney, are you pregnant?"

"What?" I gasped, the air escaping my lungs so fast that I stumbled back. She caught me, the expression on her face shifting to panic.

"I can't... It's not..."

The throwing up. The dizziness. The realization that I couldn't remember my last period.

"Oh... it's... I could be. I could be pregnant, Sophia."

The swirl of emotions had my vision blurring. Joy, surprise, terror. I felt every emotion in the book in those five seconds before my best friend snapped into action.

Sophia nodded, then gripped my arm. "Let's go to the drugstore. I'll buy a test. People will think it's for me. Then you pee on a stick."

"Soph." My voice broke.

"I know, honey. We'll figure out what to do next. Let's learn the truth though."

We bought the tests and found our way to the bookstore. I used to come here all the time growing up. I'd get lost in the thrilling pages of a mystery or a Jane Austen novel. It was romantic in a way, and right now, it was my refuge.

"Can we use your restroom real quick? Then I'm purchasing every Abby Jimenez book you stock." Sophia smiled and took charge.

Without her, I wasn't sure what I'd do. Melt. Freeze.

"The code is eight-seven-four-three," the kid at the register said.

"Thank you!" Sophia practically ran toward the door, dragging me with her. She locked it, ripped open the box, and handed it to me. "Pee."

"I don't know if I can."

"You will. You need to know if you're pregnant. We should call Connor—"

"No."

We both gasped. Questions swirled in her eyes before she cupped my face, her voice soft.

"Laney, I am with you. No matter what happens, we are friends for life. We can talk after you find out if you're pregnant, okay?"

My eyes welled up as I nodded. She stood in the corner while I did my business with shaking hands. I set the stick on the counter, washed my hands, and hung my head as I fought with what answer I wanted.

Connor and I talked about having kids years ago, but we agreed we'd try once we felt ready. Settled. Which, we were neither right now. Plus the memory from three years ago remained in my mind, where he told our neighbor that he didn't want to be a dad. I wasn't meant to hear the comment, but the way he had said it, the tone, the implication that he didn't have time for a family, stuck with me all this time.

Work would always come first. Hell, I tried divorcing him two fucking weeks ago! We weren't stable!

But I could be carrying his child.

A burst of love so strong, so powerful hit me that my knees buckled. I slid onto the floor, not caring that it was probably disgusting. I wrapped my arms around my knees and waited.

"Two minutes. Then we'll know." Sophia patted my knees, her face twisted with worry. "My sister found out she was pregnant by being dizzy. She also craved jalapeños. This girl won't even put pepper on eggs because it's too much. The spicy thing was a sure sign. That's why I even suggested it. You being dizzy could be nothing related to it."

"I was on antibiotics the week we went away. I haven't had my period since early November, Soph. I blamed the stress of leaving, of moving home. But I've been throwing up a lot, random times." A weight settled in my gut, like this pregnancy theory answered a lot of my questions.

She sighed and stood, walking over to the stick. Before reading it, she faced me.

"Are you sure you don't want to call him?"

I nodded. "I'm sure."

"Okay, momma. You're pregnant." She sighed and burst out in tears. "You're having a baby, Laney."

A sob choked me as my best friend pulled me up and hugged me, keeping me upright as I struggled to breathe. This was unreal. A baby. I'm going to be a mom.

"You're going to be the best mom, and I'm gonna be with you the entire time. My sister has all her old baby stuff. You can have it. Oh my God, Laney." She gave me a watery smile before hugging me again. "How are you feeling? You're quiet."

"Happy." I nodded, burying my face into her shoulder. "I want to be a mom, and I didn't even realize it until right this second."

She lifted my face up, happy tears falling down hers. "We need to get it together and talk out your next steps."

"I don't know what to do." My tears fell even harder. "Connor and I just found a rhythm. If he learns about this..."

"He'll be happy. He will be fucking thrilled. He'll do anything you need, drop everything to help you."

"That's the thing. I know he will. He'd do everything for the baby. He'll be the best dad in the world. But, oh God, I sound selfish."

"Good. It's time you put yourself and this baby first. No judgment from me, ever." She sniffed too as she laughed. "Wait. I'm godmother, right?"

I burst out laughing, more tears following as I nodded. "Obviously."

"Okay, now that's settled. Talk to me. What's going through your head?"

I swallowed the ball of emotion. "Let's...walk back home. I want the fresh air to clear my head."

"Deal." She threw the box in the trash and wrapped the stick in toilet paper. "You'll want to keep this. Trust me."

I pocketed the dangerous stick and wiped my face. A part of me was relieved to learn all the sickness, the dizziness, the feeling different were due to being pregnant. I obviously needed to see a doctor, to confirm and ensure things were okay. I inhaled the cold, icy air as we walked outside and let the coolness settle me down.

Sophia said she wouldn't judge me, but my stomach twisted in indecision. I could tell Connor now. I could picture his smile and the way his eyes would light up. He'd go wild buying stuff for the baby.

Yet, we had thirteen days until New Year's. Thirteen days until we discussed if we were going to stay together. A voice inside my head screamed *of course we are*, but now that I was having a baby, two things became clearer in my mind.

I wanted to raise my kid here, surrounded by family, not in the city. And second, I needed to see how things shook out with Connor's job. Although Connor and I had made progress talking through our issues, I was hit with memories of me being alone and not able to reach him.

The time I went to the ER without him. The unanswered calls for hours at a time.

My throat closed as my grip tightened on Sophia.

"You okay?" She stilled as we turned onto my childhood street. "You need to rest?"

"No." I exhaled, daring to say my decision and hope my friend wouldn't shame me. I needed to have Connor choose me at the end of the month. Not his job, not the baby. Me.

"I don't... I want to wait to tell Connor."

Sophia nodded, her expression open. "Okay, until when?"

"After New Year's." I swallowed as my eyes filled with tears. "I need him to choose me, Soph. I need to see him choose our marriage before he knows about our kid. He hasn't chosen me for years, and sure, a couple weeks have been amazing, but what if it's not long term? You remember those nights I couldn't even reach him. I'm not keeping our baby from him—I would never do that—but not telling him for two weeks isn't... I'm not horrible, right?"

Soph smiled. "You're not horrible. Not at all." She pursed her lips, her face twisting in thought. "You could spin it, so it doesn't sound like you're intentionally hiding this from him."

"What do you mean?"

"I understand your reasons, and I agree with them." Her eyes flashed for a second. "I love seeing you and Connor happy, but I remember how much he hurt you. Yeah, okay, I think you wait and see what happens on January 1. Then, whatever you decide... you share it with him for the New Year."

I swallowed the ball in my throat. "It could be a surprise."

She grinned. "Yeah, you could get a little onesie that has something cute on it."

"I love you. I don't know what I'd do without you." I hugged my best friend and hoped she could feel the love pouring out of me.

"Thank you for visiting, for being there for me, everything."

She hugged me back and said, "Sounds like, if you're having a girl, Sophia might be the middle name."

It was the tension relief I needed. I snort-laughed and pulled away. I'd tell Connor on New Year's, and figure out what this new version of our relationship looked like.

* * * *

I decided to bring dinner to Connor at the guesthouse tonight. I carried a take-out bag with chicken pot pie from the diner and two milkshakes. Maybe it was guilt about keeping something from him, or maybe I just missed him. I spent all day with Soph before she went back home, and I hadn't seen my husband at all. After all the time we'd been spending together, I wanted to be around him more.

Connor hadn't texted all day, and it had the rumblings of before, where he'd disappear into his work for days, or weeks, or months at a time. I knocked as my stomach swirled. Things were good between us. I had no reason to doubt that, right?

He opened the door, a phone pressed to his ear as his brain caught up to seeing me. At first, he frowned, but then a slow smile formed, and he bent down to kiss me while remaining on the phone.

"Ryan, I understand your concern. I plan to address that on Wednesday."

His tone was clipped, annoyed.

Connor ushered me inside, then locked the door and took the bag from my hands. His hair was messy, like he had run his fingers through it over and over. His shoulders were tense too.

"Ryan, yes—but—can I—" He shook his head and fisted his hand. "Forgive me, but it's Friday night, my wife is here, and I'll see you next week. Email me or Petra if you have any additional concerns."

Then Connor hung up and tossed his phone onto the counter. He closed the distance between us and kissed me.

"I've needed this," he whispered, cupping the back of my

head softly with one hand, the other running along my neck and collarbone. "You taste so good. Did you and Soph have a good day?"

My eyes prickled, but I hid it by kissing him back. He groaned into my mouth, his tongue sliding against mine in a familiar yet intoxicating way. He must've chewed gum at one point because the minty flavor stung my tongue, and he wasted no time deepening the kiss.

I swore I floated off the table, letting out a deep moan. All too soon, he pulled back and grinned, looking mighty smug.

"Proud of yourself?"

"Mm-hmm." He ran his thumb over my wet bottom lip, his eyes heating. "I love when you make that growly sound. Reassures me."

"How so?" I tilted my head, and his nostrils flared.

"That you're just as into me as I am into you."

"That was never in question, Connor," I said softly.

He winced, but instead of stalking off or avoiding the chat, he nodded.

"I'm so sorry that I caused you to question us." His throat bobbed as he swallowed. "I'm working on changing everything. There's a board meeting Wednesday that could be either really good, or really bad."

"Bad...how?"

He dropped his hand from my face and pocketed it. The stiffness returned to his shoulders, and a muscle ticked in his jaw.

"My dad and Dennis are going to try and remove me as CEO."

"What?" I blinked.

"It's a real possibility. I'm sick of answering to them. I'm fucking over them coming between you and me." His voice had a hard edge, one rarely used with me. Even now, he wasn't angry at me, but I felt the lingering emotion in the air.

"I wasn't sure about telling you because there are so many what-ifs, but we agreed on honesty."

My stomach hollowed out, and I choked on my own breath.

His face fell, and he pulled me into a hug, completely misreading my reaction. We'd agreed on honesty, and I was hiding something major. My throat ached. He buried his face in my hair and inhaled, his muscles relaxing like breathing me in made him feel better.

"I'm sorry I didn't tell you everything about the plan. This mandatory meeting threw me for a loop. I'm working on a backup plan, baby. If I have to start over, I'll do it. I have good connections—"

"No, you can't give in." What about the baby? What about insurance? What about bills?

He knew nothing about those.

His frown deepened, and uncertainty clouded his eyes.

"What do you mean?" he asked slowly, elongating each word and holding my gaze. Something swirled in his gray eyes—not quite confusion, but nerves, hesitation.

My guilt doubled over my omission, but I needed him to pick me. Holding off for thirteen days wasn't that big of a deal. I ignored the twist of my gut and took his hand in mine.

"You've worked so hard to get where you're at." I smiled, meaning every word as I continued, "You're not going down without a fight."

CHAPTER EIGHTEEN

CONNOR

My breath caught in my throat at her words. When Laney was on my team, I felt invincible.

"I worked hard, yes," I said, taking my time, studying her reaction. Her lips were slightly parted, and her face open, trusting. "But I want to work hard to keep you."

She blinked, and a flash of something crossed her face. She masked it, and that gutted me. Despite the last few weeks of progress, she was still hurting. My continual choice of picking work over her had left scars.

"Come here. I want to show you something."

"Wait, is this about your father trying to remove you as CEO?"

I shook my head and held out a hand. She placed hers in mine with a frown, that cute line between her eyebrows my undoing.

"I researched something today when I took a break."

"You? A break?" She nudged my hip with hers, a flash of spark in her eyes. "Unheard of!"

"Shut it." I grinned, fucking in love with her face. Her humor, smile, frown, all of it.

"I'm growing. I want to be a better partner to you." I led us to the counter where I had two pages of notes on different therapists we could visit. Therapy made me uncomfortable. Being vulnerable was hard for me. I saw it as a sign of weakness in every single way. The thought of sharing my feelings with a stranger caused hives to break out in weird spots all over my body. Yet I would do it. I could imagine my father's words, gutting me with insults. *You're not man enough. You keep your shit private. What would the company think—that you need help? You're weak.*

His power to make me feel like shit knew no bounds.

I needed therapy to deal with him.

My throat closed up, and I wanted to toss the papers into the fire. Nerves took root in my gut. "Uh," I started, my voice breaking. My face flushed as my body overheated with mortification.

This new dynamic between us was different. Laney held all the power now, and that kept me on my toes. I was used to knowing where I stood with people, both inside and outside of work, yet with her, I didn't know.

Would she love the idea of therapy?

Did she like the fact I was putting her over my job? Her eyes had widened with fear when she said I couldn't give in.

"I found a couple of therapists back home that I'd like to consider going to with you. There are options, and I know you suggested this before, and I didn't hear you."

As she nodded and chewed her bottom lip, the same unreadable look flashed across her face as before.

"What caused you to research them?"

I rocked on my heels, my hands moving to my pockets. Her tone was reserved, hiding her real feelings, and I missed when she used to share everything. Was this the wrong move? Was suggesting this now bad?

"We've been communicating better since we agreed to try, and I don't want to fall back into bad habits again. If we have a standing appointment with someone, we—I—can make sure I don't slide back."

She ran a finger over the legal pad and scrunched her nose, her cheeks pinkening before she chuckled. "You mean this."

She didn't ask it like a question. It was a statement. Pride filled me. I did fucking mean it.

"Yes, hon, I do mean this. There is no part of me that won't fight for you, for us."

"What would your dad—"

I cut her off. "He's out of our life. I know he's a pain point, and I'm sorry for that. He's had too much influence over me, and I'm done letting him get in between us."

"Connor." Her voice lowered, disbelief clouding her every word. "He's not out of your life. There's no way."

Anger flared as blood rushed to my ears. "Yes, he is. I'm choosing you."

Her face crumpled as she gripped the back of the chair. Sighing, she stared toward the kitchen, the look on her face causing my insides to tangle. Did I say the wrong thing?

I was choosing her, yet it didn't feel like it was the right move.

"What is it? Talk to me, please."

Pain flashed on her face.

"I'm struggling with how to communicate right now."

"Okay, that's okay." I fisted my hands in my pockets. The evening was not going how I had intended. I thought—foolishly—that the counseling, my dad, all of those were the right steps. I thought she'd be excited about it, not...this.

"Laney, would you like a drink? I have beer or wine."

She shook her head, not looking at me. Something had happened in the last ten minutes for her to lose the softness in her eyes, for this distance growing between us.

"Did researching the counseling upset you? We can talk it out. I can start the fireplace." I needed to do something with my hands before I panicked. Things were not going well. "Hot chocolate? Fire and a cozy drink?"

Oh my God, I couldn't stop talking. This wasn't me. I didn't ramble, yet here I was, my wife refusing to look at me while I tried not to lose my mind. "Yeah, I'll make us drinks while you continue to not look at me."

Shit.

She snapped her head in my direction, her eyes flashing with warning, but the irritation melted away as sympathy flooded her eyes.

"You're right. I'm sorry," said Laney.

I blinked. That was... "Hmm?"

There was a table between us, but in moments like this, where we weren't calibrated, it felt like a whole town. Without her as my tether, I felt lost, and I never wanted to feel like this.

"I can see you're nervous and that I caused it. I'm sorry for that."

She closed the distance between us, stopping when the tips of her shoes hit mine. I wanted to grab her hip, touch her, kiss her, but I kept my arms at my sides and let her set the pace.

"I appreciate you looking into therapists for us, but a part of me is resentful because I tried doing that before and you blew me off. I know we're in a different spot now, but those feelings are still there."

The aggressive ball of emotion returned to the back of my throat, making it hard to swallow. "Valid."

"A part of me wants to fight you," she whispered, her frown lines returning. "But that's not helpful nor really true. I think...it threw me off, and before I could figure out my thoughts on it, I spiraled."

"Are you...do you want to talk it all out? I'd like to sit with you and clarify things." My urge to argue with her dulled, and the need to figure out the root of the issue overtook my senses. She was upset. I had caused it. I needed to figure out what to do moving forward.

"How about this? I'll make us drinks, and I can show you a surprise."

"A surprise?" She arched a brow. "Do tell."

I winked, squeezing her wrist four times instead of three.

"You'll like it. Trust me."

"You know I don't need big gifts, Connor." She followed me into the kitchen instead of waiting on the couch. Like I knew she would.

"It's not a big gift, Laney." I mocked her tone and pointed to a high-top stool. "Sit there and be patient."

"That's so hard though." She groaned as I went toward the pantry where I had hidden all the materials.

Everything was in a bag, and I concealed them behind my back as I returned.

"This only cost twenty dollars, and I think you'll appreciate it."

Her eyes lit up, her radiant smile knocking me off-balance. My wife loved hot chocolate buffets, with every topping possible. It was one of her weaknesses, and I watched her as I set ten different materials all on the counter, ending with whipped cream.

"Oh!" Her grin grew as she clapped. "You bought a hot chocolate bar?"

"For you." I opened up two packets and poured milk into a pan, keeping an eye on her and her smile. She immediately reached for the sprinkles and cherries.

"I know you love them."

"Thank you. This is..." She trailed off, her voice watery. "I love it. I love you."

"I love you too." I held her gaze, hoping like hell she'd understand that my entire body and soul was put into those words. "Let me make you one. Then we can talk."

"Deal."

We ranked our favorite candies top to bottom, argued over if sprinkles added anything at all. Laney was in the firm camp that sprinkles were everything. I was the opposite. After a few minutes, I placed the steaming milk with hot cocoa in front of her, then leaned onto my arms, watching as she put all the toppings on it with an ecstatic smile.

"You're adorable." I smiled when she narrowed her eyes at me. "I love seeing you geek out over things."

"You did good then tonight." She wiggled her eyebrows and took a long sip, releasing a sexy moan. "Perfection."

"Is counseling off the table?"

"Damn, Connor, coming in hot." She chuckled and set her mug down. Her pretty fingers wrapped around the cup, her nails a bright red. "It's not off the table. I'd love if we could make a habit out of seeing someone. But the second you'd have to cancel or miss one, I'd be upset, and even now, with all our trust, I feel like you'll abandon me."

"I won't."

Her gaze grew tender.

This moment was one I wanted forever. Her sitting there all cute, a little whipped cream on her face, her beautiful eyes staring at me with love and concern. I leaned forward and wiped it off with my thumb, licking it off my finger. She gave me a gentle smile before dropping more marshmallows into her cup.

"What are you thinking?" I asked, wanting more of her honesty.

"That I love this new connection, but when we leave the bubble of Cherrywood, that it'll go back to normal. I know you're trying to figure out a way to have a lifestyle change, a change of pace, but at what cost?"

"What cost?" I clarified. She didn't understand. We could take a pay cut if it meant keeping our marriage strong. We had enough in savings.

"Yes, Connor. You getting fired doesn't help us. You cutting off your dad sounds nice, but you've been here three weeks. That's a blink of our life." She pushed off the chair and wrapped her arms around herself. "He's your only family left. He's...Do you really want him out of our life?"

"You don't like my dad." My head throbbed. I didn't anticipate tonight going like this. "Are you defending him?"

"I want us to find balance. You're going to the extremes, and that's stressful."

"Having you walk out of our condo was stressful. Seeing your left finger empty is stressful. Figuring out how to not let my dad intimidate me? Easy compared to losing you." I crossed the tile and couldn't stop myself from touching her. Hurt and uncertainty radiated from her, which was okay. I could stop it.

"You agree I need a life change, a balance, and there's no way that'll happen unless I beat the bullies. I'm standing up for what I believe in, and if they can't see my vision, then I need to leave the company."

She trembled.

I rubbed her arms up and down, noting how tense she was.

"I'll be offered a severance package for half a year, which is plenty of time for me to find a better role for us. I even looked—there are twenty jobs downtown I could apply for right now. Or if we're open to moving states—"

Her whole body tensed, and she gasped. "Move states?"

"Laney." My tone held a hint of irritation. Her face, muscles, body—all of it gave her discomfort away, yet she said nothing.

"You need to tell me what you're thinking. I don't want to guess."

She swallowed, pulling on the collar of her shirt as she chewed her lip. I hadn't seen her act like this in a while, and I wasn't sure if it was because of me, or something else. Either way, I hated it.

"Baby, tell me, please."

"I don't like that you didn't talk to me before you did all this." She sniffed, and her eyes glistened. "I don't want to move back to the city. I miss living here, in Cherrywood." She pushed away from me and started pacing.

My stomach bottomed out at her admissions, sending me off-balance and gripping the counter for support.

She continued, "I like how I feel here, where I'm surrounded by people I know and love. I'm not alone here. I'm...alone in the city, Connor."

She wanted to move to her hometown. She was lonely. My mind checked off each comment like a checklist, remaining neutral to them instead of reacting. My pulse raced as I fought the urge to argue. She had said those things before, but this time it felt real. Serious. She looked at me, already wincing, almost like she was prepared for me to freak out, and I hated that.

It hurt me that she didn't feel comfortable sharing every thought or feeling she had.

"I'm not sure I could live here when all the jobs are in the city. I could commute, but that would mean more time not at home... What's your ideal world then, hon?"

"I don't know!" She pinched her nose and her shoulders slumped. "I didn't plan to have this reaction tonight. I'm sorry. I ruined a perfectly good night."

"No, you didn't."

Fuck it. I pulled her into my arms and hugged her. Our chests collided, and our heartbeats matched, and I sank into my wife.

"I'm terrified right now, Connor, that love isn't...that just reconnecting isn't enough for us to figure out how to stay together and be happy."

My throat tightened as fear rooted me to the ground. I was terrified too, but I wasn't going to say that. I wanted to exude confidence, that I would do whatever it took to solve this. I kissed her forehead and then rested my chin on top of her head.

"We'll be happy, Laney. I know it in my soul. We're learning how to communicate again, that's all," I said, my mind already coming up with a plan. I needed to continue to date her, show her I was listening. I had the perfect idea...

CHAPTER NINETEEN

LANEY

"Can I take the blindfold off now?" I asked on Monday night—our date night. The weekend flew by with holiday activities with my parents, so this night was for us.

Connor chuckled and rubbed a reassuring hand down my arm, squeezing my wrist three times. "Nope. You know this place too well so it's more of a challenge to surprise you. Blindfolding was the only way."

"When I agreed to dating this month, kidnapping wasn't on the list."

"So funny, so clever."

He made a left turn for a bit, then right. If I tried paying attention the entire drive, I could possibly figure out where we were going, but I was too nervous. Butterflies fluttered deep in my gut. "Almost there, Laney."

He changed the music to one of my favorite holiday songs and patted my knee, humming along in his deep tone. Maybe it was the fact that one of my senses was blocked, but I really took in the moment. The way Connor's cologne smelled spicy, the way he kept finding small ways to touch me, and the fact he'd planned whatever tonight's surprise was. It showed he was listening to me. That he'd truly heard me when I said I didn't want gifts. I wanted time together, that was it. It was almost like we'd tossed his work stuff aside and were focusing on us—which was the entire point of this month.

"This isn't something extravagant, right?" I asked, cracking my knuckles on my left hand.

"Nope."

"And I'll enjoy it?"

"Yup." He lifted my tense fingers and kissed the back of them, the scruff of his beard contrasting with the softness of his lips. My heart skipped a beat at the gesture, and my breathing picked up.

I turned into a puddle when Connor was sweet. A complete puddle.

The car stopped, and he undid his seat belt. "I'll come and get you. Stay put, beautiful."

Heat tickled my face from his compliment. It was strange to be with him for so long but still feel giddy. *What about when he finds out you're pregnant?* I shoved the voice away. Tonight was about him and me, and that was it.

"Alright, I did my best for tonight," Connor said, undoing my seat belt and gently kissing my temple. "We only get it for ourselves for twenty minutes."

"Get what?" I stood on asphalt and dug my toes in. Sounds of laughter and smells of fire and cinnamon and hot chocolate were around us. "Okay, we're in the center of town."

"Correct." Connor guided us for a minute, the asphalt shifting to a smoother surface after a few steps. "Shit, okay, I suddenly got nervous."

"Connor," I said, reaching around until my hands landed on his chest. I smoothed them over his heart and then over his shoulders. "This could be the worst idea you've ever had, but I already love it."

"Pretty sure the worst idea I ever had was that year I thought we could *wing* a vacation."

I snorted. "Oh, that remains the top spot. We slept in that shared hotel room, and the bathroom was disgusting."

"I can't believe we did that, but hey, thanks for reminding me."

"Anytime." I grinned and scooted closer to him. "I'm going to love it. Please show me."

He sighed. Then he removed the blindfold, and I found him staring intently at me. His jaw was tight and his eyes wide, a sure sign he was feeling hesitant. "Okay, you've always said how much you loved ice skating here growing up, but we never found the time to do it the last few years." He swallowed and glanced over my shoulder. "We have the rink to ourselves for twenty minutes. I want to watch you skate, baby. The town can watch you."

My chest ached with how much I loved this. "Connor," I said, breathless as I stared at the completely empty rink. People were everywhere, walking and enjoying the countless other holiday activities, but the rink was empty. "You did this for me?"

"For us, yes." His voice was tight. "Do you like it?"

"This is so sweet." My eyes watered, and I clutched my hand over my stomach. "I love that you did this, Connor. I love you."

The relief on his face was evident, and it was like he needed that one moment of validation. My confident, sexy husband returned. He smiled, his gray eyes crinkling on the sides as he took my hand and swung our arms in the air. He had never once swung our arms like we were kids, and it was clear that any remaining nerves had disappeared.

This was *us*. Goofy, trusting, fun.

Connor led us to a bench where skates in my size were already placed. He also suddenly produced earmuffs and a bright green scarf. "Some woman named Nancy heard me making these plans and insisted I buy you a new scarf and earmuffs. Her grandma knits them, so they are all handmade."

I sat on the bench, and he lowered to the ground, sliding off my shoes and helping me lace my skates. "How did you even plan this? Seriously?"

He winked. "I'm not revealing my sources."

"Oh, I love a good wink." I laughed as he finished both my skates. "I am honestly so excited right now."

"Good." His wide grin matched mine.

It was precious how happy we both were in this moment. Sure, it wasn't real life, and it was just a snapshot of our month of dating, but the thought he put into this? This was all I wanted. The earmuffs and scarf? "This might be my favorite date ever."

"Yeah?" He arched a brow as he tied his own laces, pride radiating off him. "We haven't even skated yet."

"Doesn't matter. We could sit here on this bench and watch the crowd and talk about nothing, and it'd be the best."

He stood and held out a hand, his grin both challenging and reassuring. "Our time is counting down. Skate with me, baby."

The cold air nipped at my cheeks, but it was nothing compared to the warmth spreading through me as I glided across the ice. This was my sanctuary, the place where I'd always felt most free as a kid. The rink was set in the heart of town and was surrounded by snow-dusted trees strung with twinkling lights. Booths from the holiday festival lined the perimeter, the air filled with the sweet scent of roasted chestnuts and spiced cider. The cheerful sound of a local quartet playing carols floated across the square, which blended with the laughter of children making snow angels nearby.

I glanced over my shoulder and couldn't help but smile at Connor, who was wobbling his way toward me, his arms flailing like a baby deer learning to walk. "You've got this!" I called, skating backward with ease, my legs moving in perfect rhythm.

Connor let out a laugh, half amused, half embarrassed. "You didn't tell me you were a pro!" he shouted, just as he nearly lost his balance again. I reached out and caught his hand before he could fall, pulling him closer until we were both laughing. His cheeks were pink from the cold—or maybe from the way I was looking at him.

"You're doing great," I teased, tugging him gently along. The crisp air carried hints of pine and the distant crackle of a bonfire, grounding us in this perfect winter wonderland. For a moment, the world fell away, and it was just us, the sound of skates slicing through ice and the glow of the holiday lights above. It wasn't just the ice that felt like home tonight—it was him.

I could see our future now, date nights like this, raising our child, joining the small-town life. I wanted it. I wanted it desperately, but the only issue in the scenario was Connor.

Could he be happy here? Or would he move here and then resent me later? My heart thudded hard against my ribs, and I rubbed the pang. I wanted to enjoy the night, not overthink everything. These were problems for later.

"Next challenge for you." Connor skated closer to me. "I've been told the special-crafted hot chocolate at the booth is one of the best."

"You mean that I will have to drink and skate at the same time?" My eyes bugged out. I felt more confident skating, but that would be too much. "Connor, *no*."

"You can do it." He smiled and kept his gaze on me. That's when it hit me.

Connor was happier here. He didn't have stress lines on his face or look constantly on the state of collapse. His eyes were brighter, his shoulders less tense. I wanted to convince him this place was better for him, for us.

"...pregnant?"

Hushed voices carried over the light breeze, and I snapped my attention behind me. A group of older women huddled together, all wearing various colors of green and red. They whispered, but it was loud enough to reach me.

My stomach bottomed out.

Were they talking about *me*?

"Drugstore...snuck out but the box was in the trash."

Shit. That was me. My face heated. I had to get away from them. There was no way they knew it was me. Soph didn't tell anyone, but this small-town grapevine was the worst. You couldn't hit a curb on the other side of town without everyone hearing about it and checking your hubcaps as you drove by. (True story.)

I didn't want Connor to find out. I couldn't. I had a plan.

We skated for the duration of our solo time, smiling and laughing as I skated circles around him. When he sighed, glancing at his watch, I headed toward him.

"So there is one part of the deal that I never mentioned," he said, eyes twinkling.

"What...deal?"

"How I got the rink for twenty minutes on a busy night before Christmas." He grinned, a playful glee coming off him. "I'll show you. Come on, wife."

CHAPTER TWENTY

CONNOR

The Zamboni was larger—and more complicated—than I'd expected. Its controls looked like something out of a spaceship, with levers, buttons, and knobs that all seemed equally important.

"Are you sure about this?" Laney asked, her arms crossed as she stood by the rink, her eyes dancing with amusement.

"I'm a CEO," I said with mock confidence, climbing into the driver's seat. "How hard can this be?"

She snorted. "Running a company doesn't exactly qualify you to drive a glorified ice-cleaning tractor."

"Details," I replied back. I patted the seat beside me. "Come on, baby. You're riding shotgun."

Laney hesitated for a moment before climbing in, her body brushing against mine as she squeezed into the narrow space. "If we die, I'm haunting you," she said, her voice teasing.

"Noted." I fiddled with the controls, squinting at the buttons. "Okay, so this lever...should make it go forward."

The Zamboni lurched to life, and Laney squealed, grabbing

my arm for balance. We rolled onto the ice with all the grace of a baby elephant, the machine swaying slightly as I over-corrected the steering. When I made the deal to *clear the ice* when we were done, I figured there would be a guide or something. I never expected to wing it.

"Connor!" Laney shrieked, half laughing, half panicked. "Watch out for the wall!"

"I've got this," I assured her, even as the Zamboni veered dangerously close to the boards. A group of kids scattered on the other side, their giggles echoing across the rink.

Laney doubled over laughing. "You're terrifying! How are you worse at this than skating?"

"It's all part of the experience," I said, grinning despite the sweat forming at the back of my neck. "Hold on—we're going to pick up speed."

"Pick up speed? No!" Laney protested, but her laughter betrayed her.

I pushed the throttle, and the Zamboni surged forward, gliding faster across the ice. For a moment, it felt like I actually had control. Laney leaned into me, her laughter bubbling up again as she pointed toward the other side of the rink. "Turn, Connor! Turn!"

"I'm turning!" I yanked the wheel, but the Zamboni responded a beat too late. We started spinning, the machine pivoting in slow, looping circles. Laney's laughter turned into breathless gasps as she clung to my arm.

"Connor! We're going to—"

The Zamboni slid toward the rink's edge, its massive frame gliding straight for the hot chocolate bar. My stomach dropped as I frantically twisted the wheel, trying to correct our course.

The Zamboni jerked to a stop, its nose mere inches from the steaming pots of cocoa and the wide-eyed vendor.

For a moment, everything was silent. Then Laney burst into laughter, her head falling against my shoulder. "Oh my God. We almost destroyed Christmas."

I couldn't help it—I laughed too, the sound rolling out of me in waves. "I'd like to point out that we didn't though. No hot chocolate was harmed in the making of this moment."

Laney lifted her head, her cheeks flushed and her eyes sparkling. "That was the worst—and most fun—ride of my life."

I reached over, brushing a strand of hair from her face. "I aim to impress."

She rolled her eyes but smiled, her fingers still gripping my arm. "Impress, huh? You almost killed Santa's hot chocolate supply."

"Details," I said, smirking. But as our laughter faded, I realized I didn't want the moment to end—the closeness, the sound of her laugh, the way her eyes danced even in the chaos. It felt... right.

"Kiss her!"

I glanced up at the group of townspeople who were watching us. "Kiss Laney!"

My wife stared up at me with cheeks pink and lips parted. "We should probably do what they ask, right?" she whispered.

"Hmm, yes." I cupped her face and pressed my lips against hers, taking in how soft and full they were. She tasted like mint, and when she made a small moan, I deepened the kiss, not caring that everyone was around us. I loved this woman so much, and I had almost lost her. I'd skate or drive this Zamboni or kiss her in front of an audience every day if it meant I got to keep her.

I pulled back, admiring the way her lashes fell on her cheeks, the slight flush of her skin. She blinked up at me, her eyes a little dazed. "That kiss was…"

"I know."

The magic of the night hit me hard. This place was like a snow globe. Laney covered her face with her hands, groaning. "Oh my God, everyone will be talking about us now."

"Let them be jealous."

The cold air nipped at my face as Laney and I stepped off the ice, our laughter echoing. My legs felt a little unsteady after the Zamboni adventure, but it was nothing compared to the way my chest felt lighter than it had in years. I glanced at Laney and the way she smiled made the rest of the world disappear.

"That," she said, wiping a tear from the corner of her eye, "was the single most ridiculous thing I've ever done."

"You're welcome," I said, smirking. "I aim to make memories."

"Let's just agree you're banned from heavy machinery for the foreseeable future."

"Fair." I chuckled, looking back at the rink.

Once we were on solid ground with our shoes on, Laney laughed again. "I still can't believe what just happened. We were almost a headline, Connor. One of those feel-good small-town news stories. *Wife and husband almost take out hot chocolate bar.*"

The lights shimmered on the freshly polished ice, and kids were already skating again, laughing like they hadn't been about to get run over by the Zamboni. It was somehow perfect despite our horrible job.

As we reached the first set of small booths, a voice called out. "That was some fancy driving, city guy!"

I turned to see an older man in a thick sweater and worn red coat waving us over. He had the kind of friendly face you'd expect in a town like this—one where everyone knew everyone.

"I swear, the Zamboni had a mind of its own," I said, raising my hands in mock surrender. Not that the city guy comment annoyed me, but I deserved it.

"You gave the crowd a good laugh," the man said, chuckling as he handed me a cup of steaming cocoa. "Always good to have some excitement around here. I'm Sean Hastings, by the way. I run the grocery store."

"Connor," I said, shaking his hand. "Appreciate the cocoa. And I'm just glad I didn't take out the stand."

Sean grinned. "Small miracles. Though, I bet if you had, the chamber of commerce would've sent you the bill."

"The chamber of commerce?" I asked, taking a sip. The cocoa was hot, sweet, and exactly what I needed after the chaos. Laney held hers up to her mouth after a sip, the marshmallows coating the top of her lip.

"Yeah," Sean said, gesturing toward a few other people gathered nearby. "We're just a bunch of local business owners trying to keep things running. We're the ones who keep this rink open, organize the holiday market—things like that."

Laney raised an eyebrow, her voice teasing. "And handle damage control after near–Zamboni disasters? I'm sure that's in the job description too."

Sean laughed. "Something like that. You two have a good night. Tell your parents I'm expecting them to bring dessert next bridge night, Laney."

"You got it, Mr. Hastings."

"Mr. Hastings." The older guy rolled his eyes. "You can call me Sean, Laney. You're an adult now."

"Some things never change." My wife grinned and gave him a half hug before he headed back to the group.

Laney nudged me with her elbow. "You okay? You seem thoughtful."

I stared out at the rink, watching a group of teenagers race each other across. Their laughter echoed in the crisp night air, and for a moment, I just stood there, taking it all in. This small-town life had a lot of perks that I never realized. Even now, how Laney knew Mr. Hastings felt special.

Mr. Hastings was on Cherrywood's chamber of commerce? A flicker of interest hit me. How did that even work? "Yeah, just...thinking. I didn't realize how much effort goes into keeping a town like this running."

Laney tilted her head, studying me like she always did when she knew there was more I wasn't saying. "It's not exactly glamorous, is it?"

"No," I admitted, a smile tugging at my lips. "But it's...honest. You can see the impact. Everyone here knows each other, looks out for each other. There's something refreshing about that."

Her gaze softened, and she slipped her hand into mine. The gesture was small, but it steadied something in me I hadn't realized was off-balance. "You sound like you actually like it here."

I laughed, though there was more truth in her words than I was ready to admit. "Maybe I do."

It was the place where my wife had fallen back in love with me. It was the place she was happiest. I'd been so focused on hustling, making a name for myself, forgetting what life was about. When Petra admitted how she had forgotten how to live, that hit me too. Was it really living when I spent all my time at work? Was it living when all I felt was stress and worry?

It was the moments like tonight, like Laney holding my hand and smiling up at the stars that brought me back. What if every night could be like this? The thought remained with me as we shopped the small booths.

Later, as the rink cleared, I found myself near the hot chocolate stand again where Sean and a few others were chatting. He waved me over, and I joined them, nursing the last of my cocoa.

"We were just talking about our struggles with the off-season," Sean explained. "December's great, but after that, business slows to a crawl. Half of us barely scrape by until summer."

Another shop owner chimed in. "We've tried promotions, events, you name it. But it's hard to bring in steady traffic."

I listened, my mind already racing as Laney stood a few feet away, deeply engaged with a group of women her age. Maybe she knew them. Maybe they just met. With her in my peripheral, I spoke to Sean. "What about digital marketing? Online promotions? You could attract people from nearby cities."

Sean shrugged. "We don't have the resources for that kind of thing. Most of us are lucky if we can keep the lights on."

"What if you pooled your resources?" I said, the idea forming as I spoke. "Create a unified strategy to market the town as a destination—not just in December but year-round."

The group exchanged skeptical glances, but I caught a flicker of interest in Sean's expression. "That's a nice idea," he said, "but who's got the time—or the know-how—to make it happen?"

I didn't answer right away. Instead, I glanced at Laney again, her laugh carrying over the ice. For the first time in years, I felt something shift in me—not ambition, not obligation. Purpose.

And maybe, just maybe, this little town had more to offer than I'd ever expected.

CHAPTER TWENTY-ONE

LANEY

The warm glow of the town's Christmas lights reflected off the ice as Connor and I strolled hand-in-hand, still buzzing from the Zamboni chaos. I thought we were heading back to my parents' house, but before we could turn the corner, a woman dressed as an elf stepped in front of us, holding a clipboard and grinning ear to ear. She seemed familiar but wasn't someone I went to high school with.

"Ah! You two are perfect!" she exclaimed. "We need more participants for the Holiday Scavenger Hunt. You're officially drafted."

Connor raised an eyebrow. "Laney, this is all you."

"Don't you 'this is all you' me," I said, poking him in the side. "You're doing this with me. We can't let the elf down."

"No, you can't. Plus, Laney, your mom told me you've been taking photos of all the events the last few weeks and haven't participated in them." The woman winked. "She may or may not have told my mom to find you."

"And your mom is..." I asked, trying to see why she seemed so familiar.

"Becky."

"Ah yes. You're Katie!" I beamed. "You just had twin girls. Congrats!"

"Thank you." Katie blushed as a radio crackled. She held up a finger and responded. "I found two more, so we have at least twenty now."

"Ten-four, Buddy."

Katie rolled her eyes. "They called me Buddy because of the yellow tights, which is my fault. I chose this outfit." She paused and smiled again. "Thank you both for doing this."

"Did we have a choice?" Connor asked, his tone playful.

"Nope." Katie laughed, then her gaze filled with warmth. "Speaking of babies, you look like you're glowing, Laney."

"What? No. I'm not...glowing?" I barked out an awkward laugh and pulled at my scarf. "Not glowing."

Shit. There was no way she could know. No way she could tell! Did Connor notice? Did he think something was different? My heart raced and my palms sweat, and did the temperature rise somehow?

"You're happy." Connor pulled me under his arm, kissing my temple again. "That's what she means."

Katie nodded. "He's right. You look happy. Have fun tonight. I'm gonna be running around all night playing emcee, host, and trash pickup."

"Wait, why are you doing all three? Shouldn't you be home with your babies?" Usually there was an entire crew helping with these events. Now that she mentioned it, there were significantly fewer people out in the town center than normal.

With Christmas nearing, there should be hundreds of people here.

Katie shrugged. "Short-staffed. Can't afford to pay people as much. Every year the events get smaller."

"That's...so sad," I said, the weight of Katie's words settling heavily in my chest. "Cherrywood without the festivals wouldn't be the same. So the town is losing money?"

Katie nodded, her expression tight. "Small businesses are really struggling. My uncle had to pick up another job because the shop wasn't bringing in enough. And he's not the only one."

I frowned, glancing at Connor. He stood beside me, his hand resting lightly on my back, and I could see the gears turning in his head. The CEO in him never switched off—not that I wanted it to right now. This was the kind of thing he could actually help with, wasn't it?

Connor's voice broke through my thoughts. "What's the biggest challenge for the businesses?" he asked Katie, his tone calm but probing. "Is it competition, fewer visitors, or something else?"

Katie let out a sigh, crossing her arms against the chilly evening air. "It's everything. The big stores out on the highway make it hard to compete on price. And after the holidays, we just don't see enough people coming through town. Summer tourists help, but the other seasons are tough."

"That makes sense," Connor said, his brow furrowing. "Have you thought about ways to draw people here outside of the holidays? Cherrywood has so much charm—it feels like the kind of place people would love if they knew about it."

I couldn't help but smile a little at how natural he sounded, like he'd been part of Cherrywood for years instead of just a couple of weeks.

"We've tried a few things," Katie said, her voice hesitant. "Like promotions and sales. But most of us don't have the time or money to do much more. I know for me, the gardening shop takes everything I've got to keep it running."

Connor nodded, his gaze sharpening. "You wouldn't have to do it alone. If the businesses worked together—shared costs and responsibilities—you could make it work. A little collaboration could go a long way."

Katie looked at me and then back at Connor, her lips quirking into a small smile. "You sound like you've thought about this before."

"He's full of ideas," I said, unable to keep the pride out of my voice.

Connor shrugged, his focus still on Katie. "It's about finding ways to make Cherrywood's charm work for you. This town has so much heart—people just need to see it."

Katie let out a thoughtful hum, her gaze distant as if she were already imagining what that might look like. "It's a nice idea, I'll admit."

My stomach twisted at her words. It was subtle, but I could see the flicker of something in Connor's expression. He didn't respond right away, his eyes drifting over the festive lights and the town square. For a moment, I wondered if he was picturing it too—a life here, building something for Cherrywood.

I reached for his hand, squeezing it gently. He looked down at me, his gray eyes softening, and for the first time that night,

I let myself hope. As Katie excused herself to check on her booth, I leaned into him, my cheek brushing his shoulder.

"You really think something like that could work?" I asked quietly, my heart pounding just a little harder than I expected.

"It makes sense. Transitioning to more modern marketing techniques is what makes or breaks towns like this. The tourism is going to keep it going but how to show it off? There could be a whole rental business here, the whole Airbnb thing. This is the perfect getaway for those who live in the city and want to escape." He rubbed the back of his neck, his gaze continuing to move up and down the street. "Anyway, if they focused on the future, they could turn this town into a destination spot."

I shivered. I loved hearing him talk about saving Cherrywood. He frowned and rubbed his hands up and down my arms. "Are you cold? Do you want to head back?"

"And not do the scavenger hunt?" I arched a brow. "That would put us on the front of the town paper."

"Honey"—he laughed and tugged one of my curls—"we're already gonna be on it. We almost destroyed the rink, or have you already forgotten?"

Snorting, I stared at the list Katie handed us. "Wow."

"What is it?" He leaned over, his breath hitting my cheek and making me warm head to toe. His hand still rested on my back as he laughed. "This list is something else."

1. Guess the Weight of the Gingerbread Baby—Head to the local bakery and guess the weight of the giant gingerbread baby on display. Bonus points for taking a silly photo pretending to cradle it.

2. Snap a Photo with a Baby Reindeer—Find the baby reindeer (it's probably a dog or goat in a reindeer costume) and take a creative selfie with it.
3. Find the Elf on the Shelf—A cheeky elf doll is hidden near the Santa sleigh. You must locate it and re-create its pose for a photo.
4. Create a Christmas Fashion Statement—Assemble the most over-the-top holiday outfit using props from local vendors. You must wear it for the rest of the hunt—or at least until the next task.
5. Perform a Dramatic Reading of "'Twas the Night Before Christmas"—Find a public spot (preferably a gazebo or fountain) and read the poem out loud with your partner. Bonus points for exaggerated gestures and voices.
6. Reindeer Ring Toss—Locate the game booth and land three rings on the inflatable antlers of a volunteer "reindeer" (probably another participant or a town local wearing antlers).
7. Decorate a Snowman in 90 Seconds—Using a kit provided at the town square, dress up a small snowman with three ridiculous accessories.
8. Find Santa's Missing Mitten—Santa "lost" his mitten somewhere in the fountain. Bonus points for returning it directly to Santa and convincing him to give you a candy cane.
9. Sing a Carol to a Stranger—Pick a holiday tune and serenade an unsuspecting shopper in the square. Bonus points if the stranger joins in.

10. Balance the Christmas Package—Stack 5 wrapped gifts on your head and walk 10 steps without dropping them. Bonus points for an epic balancing photo.

"Should we go hold a gingerbread baby?" Connor asked, a teasing grin spreading across his face as he pointed at the scavenger hunt list.

"Wait, what?" I barely managed to get the words out, my breath catching in my throat.

Connor's grin only widened as he tugged me closer. "You know I've got to start at the top. I can't go out of numeric order. So let's head to the bakery."

He reached for my hand, but paused, his eyes softening. "We can head back if you're not up for it. I just like spending time with you."

I swallowed hard, trying not to panic. "No, yeah," I said, my voice cracking. "Let's... start from the beginning."

His smile returned, and he laced his fingers through mine, guiding me toward the bakery, where the gingerbread baby guessing booth was set up just outside.

The scent of gingerbread and frosting hit me like a sugar-filled cloud as we approached the booth. Front and center, a giant gingerbread baby lay cradled in a display cradle, complete with icing eyes, a gumdrop nose, and a frosting bow on its head. A sign overhead read, GUESS THE WEIGHT OF CHERRYWOOD'S SWEETEST BABY!

Connor let out a low whistle. "That is... both impressive and terrifying."

The baker behind the booth beamed at us, clearly enjoying

our reaction. "Careful now," she said, wagging a spatula at Connor. "This is my pride and joy. Don't let her hear you calling her terrifying."

"She's perfect," I said quickly, desperate to avoid drawing more attention to us.

"You have to hold her to really get a feel for the weight," the baker said, gesturing toward Connor. "Go ahead."

Connor didn't hesitate. He stepped up, carefully cradling the gingerbread baby in his arms like it was a real newborn. "Wow," he said, rocking it gently. "She's heavier than she looks."

"You're holding her like you've done this before," the baker said with a wink. "Practicing for the real thing?"

I choked on my own breath. "Nope! Definitely not! No babies here!" My voice shot up an octave, and I cleared my throat.

Connor raised an eyebrow at me but didn't say anything. Instead, he turned back to the gingerbread baby, frowning in concentration. "I'd say...twelve pounds."

"Twelve pounds?" I hissed. "That's absurd! No gingerbread baby weighs that much!"

"Okay, Ms. Expert," he said, grinning. "What's your guess?"

I glanced at the gingerbread baby, my palms sweating. "Uh...seven. Seven pounds."

The baker laughed. "Well, one of you is closer, but you'll have to wait until the end of the night to find out who wins. Don't forget to take a photo with her before you go!"

Connor handed the gingerbread baby back to the baker, but not before holding it up to my face like Simba in *The Lion King*. "Should we name her?"

I shoved him, laughing nervously. "Let's move on."

The baby boutique was set up with string lights and holiday décor, and the window display featured tiny reindeer onesies, elf hats, and miniature mittens. Connor stopped in his tracks, pointing to a pair of fuzzy baby booties. "Look at those. Tell me those aren't the cutest things you've ever seen."

I was pretty sure my face was about to catch fire. "They're... fine."

"Fine?" He turned to me, incredulous. "Laney, they're tiny boots. For tiny feet."

Before I could stop him, he stepped inside, pulling me along. The boutique owner greeted us with a cheerful smile, holding up a holiday-themed diaper bag. "We just got these in! Perfect for new parents."

Connor slung the bag over his shoulder, striking a pose. "Do I look like a cool dad?"

I grabbed his arm, yanking him toward the door. "Connor, we don't need a diaper bag."

"But it's on sale," he said, grinning. "And it's practical."

"For... o-other p-people," I stammered. "We don't have a baby!"

The boutique owner tilted her head, clearly confused. "Well, you don't need a baby to shop here. Plenty of people buy gifts for friends and family."

Connor smirked, grabbing a pair of the fuzzy booties. "Great idea. These will be perfect for... the future."

I snatched the booties out of his hand, practically throwing them back on the shelf. "Nope. We're not doing this. Next scavenger hunt item, let's go!"

He laughed, raising his hands in surrender. "Okay, okay. No

baby boots. But you're acting a little weird, Laney. Everything okay?"

"Perfect!" I said, my voice a little too chipper. "Let's go find the reindeer."

I could feel Connor's eyes on me, his curiosity growing. I looped my arm through his. The sooner we got to the next task, the better.

As we stepped back out into the bustling street, the lights twinkled overhead like tiny stars, and laughter from the square filled the chilly air. Connor reached for my hand, lacing his fingers through mine, and gave it a gentle squeeze.

"You're quiet," he said, glancing down at me. His gray eyes softened, searching my face. "Are you sure you're okay? We can head back. Just say the word."

I smiled, this time more genuinely. "I'm good. Just...taking it all in." That much was true. I was internally sweating about him nearly finding out the truth, but other than that, I was swell. Great, even.

He nodded, his gaze sweeping across the square, the warmth of his hand steadying me. "It's a good night. I can see why you love this place so much."

My chest tightened—not in panic this time but in a sweet ache that made me want to laugh and cry all at once. This man, my husband, who had once thrived on skyscrapers and high-stakes deals, was falling in love with Cherrywood. And, whether he knew it or not, with the life we *could* build here. If he would try it.

I glanced up at the clock tower in the square, its face glowing faintly in the night. Just ten more days until New Year's. Until the moment I could tell him everything—about the baby, about how I wanted this town to be part of our future, about how I could see us raising a family here. He had to get through the board meeting though. That was step one. Then...we could figure it out.

For now, I'd hold on to this perfect moment, to Connor's hand in mine.

CHAPTER TWENTY-TWO

CONNOR

I couldn't stop smiling. It was Tuesday morning, the day before the board meeting. I should be a nervous wreck. I should be stressed and going over the presentation a million times, but I wasn't.

My wife was back. We had had the perfect date night, and even though I should be thinking about what to say, my mind kept going back to the skating rink and scavenger hunt. We didn't win, but we laughed. We didn't get back until midnight, and even though Laney had stayed the night, my tired mind raced with ideas.

This town needed someone to help it.

"I cannot believe you are on the cover of the *Cherrywood Times*. You. Of all the grinchy people I know." Petra rolled her eyes as she pointed to the papers on the table. "You almost took out a stand *and* went all out for the scavenger hunt. How do I know this, you might ask? Because Matt told me. He heard it from someone who saw the Zamboni incident, and this town is just wild. Why does everyone know everyone's business?"

Petra had stayed in Cherrywood preparing with me, and the town was wearing on her. She wore a sweater that was clearly handcrafted. I wouldn't mention it, but it made me smile.

"Because they all like each other." I checked my phone to see how Laney was doing. The town's events were picking up with Christmas nearing. Today was a Christmas tree farm celebration. She'd be outside all day, so I made a note to bring her more hot chocolate and find an extra blanket for her.

Plus, a part of me wanted to talk to the owner of the farm and see how they were doing. After a quick search into the town, it was clear they needed help or they'd continue to lose visitors. The thought of Laney's parents unable to keep business at the hardware shop gutted me. I couldn't get the idea out of my head. If they had someone in charge of improving the local economy... it'd help save a community. Jobs and lives.

"Connor, what do I say? Matt is texting me *again* about grabbing dinner. He's going to take me to his grandma's house! That's ridiculous, right?"

I hid my wince. Matt could be a decent guy, but I still didn't want him around. At least he was texting Petra and not my wife. "Uh, do you want to get dinner with him?"

"Yes. Maybe?" She groaned and covered her face with her hands. "No! My career is on the line with you. My ex is an asshole. Your father is a bully. We can't find the link between Dennis and the attack, nor my ex. I cannot have a puppy dog of a man interested in me."

My lips twitched as I stared at my assistant. "You're a mess."

"Oh, fuck off. You were a mess like three days ago."

"Still nothing on the connection to my dad, or Dennis and the data breach?" I scrubbed my jaw. That piece of evidence would really tie our presentation together. "Let's say we can't find anything. Our presentation is still strong. It still shows why you deserve this role."

"I'm a woman, Connor. These men are not as forward thinking as you are." Her eyes were the only indication she was sad. "If we can attack and—"

"No attacking. That's giving away our hand. We remain stoic. Take the high road." I thought about Laney, about her hope in me, in us, and my heart skipped a beat. I had to get this right, and for the first time in my life, I was nervous. Fucking rattled. Yet, I couldn't show Petra that. "You have to remain neutral. Whatever they say, or insinuate, you keep your face the same. Now let's walk it through again."

We practiced our opener: our current landscape, Petra's new role and how it would elevate us, everything Petra has initiated, led, or completed over the last seven years, and then data. How we have increased profit, our plans to double it, the companies we're acquiring because of Petra's connections. How she'd taken data and created plans around it, executing major deals with her insights.

I told Petra we had to take the high road, but that was slightly a lie. A fib. She had to take that path or she'd get blasted by them. Me though? Nah. This was my attempt at righting my life, and I'd use every card possible. I didn't want to resort to revenge, but I would be prepared regardless.

I remembered exactly how my father said I should forget my wife and let her leave. I'd pull up old texts he'd sent over the years, berating me for picking my wife over the company. The three board members who I was good with all had families. I'd play into that, share that Laney and I had an emergency come up and that mattered more. And that part of the motivation for moving Petra into a role with more power would be to focus on my family.

The resolution to the mess I had created was all right within reach. Things just had to go my way.

"Jen sent us an email, dude. This could be…" Petra trailed off. "Connor. Check your email now."

Shit. I fired open my browser, my heart racing, as I clicked the email from our CTO.

> I wanted to inform you that we have successfully identified the source of the recent breach. Our investigation revealed that the breach occurred due to a compromised internal account, that of Nate Smith.
>
> Additionally, we discovered suspicious messages between Nate and several influential members of our company. These communications suggest a potential internal collaboration or, at the very least, serious security lapses that need immediate attention.
>
> I recommend an urgent meeting to discuss the next steps, including tightening our security protocols and addressing the involved parties. I will clear my schedule to fit yours.

"'Influential members of our company'?" Petra repeated the words that I stared at.

"Does she mean—"

"My father, our board. Either option is possible." My gut churned with the reality crashing over me. "We have to head into the office. We need to speak with Jen."

"I can be ready in five minutes." She shut her device and had quickly stacked the papers into a pile. "Connor, I know Jen. That last paragraph... she's stressed."

"Yeah." I gripped the back of my neck, the thought of leaving Laney almost unbearable. I could drive there now, come back tonight, leave again tomorrow morning. "Call Jen, have her meet us in her office at one."

"One?" She arched a brow. "What about eleven?"

"I need to tell Laney what's going on. I planned to see her later and can't back out."

Petra nodded, but her retort was right there on her face. "I think she'd understand—"

"I know she would, Petra, but I'm not fucking chancing it." I narrowed my gaze, lowering my voice as my pulse raced. "These are the moments I need you to be better for me. A two-hour difference won't matter."

"Yes, it could. If someone found out that we know, they could cover their tracks. If it's your father or Dennis or someone else, they could be monitoring our emails."

"Jen would know if that was true."

She shrugged. "If I'm going to be your COO, you have to trust me. I have a feeling that Jen sending that email set off a chain reaction from the people who want you gone. I'll set the meeting for noon. That gives you forty minutes to talk to Laney, get your shit together, whatever."

My jaw tightened as Petra's words hit me in the chest. Forty minutes would work. The tree farm was twenty minutes from here toward the city, and I could grab her lunch before.

"Done. Get moving. I'll call Jen and tell her to remove the email."

It was a whirlwind before Petra left the house and I was in my SUV. Jen answered on the first ring, her voice nervous. She was never nervous.

"Talk to me, Jen."

"I think—"

"Wait." I pinched my nose as someone pulled out ahead of me. "Are you in the office?"

"I am, yes."

"We'll meet off-site. Petra will send you a location. Do not tell anyone what you found, delete your email to me, and leave your phone at the office."

"Do you think we're being watched?"

"I think someone is fucking with me, and I'm over it." I passed an old sedan, annoyed that people didn't know how to drive the speed limit. "And I don't trust anyone but you and Petra right now. Bring everything you found and refuse any requests from the board."

She gasped. "How did you know?"

I laughed darkly. "Put in PTO right now. Say something came up at home. Then go to the soup place down the block. Something isn't right."

"Okay, Connor. Be safe."

I hung up. My adrenaline was the highest it had been in a while. If the board—or my father—was watching us, that broke so many laws. But why had they wanted an attack? It had brought only bad press and loss of sales, and dragged my name through the mud.

Dennis and my father were the only two who were evil enough to do it, but why?

I drove a little too fast toward the tree farm, the urge to head to the office overwhelming me. I felt responsible. This was my company, and I had to protect it, protect everyone.

Sweat beaded on my forehead despite the frigid wind. I parked, then scrubbed my face over the fact I had forgotten her soup. So I was just gonna say goodbye in person? I groaned as my stomach fucking twisted into a pretzel. Laney might not understand my reason for leaving, and I really needed her to.

Even if she does understand, will she accept it?

I'd be choosing the company over her tonight. That's what she'd feel, but I didn't have a choice. This wouldn't be the last time this happened, and that reality hit me like a truck. There would always be *something* that came up at work. She might forgive me tonight, or the first few times it happened again, but what if emergencies kept resurfacing? I didn't fucking want that.

"Fuck." I pinched my nose and took deep breaths before someone tapped on my window. My wife stood there, red-nosed and with a small smile.

"Laney," I whispered, in awe of how damn pretty she was. I opened the door, and her smile grew.

"What are you doing here?" she asked, a little breathless.

"I wanted to see you." I pulled her into a hug, squeezing a little too tight. She smelled like cinnamon and the wind, which brought the scent of all the pine trees around us. "Are you warm enough? Do you want my jacket or gloves? How are your ears?" I checked them, rubbing her lobes to make sure they weren't frozen.

"Connor." She giggled against my chest before standing on her tiptoes and kissing me. Her lips were cold and she tasted like Christmas—like mint, warmth, fire, and tea. She ended the embrace way too fast, and I rocked toward her, not wanting to let our connection end.

"I'm doing great. This place is amazing, and the photos I've gotten? Holy cow. They are incredible. Do you want to see them? If you can take lunch with me, I can show you!" She spoke so fast, so joyfully. She loved this stuff.

My heart broke. She was so happy, and I couldn't... burst it. My throat bobbed as emotion choked me.

"I can't do lunch, baby, but I want to see a few."

A little line formed on her face, her knowing gaze assessing me. "If you're not here for lunch, what's going on?"

I hated this. I hated doing this to her. Taking her hand, I kissed the back of it and hoped she felt the guilt, the worry from me.

"I have to head into the city today. My CTO found evidence that someone, probably the board or my dad, planned the data breach as a way to hurt me. We think they are monitoring us, so we have to meet off-site to talk."

Her eyes widened and her lips parted.

"I am so fucking sorry. I planned to bring you soup and massage every part of you to make sure you weren't too cold today." I squeezed her hand, fully aware that mine trembled. "I have to do this, baby, and I hate that I feel like I'm letting you down. I'm only doing—"

"You're not letting me down." She smiled, squeezing my wrist five times. That was new. I didn't know what five squeezes meant. Her initial shock wore off, and she stood straighter, her voice stronger. "You told me. You're including me." She sighed, and the cloud of her exhaled breath surrounded us.

"You need to put on another scarf if you're going to be out here all day," I muttered.

She cupped my face, her soft fingers grazing my jaw as she forced me to look at her.

"Thank you for letting me know what was going on. The old you would've texted something like, 'a work thing came up, have to cancel,' and it'd feel like a gut punch. You driving out here? Telling me in person?" She gave me a watery smile. "This feels good. This feels like you understand what I want."

"Wait, really?"

She nodded. "I hate that you're leaving, of course, but this is huge. Finding a connection to the board? Wild. You need to be there for your people and get justice."

"You don't think this is me choosing work over you?"

There. I asked the one question that had gutted me since I learned I had to go into the office.

Laney rubbed her lips together, a thoughtful expression on her face.

"No. I don't. Not today."

"If I can wrap it up fast, I'll drive back tonight, okay?"

"Sweetie," she said, her lips curving, "you need to head there tomorrow anyway. You should stay, focus on your presentation."

Spend a night away from her? Two nights away? Not see her tonight? No. Unless...she wanted space?

"You don't want me to come back?"

"I want you safe and prepared. Tomorrow is big for you, for us."

"What are you not saying?" I whispered, unsure why I felt the need to hold her tighter, closer. She had said the right things, touched me, smiled, yet something felt off. Maybe it was the anxiety of the meeting, but panic clawed at my throat.

"Laney, please."

"I promise you—I'm okay. I'm not upset with you." She held my gaze as someone called her name from across the parking lot. "I would offer to go with you, but the events tonight and tomorrow are big deals."

"Yeah."

"I need my husband—you—to focus on nailing the bastards who are messing with the company you've run for years. I'm telling you to not worry about me tonight or tomorrow. After? Yes. You better get your ass here, and we can talk about next steps for us, but not tonight, and not tomorrow."

"I won't be able to sleep tonight without you."

"Then call me. We can fall asleep talking." She squeezed my forearms, pure determination and encouragement on her face. "I need my dominant, take-no-shit husband right now. The one who obliterates anyone who lies or cheats. He's a little scary and a lot hot."

I nodded, the grip on my throat loosening. I placed my hand on her shoulder, rubbing her collarbone with my thumb, squeezing three times, and taking a few deep breaths. Touching her calmed me.

"I can be him for a little bit."

"Good." She grinned before pulling the collar of my jacket and dragging me down for a kiss. "Now kiss me goodbye, properly."

That, I could do. Her full pillow lips pressed against mine, and I moaned at the contact. I fucking loved her mouth. The sassy comments, her intelligence, the way she leaned into the kiss like she couldn't be close enough to me. I slid my tongue against hers, shuddering at how good she tasted. She nipped my lip before pulling back, a wicked gleam in her eyes.

"Brat," I teased.

"Gotta give you something to think about while you're gone." She licked her lips, then pointed over her shoulder.

"I gotta get back to work. Be safe, okay?"

"I will. You too."

She waved and winked at me before going to talk to someone in a huge green winter coat. I wondered if he was the owner of the farm—but that wasn't a question I could ask right now.

I had to focus on my job. My wife was okay. She'd given me permission to leave. I'd throw myself into work to distract myself from missing her and shove down my curiosity about this town. My gut churned like something was off, but Laney told me once it wasn't worth stressing before something happened, because then you're stressing twice. While it was true, I couldn't stop the stress.

Laney and I are good.

I repeated it over and over and chose to believe it. Once the board meeting was over, we'd handle what came next.

CHAPTER TWENTY-THREE

LANEY

"Have I told you that you're pretty?"

I blushed. Connor was speaking to me over FaceTime. He had set his phone up against a lamp at his desk at work and insisted we talk for an hour this morning. It was wonderful.

He called me last night and updated me on what they'd found and their plan. For the first time in years, I felt included. I felt important. It was magnificent. I still couldn't believe the way his face had crumpled when he told me he had to leave yesterday—that emotion couldn't be faked.

He'd chosen me. That's all I wanted. It's all I wanted the last few years, ever since I became an afterthought.

"Stop, you're already married to me," I teased back, rolling over in my childhood bed to see him better. The tree farm event had gone late. My legs were tired, and my arms ached—something I wasn't prepared for. My head also throbbed. I rubbed the spot between my eyebrows and made a mental note to take some Tylenol. Could I? I had to look up if I was able to anymore. Even thinking about the secret I held weighed me down, and I winced.

I'd tell him soon.

"What's wrong? Do you have a headache?" Connor frowned. "I can send some stuff to you. Or call your mom."

"I'm okay." I sighed, unable to fight a smile. I love having him take care of me. "Just a little headache. I didn't realize how much I was on my feet yesterday. Wore me out."

"Baby, you should rest all day then, before the event tonight. Is someone going with you?"

"My mom is stopping by. My dad has a booth, so he'll be working." I yawned, stretching my arms over my head. The motion caused my head to spin, and I waited a few seconds for it to settle. That was...weird. The dizziness had stopped last week, but this episode was worse.

"I don't want you working again alone if you're not feeling well." He rubbed his jaw. "I could try to be back by seven—"

"I can handle one night, Connor." My voice came out strong, and I pointed a finger at him. "You need to focus on saving the company from assholes."

"Sure, but I also need to focus on making sure my wife is healthy."

"It's kinda hot when you say *my wife* like that."

His eyes lit up, and my giant grump smiled. "I love saying it. Call me possessive or jealous, but yeah, knowing you are my wife gets me through some tough times."

I smiled. It was weird how nothing, yet everything, had changed since finding out I was pregnant. I wanted to wait to tell him, to ensure he'd choose me. But then yesterday happened, and I saw firsthand the torture it was for him to go to work. He had practiced his presentation with me. I wasn't an outsider when it came to his business anymore, and that had been the missing piece. I wasn't going to wait until the New Year to tell him the news.

I'd do it the next time I saw him. Tomorrow. That way it wouldn't be a distraction and instead be a celebration. Even if the board meeting went to hell, this was a highlight, a future for us. Thinking about his reaction made me giddy. Because despite how the board meeting went, we'd find a way to be okay. Connor had sent me three job openings in the suburbs that he'd apply for if everything went south. They were only an hour outside of my hometown. That was close for me…not ideal, but it was better than where my mind went last week.

He had even shared his backup plan with me. The man was prepared.

"You sleep okay?" I asked. "You ready for tonight?"

"No." He chuckled. "My personal pillow was gone, and I don't want to let you down tonight."

"Connor," I chided, "you're standing up for yourself to the board. That's admirable."

Even if he got fired, they'd have to give him a severance package, and that would allow insurance for a while. Plenty of time for us to figure stuff out. Once I learned that, the urgency and fears had lessened.

"Regardless of what happens, you won't let me down."

"That's not true." He took a sip of water and cleared his throat. "There's a lot that could happen that would let you down, Laney, but I'm avoiding them at all costs."

"Have you seen your dad yet?"

His gaze darkened. "No. He's coming an hour before the meeting to speak with me."

My stomach clenched. "I hate that I'm not there with you."

"I wish you were, but the thing with my dad needs to end. It has to be me." He rubbed his temples as someone knocked on his door. "I gotta head back, but rest before the event tonight, okay?"

"I will. Good luck."

"Thank you, Laney." He held my gaze, his jaw working, before he smiled. "I love you."

"I love you too, husband."

His face lit up, and that was the image I wanted before hanging up. Connor happy. Today would suck for him. He could be removed from a job he loved, betrayed by his father.

It was weird how walking away seemed like the only option for him, even if that one was the most stressful. His dad was influential and assertive, and if Connor truly did cut him off, it wouldn't go over well.

The same dizzy feeling returned with a weighted lead in my stomach. I felt a prickle of awareness, like something was going to happen.

I frowned, sending him a quick text for good luck.

Laney: You totally got this, Connor. I love you. Can't wait to see you tomorrow. I have news!

Connor: Me neither, baby.

I got up and stretched, then called Sophia while I got ready and updated her on everything that had happened this weekend. My best friend analyzed every interaction.

"So you're going to tell him tomorrow?"

I nodded. "This feels right."

"You gotta trust your gut." She yawned and took a large sip of her coffee. "This actually makes me feel better. Again, always supporting your choices, but he should know. And waiting for the presentation to be over is perfect. He doesn't need the distraction or worry."

"Exactly." I nodded, the butterflies in my gut settling. "We'll know our future and can plan it together."

"Be prepared for him to be upset though, Laney. He might be upset you kept it from him, and he's usually a little overbearing. Just mentally prep for ways to reassure him."

I chewed my lip. She was right, but I was confident Connor would be overjoyed to learn the truth. "I'll be able to handle it."

"I know you will, girl. Now, what are you wearing to this gala event tonight?"

"Ha." I groaned. "It's outside, so it's not like you can look super cute while freezing."

"Disagree. You have those cute jeans and boots, and the bright red coat. Cherrywood is magical, I swear. Send me pictures of the event, would ya? I want to live through them."

"You could come?"

She made a face. "I wish I could, but my damn boss has a team dinner tonight for the holiday gift exchange. I picked him, which...I got him coal."

I snorted. She probably wasn't kidding, and I loved that about her. "I'll send you some photos when I can. Thank you for everything the last few weeks." A rush of gratitude washed over me. "I couldn't have gotten through this without you."

"That's what besties are for." Soph smiled warmly at me. "Remember this when it's my turn. When my super-hot and rich and famous husband tries to leave me, and I'm devastated."

"No man would leave you."

"No man wants to date me," she corrected. "Okay, my boss is calling. Let me know how tonight goes with Connor, okay? Love you!"

"You too!"

I wanted to spend the morning prepping for the event, getting my gear ready, doing my hair, and enjoying the atmosphere. In the days before Christmas, the joy was infectious. Music was everywhere, people smiled even more. My dad hummed "Frosty the Snowman" as easily as he breathed, and I swore the air smelled different. As if so many residents baked cookies at the same time that the atmosphere changed.

Ignoring the twist in my gut, I tried eating a few snacks and...nope. Wouldn't stay down. Tried a soda. That wouldn't either.

After a quick scan online, I learned that morning sickness was totally normal. I would keep going and try eating later, as a website had suggested.

Morning shifted to afternoon, then to the evening, and it was showtime.

"Laney, Laney, can you cover the Christmas movie night in the park?"

I waved and nodded to Becky, the event organizer. The wind had let up for the event, and kids' laughter, music, and cheers echoed across our town center. There was a live nativity scene near the church, carriage rides near the bank, and then a holiday movie projected on a screen at the baseball field. *A Charlie Brown Christmas* was playing. It truly was an incredible night filled with joy.

I captured the way the streets were lined with lights and

ornaments, the way wreaths hung on every door, and if there was space, a tree was put up. The green and red lights lit up the night sky.

"Hi, Laney!"

"Hi, Laney-girl!"

I smiled as neighbors greeted me. Travis and Tessa had volunteered to bartend at the end of the road, and they yelled my name as I approached. The baseball park was to the right of them, where pallets held fuzzy blankets that could be rented.

"Hey, you two."

"Look at you with that camera." Travis winked. "Want a drink to go?"

"No, I'm alright." I held up the device, hiding my wince as another bout of vertigo hit me. It could be stress. Connor met with his dad an hour ago, and the board meeting had started. I hadn't heard from him since.

I didn't expect to. Well, maybe a text update or something, but my damn stomach was a mess. Between the nerves and the baby, I wanted to curl up in warm pajamas and sleep.

"This place is still the same." Tessa's voice was filled with pride. "We've grown as a town, but the stores still go all out. The owners' association has less drama now that Kelly moved out of town."

I snorted at their banter and snapped a few photos of them. The tilting of a glass, the light reflecting off Tessa's eyes as she smiled. Travis standing with pride, a towel hanging on his shoulder as he stared at our town. Grinning, I showed them the shot.

"This is a good one."

"I look hot." Travis winked, and I rolled my eyes.

"You are also still the same," I teased. I left them at the bar and was immediately hugged by my mom's best friends. They smelled like vanilla and vodka, still, which was why I called them the ViVs. They thought it was hilarious.

A deep longing rooted in my chest as I talked to everyone and took pictures of them. I loved knowing the town's history and people. I loved how they knew me, and despite not being here for ten years, they embraced me like I had never left. Sneaking out my phone, I sent a picture to Sophia, and then Connor.

"You look happy."

Matt leaned against the fence, his cheeks pink and his smile wide. He wore a ridiculous hat shaped like the Grinch. I joined him, snapping a few shots of the kids cuddling before the movie started. There was a family in matching jammies that were adorable.

"I could say the same about you."

"I'm always happy." He rolled his eyes. "You know this. It was my hippie mom and lunatic father. Every day we choose to be happy. Some might say it's a curse."

"They are wrong. Never change." I reached out for a streetlight as another wave of vertigo hit me. I wish I could've taken some meds, but that meant keeping liquids down, and I couldn't. I swayed a little but righted myself before anyone noticed.

"This place is still amazing."

"It really is. My niece is out there right now. She's the five-year-old going on thirteen." He leaned closer to me and pointed.

"How cute," I said, not caring that half my body pressed against his.

"Whoa, Laney, are you alright?"

I nodded, but the movement caused my head to spin. I wasn't sure, but it looked like he winced when he stared at my face.

"Sit. You need to sit down."

"No, I need to take photos." My mouth was so dry and gross, and my lips were so chapped. Where was my water? "Becky needs me too."

"Everyone has a phone. She can create a contest or something for people to submit their photos."

"Oh, that's a jolly idea, Matt." I giggled as he put an arm around me. "You're so warm."

"When was the last time you ate?"

"Probably yesterday morning?"

He walked us toward the nearest bench, setting me down and gently placing his hands on my forearms.

"Laney, you need to eat. What about water?"

"Can't keep it down."

"You're so pale right now, it's freaking me out. Where's your mom? Your husband?"

"Busy." My eyes prickled.

"Do you have a drink?"

"We should take you to the emergency room, just to be safe." He ran a hand over my forehead, his lips turning down in a frown. Matt never frowned.

"Where's your phone?" he asked, his tone urgent. I handed it to him. He was a teacher and knew how to take charge.

"Connor, yeah?"

I nodded.

He dialed, but no answer. Shocking. He tried again, the concern and worry in his eyes growing.

"He won't answer."

"Then I'm leaving a message." This wasn't the Matt I knew from high school. This one was different. "Hey, Connor, this is Matt. I'm with your wife, and she can't even stand up straight. She's swaying, said she hasn't eaten or drank in a day. I'm going to try to find her mom to take her to the ER here, but I'll take her if I have to. Get your ass back here."

"Whoa. That was very un-Matt-like."

"Well, your husband should be here with you."

I winced and rubbed my forehead. "He has a busy board meeting tonight. It's a big deal."

"Sure, but if he knew how you were feeling, he shouldn't have gone."

"He doesn't know," I whispered. "I was gonna tell him about the baby tomorrow." My stomach tightened at sharing the news with him.

Matt reared back, his eyes wide with something. "Okay, we're going right now."

"What?" I blinked, but my world spun too fast. I gripped his arm as I swayed left and then right. Then everything faded to black.

CHAPTER TWENTY-FOUR

CONNOR

"You're a fool."

My eye twitched when my father waltzed into my office and slammed the door. His nostrils flared in disgust as he stared at me, then the wall, and then back at me.

"Nice to see you too, Father."

"Hanging up the phone on a board member? Not coming into the building in weeks? I don't know what Laney, or your marriage, has to do with this job, but you're about to lose it."

"Don't talk about my wife." I stood up from the old black chair I had inherited. It squeaked as it rolled back, the only sound in the room despite my breathing. Adrenaline coursed through me, heightening every sound or movement. Sweat beaded on my dad's forehead. His hands were in his pockets, but his shoulders were stiff. His chest heaved, like he'd ran up the stairs instead of taking the elevator. A tense, horrific hate clawed at my throat at seeing him in my office, glaring at me like I was a disappointment.

I worked hard. I paid taxes. I tried to be kind and do good, and I might've lost my way when it came to Laney, but I was back. The lens through which I saw my dad shifted. Maybe it was hearing Laney cry or knowing what the pain of her leaving felt like, but my father's opinion of me didn't matter anymore.

"Also I didn't say you could walk in here."

"Do I need permission to speak to my son now?" He barked out a horrid laugh.

"Yeah, I'm thinking you do." I kept my hands on my desk, refusing to clench them into fists. Images of Laney, of the fireplace, of our home replayed in the back of my mind.

"You're not invited to the board meeting, so why are you here?"

"You haven't answered a single one of my calls. When Dennis and Ryan said you've been acting irrationally, I vouched for you. I put my trust in you, and you're embarrassing me by gallivanting in some suburb instead of doing your job? You had a data breach from inside the house. What CEO leaves when that happens?"

I eyed my watch. Petra and I were meeting in ten minutes to set up in the conference room, and the last thing I wanted to do was talk to my father. Shaking my head, I sighed. I'd practiced what I wanted to say the entire drive over yesterday, yet the words did come out heated like I expected. I was calm and ready to cut this chapter from my life.

"I don't have to answer to you. I'm not your punching bag anymore. I don't want you in my life if this is how you're going to act. You also shouldn't know about the data breach being inside the house. That's further proof Dennis shouldn't be on the board."

"Don't answer to me? How do you think you got this job?"

His words were harsh, and spit flew from his lips. "You're so ungrateful—"

"I'm not. I worked hard. I'm going to ask you to leave before I call security because, despite your and Dennis's opinion, I'm in charge of this company." I ran a finger over my wedding ring, making sure I didn't forget the end goal.

I wanted to have more balance at work. That meant not letting my dad or Dennis pressure me. Meeting his gaze one more time, I swallowed and steeled myself.

"You raised me as a single father, and that's hard, and I'm glad you did. But I don't know what you want now. I don't get it. Why are you so indebted to Dennis? Why are you picking him over your son? I'm done with your games, Dad. If they fire me tonight, then so what? I love this job and am good at it, but tonight changes things."

Without waiting for his response, I grabbed my laptop and phone and marched past him. Petra glanced up from her desk, immediately stood, and fell in step with me.

"How was it?" she whispered, not giving anything away.

"No fucking idea, but it's done." I kept my face impassive despite the thunderstorm underneath my skin. I bit the inside of my cheek to distract from my inner turmoil. How fucked was it that I was scared to stand up to my dad at thirty-five? That it took Laney almost leaving to knock some reality into me?

The company had therapy services that I'd look into if tonight went as planned. It wasn't fair to myself, or my wife, if I didn't work through these workaholic, obsessive tendencies.

"Board is scheduled to arrive in thirty minutes. Everything is prepared like we planned. Folders printed and set up." Petra pushed the large conference room doors open and propped one of them open with the door stand. A blast of warm air rushed at us, and she coughed.

"Okay, how hot is it?"

"We can adjust." I gripped my tie, sweltering in the heat.

"You figure out the heat. I'm going to go over our notes."

The next thirty minutes to an hour flew by. The board walked in, three of them glancing at me with sympathy in their eyes. That didn't feel great, but I stood tall and shook all their hands.

Margaret has two kids, has been married for ten years, and started her own tech company decades ago. George was conservative with money but progressive in innovation. Bruce was big on security. Ryan was hit or miss with big initiatives, and Dennis was corrupt.

Once they were seated, Petra pulled up the agenda and began. "Thank you all for coming to an emergency board session called by Dennis. You can see on the schedule that we have agenda items to discuss."

"Is the first one really necessary? Pretty sure it'll be voided after we make a vote on the ability of Connor to remain as CEO." Dennis smiled and raised his hand in the air, waving it toward me. "Why discuss the position if it won't exist depending on the vote?"

"Dennis," Bruce chided, his brows furrowed, "we follow the order."

"But if we vote on the new position, then remove Connor as CEO, it doesn't matter."

"That's actually not true." Petra stood, looking like a total badass. She didn't flinch or acknowledge Dennis's petty behavior. She clicked on the PowerPoint.

"In the company bylaws, section eight, about the creation of new positions, it states that the board has the power to vote on executive positions. I want to reiterate that the CEO might present the idea, but the board has final voting power on the role. Our bylaws also say that meeting agendas are set twenty-four hours before and are not to change. Connor, would you like to start?"

Dennis's face turned red as he glared at her and then me. Ryan noticed the exchange but just frowned. This was go time. I went into detail, explaining the job duties, description, and how making Petra COO would increase our company's productivity, revenue, and culture. I spoke on the role it would play between departments and external relationships.

I spoke for thirty minutes before they pounded me with questions. Financial ones, long-term ones. My phone buzzed, but I ignored it.

"You think your assistant has the qualifications to do this job?" Dennis scoffed. "There's no way. She's a glorified secretary."

"We're going to have to disagree on that, and I demand you show her respect." I lowered my tone. "Over the last seven years, she has dealt with every facet of this company, and that's what a COO does. Deals with everyone and every detail. She is the only person for this role, and I welcome any questions that are not an insult to her."

"She can't handle the responsibility." Dennis stood and gripped the back of his chair. "Team, Connor is losing it. I know we're not voting yet, but he left his post the last few weeks because of his wife—"

"Is Laney okay?" George asked before glaring at Dennis.

"We knew he was remote, and it's not like work didn't get done, Dennis."

"A CEO should be here. At the office. I mean, fuck, there was a cyberattack! That could've killed the company, and instead of being here, he was worried about his wife."

"First off, Laney is fine. Thank you, George. My priorities were shifted for a moment, but I trust Jen, our CTO. She handled the tech aspects, where our legal team handled the rest. That is their roles and they handled them perfectly. We could get into how we had one, but I'd like to focus on the subject at hand, back to Petra being named as chief operating—"

"She's not going to have that position!"

"Oh, because you want it to go to your nephew, right?"

The air in the room dropped five degrees. I hadn't wanted to bring up Dennis's nephew because it felt too dirty. I didn't like stooping to his level, but it was time.

"Do you want me to update the board on our conversation, or would you?"

"What is he talking about, Dennis?"

"He's full of shit! Look at him. He's panicking because he knows he's being irrational with this ask."

I, in fact, was not panicking. I was in control. My phone vibrated again, but I hit the side button. This was the moment that had been years in the making.

"When I spoke with you all about the idea of having Petra as a chief operating officer, Dennis opposed it aggressively and told me the only way I'd get his vote—and all of yours—was if I hired his nephew, who not only isn't qualified but also hiring him would go against the bylaws prohibiting family members of the board from working here."

"That isn't true!" Dennis shook the chair, his eyes bugging out of his head. "You're lying. You're making this shit up."

"He's not." Petra stood and clicked to the next slide. "We have evidence."

"You recorded me?" he roared.

"Yes." I stood on the other side of the podium and met Petra's eyes for a beat. "I can play the video, which would be embarrassing for you, Dennis, but enough is enough. Petra is qualified. The job should be hers. Let's vote on it."

Margaret motioned first. "I move to approve the new position with the role being filled by Petra Swarski."

"I second." Bruce nodded at us before frowning at Dennis. "All in favor?"

"Aye," Ryan said.

Margaret nodded, saying, "Aye."

"Aye," George agreed, securing the vote of the majority. I couldn't hide my smile as Petra beamed.

"Aye," Bruce added, making four of five to confirm her.

"No." Dennis swallowed. "I vote no."

"Your vote is noted for the record, but the motion has passed. Petra will be named the new chief operating officer in four months' time, giving Connor enough time to prepare her replacement," Margaret said.

"Thank you, all. I won't let this opportunity go to waste. Let me prepare the next agenda item."

While Petra switched over the slides, I pulled out my phone to see a text and a few missed calls from Laney. My stomach tightened, fearing the worst. The voicemail-to-text feature popped up.

> Hey, Connor, this is Matt. I'm with your wife, and she can't even stand up straight. She's swaying, said she hasn't eaten or drank in a day. I'm going to try to find her mom to take her to the ER here, but I'll take her if I have to. Get your ass back here.

"What?"

My body didn't feel like my own. My skin prickled. She wasn't well. Matt was gonna take her to the ER, not *me*.

I'd missed the call. What if she'd tried calling me? Fuck. Fuck.

This had been her entire point. Work always came first. Oh my God.

"Petra, I have to go."

"Right now?" Her eyes widened.

"Laney...ER..." I couldn't breathe. "I need to—"

"Go right now." She swallowed and faced the board. "I'll handle the next part without Connor."

"We're gonna vote on your job, and you're running? Are you fucking serious?" Dennis laughed. "Oh, this is so much easier."

"My wife is in the ER right now, an hour away. That is where I should be. Not here, defending my work to you of all people. I do a great job, but I don't care—remove me. Petra can run this place." I didn't even wait for a reply before running out the door with my phone to my ear.

It rang and rang and rang, but Laney didn't pick up. Fuck. I punched the elevator button, but it took too damn long. I needed to go, right now. I barged through the stairwell doors and took them two at a time as my mind raced.

Did she pass out? Was she with her mom? I didn't know. My ears rang, and my throat closed up to the point I couldn't breathe.

She was with Matt, of all people.

"Connor, wait!" Petra had her heels in one hand as she darted down the stairs toward me. "I'll drive you!"

"What about the thing?" Two more steps each second. One more floor to go.

"Fuck that. If they can't see that family matters more, then I don't want to work here. Plus, didn't want to get you all pissed, but if they let you go, I'm leaving too."

"Petra," I scolded, but almost laughed, "admirable, but you don't have to do that."

"Where did you park?"

"Floor A in the garage."

We ran together, and she hopped in the front seat, giving me the passenger so I could call everyone. I tried Laney again, and my stomach soured. I traced her location, which showed her at the hospital.

"Fuck. She's at the ER and not answering."

"She could not have her phone with her."

"Matt took her. Her fucking high school ex." I scrubbed a hand over my face. My jealousy was overshadowing my concern. "I need to try her mom."

"Good idea." She swallowed as she pulled onto the road that led to the interstate. It was late, so there wasn't as much traffic, but it was still too much. "Ugh, shitty drivers."

The phone rang in my ear as I dialed her mom. It rang without an answer.

"Why is no one answering their fucking phones?"

"You could try Matt."

"I don't have his fucking number."

"Uh, well, see...I do?" She cleared her throat, her voice shaking a little toward the end. If I wasn't freaking the hell out about Laney, I'd want to dive into that, but it was not the time.

She tossed me her phone and I scrolled for Matt, then dialed his number. He answered on the second ring.

"Petra?"

"Is Laney okay? What's wrong? Where is she?"

I heard a beeping sound. Was that from a machine? Was he at the hospital? I loosened my tie since each breath took effort.

"She's okay, yeah." Matt sighed before a muffled voice neared him. "I'm gonna step out for a minute."

"Are you speaking to Laney? Put my wife on the phone."

"Connor." Matt spoke softly but firmly. "That was the nurse. Laney is doing fine. She passed out due to dehydration, so they have her hooked up to some IVs and are monitoring her. They want to check...make sure she is good." He cleared his throat and hesitated. "Are—are you en route?"

"Yes. I'm en route. Now can I speak to her?"

"She's sleeping. She's safe. We're on the second floor of the hospital. They'll buzz you up."

There was something about his tone that had me on edge. He was hiding something. I could smell the lie through the phone, and I gripped the car's grab handles so hard that my knuckles whitened.

"Why aren't you letting me talk to her?" I barked out.

"Because she's resting. Because you're really emotional right now and won't help her. Let her feel better before you barge in here. She needs you calm."

"Are you Laney's husband?" A kind, authoritative voice spoke to Matt, which carried through the phone.

My vision blurred. I saw red.

"Connor, I'm going to try to see if the doctor will give me any information. Her parents are on their way. Just take some deep breaths and get here. You acting frantic won't help her at all."

Then he hung up.

My pulse skipped a beat, the pressure in my chest tightening and doubling with each breath. Placing a hand on my chest, I pushed into it, hoping that would ease the pain.

"Breathe in slowly, Connor. Count to seven, then exhale. We'll get there, okay? It sounds like she's okay."

"They asked if Matt was her husband."

She sucked in a breath. "You should be thankful he helped her. He's not the issue."

"I know he's not the fucking issue. If I wasn't obsessed with the board meeting, I could've answered the first call." My eyes stung, and my throat closed. "I don't know what to do."

"You breathe. You calm the hell down. Call her mom or dad, talk to them."

"Yeah, okay." I dialed her dad. No answer.

Forty-seven minutes until we arrived at the hospital.

Forty-six.

Forty-five.

Each minute passed excruciatingly slowly, and each second, I vowed to never let this happen again. Whatever it took, I'd put Laney first.

If she'd still have me after this.

CHAPTER TWENTY-FIVE

LANEY

"Well, this is weird."

My mom's head snapped toward me, along with my dad's and Matt's.

Matt was in the room with me... why?

"Did I travel back in time? Am I in high school?"

"Now is not the time for jokes, missy." My mom squeezed my forearm before resting her head on the spot next to my stomach. "You scared us."

My dad's face was tight with worry. Despite wearing bright green Christmas overalls, he glared at me. "You are staying under my roof, and we didn't even notice how sick you've been. Honey, what is going on?"

Flashes of the night came at me fast. Feeling dizzy. Taking photos. Matt. Matt demanding I go to the ER. I moved my attention to him. He stood in the back, hands in his pockets and a grim look on his face.

"Did you drive me here?"

"You passed out against me. We rode in an ambulance, Laney."

Shame flamed my face. I should've listened to my body more. All day, I'd felt weird but pushed through it because it's what I always did. It had been selfish of me. I couldn't just think about myself anymore. Immediately, my hands went to my stomach, and I gasped.

"I-I need to talk to the doctor."

"We can page the nurse, sweetie. Are you in pain? What do you need?"

"I need..." My eyes welled up as panic clawed at me. What if my neglect hurt the baby? Oh my God. Connor.

"Where is my phone?"

"I think it's in your bag, but Laney, I haven't told them." Matt's face was more serious than I had ever seen it. No smile or quirk of his lips. "I'll try to find the nurse for you."

He stepped out but left the door open. Something shuffled outside the room—loud footsteps.

"What is he talking about?" My mom sat up straighter, her gaze narrowing on my face. "Laney, please."

"I haven't had a chance...Connor..." I squeezed my eyes shut as guilt and pain and stress swirled into one ball of emotion that closed my throat. I couldn't breathe or swallow. I had to tell them the truth, even before I could tell my husband. "I'm pregnant."

Neither of my parents spoke. They stared at me, wide-eyed.

"I'm pregnant. I found out a few days ago. It's why I've been so sick, not able to eat." I sniffed as tears rolled down my face. "I didn't know how bad it had gotten."

"Does Connor know? You could've told us. We could've helped. Oh, honey." My mom hugged me tightly. "I have so many emotions, I don't know how to deal with them."

"I'm gonna be a grandpa." My dad clapped his hands and laughed. "Holy shit."

"Laney."

I jumped at the deep voice at the door. Connor stood there, lips parted, as I stared at him over my mom's shoulder. He looked terrible. He had done a full one-eighty since our FaceTime just hours ago. His styled hair was disheveled. His tie hung half undone, his shirt untucked. His jacket wasn't buttoned. He looked so messy and distraught that my heart broke for him. His mouth parted as he ran a hand over his face. Then he neared me and kneeled on the floor. Even on his knees, his height matched me in the bed, and he rested his forehead on my stomach.

"You're okay. You're okay."

"I'm okay, yeah." My eyes prickled, and I ran a hand through his hair, digging my fingers into his scalp as his shoulders shuddered. "How are you here?"

"We're gonna step outside to grab a coffee, okay, honey? You two should talk." My mom patted my shoulder and then squeezed Connor's before leaving and shutting the door.

Once the handle clicked, absolute silence greeted us, and it suffocated me. I had kept the pregnancy from him. He would hate me. This wasn't what I had planned.

"Connor...I—"

"I'm so fucking sorry." He spoke into my abdomen, his voice muffled over the hospital sheet. His shoulders shook, and he gripped my hand in his and squeezed it hard.

My own tears spilled over at the devastation in his voice.

"Connor, I'm sorry."

He stilled and lifted his face enough to meet my gaze. His eyes were red, and he licked his lips twice before shaking his head.

"You have nothing to be sorry about except not taking care of yourself. I wish you would've told me you weren't feeling well."

"What would that have done?"

"I would've known! I could've stayed here, helped you."

I smiled, but he didn't match it.

"I've been sick before. I'm a grown adult, and yeah, I could've told my parents or stayed home, but I loved the festival. I didn't want you to worry about me or stress about it when you had to focus." I swallowed, broaching the topic that had me twisted up. "Did you hear—"

"I fucking hate that you're putting my job first." He scrubbed his hand over his face. "We agreed on honesty. I'm upset you kept this from me."

"I was gonna tell you tomorrow." I sniffed as I placed my hands over my stomach. "I really didn't want you distracted, and yet here you are. Is the meeting over? How did it go?"

Knock, knock.

"How is our sweetest patient this evening?" Kelly, a cheery nurse, walked in with a smile. "Oh, hello. Now, is this your husband?"

"Yes," I said proudly.

"Good for you. Two attractive men in one night."

Connor stiffened and flexed his jaw, and my stomach dropped.

"I need to check your vitals, okay, hon? Do you mind moving over there for a few minutes, handsome?"

Connor nodded and awkwardly released my hand to sit in the chair my parents had been in ten minutes ago. While Kelly took my temperature and checked the machines, I stared at my husband.

His gaze never left mine, and he kept swirling his wedding ring around his finger over and over, like he was thinking hard about something. I couldn't be certain whether he knew about me being pregnant. But I knew I had to tell him now.

"All looks good. Now that your vitals are settled, do you want to try eating anything?"

"Yeah," I croaked out. "That'd be good."

"They have you staying overnight for monitoring, and then we'll get an ultrasound in here as well, to ensure the fetal heartbeat." She smiled at me and then Connor. "Someone will be back in a few hours. Our vending machines are down the hall, and I know we have saltines in there."

"Perfect," I said, my pulse skyrocketing. Connor wasn't stupid. He had to have heard the fetal heartbeat comment.

Kelly left, once again leaving the two of us alone, and I was nervous to look at Connor. How could I have thought it was a good idea not to tell him? I played with the bedsheet, my head spinning with indecision. What could I say? How do you speak when you're clouded in guilt?

"I'm sorry I didn't tell you." I faced the wall near the bathroom. My voice was all watery and weak. "I had a plan—"

"We're having a baby," Connor said, his voice just above a whisper. There wasn't heat or anger in his tone. Just... wonder.

I snuck a glance at him, and my breath caught in my throat. He was smiling.

"We're having a baby, Laney." He barked out a laugh and put a hand over his chest, his eyes lighting up in a way I hadn't seen before. Then his face shifted into a frown. "Wait, you...you want to be a mom, right? You want this...with me? If you don't...I'll—I— What do you want?"

Goddamn, I loved this man. This confident, badass leader who strutted into rooms was falling apart over me and our potential family.

"Yes. I want it all, but—" I held up a hand, and he nodded, waiting for me. "We still have so many things to talk about."

He swallowed, his throat bobbing with the movement, and he jumped off the chair. "I need you closer to me. I can barely breathe right now."

I snorted as he gently wrapped his arms around me, pulling me into a tight hug. He smelled like home, and the embrace put all my stress at ease. Running my hands over his shoulders, I massaged a knot as the hug continued without talking.

I had questions. Lots of them. I'm sure he did too. But right now, this was enough. Us safe and together.

"You need to eat." He broke the hug and kissed my forehead, lingering before he smiled down at me. "Saltines and Sprite?"

"My favorites."

"I'll get you some and be right back. Are your parents still here?"

"I actually don't know." I shrugged and reached out to grip his hand. "I'm so glad you're here, Connor."

His answering smile melted my heart.

"There's nowhere else I'd rather fucking be." He kissed the

back of my hand, handed me my bag with my phone, and went to the door, stopping and staring at me with an unfocused look.

"If you thought I was overbearing or protective before, you have no idea what I'm gonna be like now that you're carrying our child."

"Oh."

Heat stung my face before he winked and said he'd be right back.

I nodded, and he left. Exhaustion plagued me, but I knew I had to eat a little before they'd release me tomorrow. My phone had ten missed calls from Connor, frantic texts from him as well.

> **Connor:** PLEASE tell me you're okay.
>
> **Connor:** LANEY. Fuck! I'm so sorry. I'm on my way.
>
> **Connor:** I love you so fucking much, please be okay.
>
> **Connor:** I hate that Matt is with you.

My stomach tightened. Yeah, having Matt take me here wasn't ideal, but it wasn't like I chose to pass out on him. I went to his contact information and quickly sent him a thank-you-for-everything text.

He responded with **anytime**.

Then I texted my mom and dad in our group chat.

> **Laney:** Connor is gonna stay with me through the night. You are dismissed from your duty. Clock out.

Mom: Your dad has already ordered ten baby outfits. He's out of control.

Dad: Why are you ratting me out?

Mom: So she can talk sense into you!

Laney: Okay, I'm silencing my phone. I'll text you when I leave tomorrow.

Mom: Love you!!!

Dad: If it's a boy, you're naming him after me, right?

Chuckling, I tossed my phone back in my bag and relaxed into the hospital bed. It was more comfortable than I thought, and I yawned just as Connor walked in with a soda and a sleeve of crackers.

"Thank you." I reached for them, and he pulled the chair closer so he could touch me while I ate. His face seemed different from when he had walked in the door, and I leaned over, running my hand over his jaw.

"I want to explain some things to you."

"Not until you eat." He opened the package and handed me a cracker, one eyebrow arched like he was prepping for an argument. "Don't test me."

"Yes, sir." I chewed the cracker and chased it down with the soda.

"Delicious."

"I know you're not kidding either." He chuckled and ran a

hand down my leg, squeezing it under the sheet. "Only you would claim this as your top-five favorite snacks."

"It's my truth." I ate another and sighed at being able to swallow without the urge to throw up. "All those days I was dizzy or throwing up? It was the pregnancy."

He nodded. "I looked up all the common symptoms while I got the food. We can battle them and make sure you're comfortable."

"You're being so patient about this, Connor." My eyes prickled as I swallowed a bite. I couldn't eat anymore until I said my piece. "I found out a few days ago and chose not to tell you. I'm sorry. I-I feel terrible keeping that from you. When that felt weak, I realized the truth. I was so worried that you'd change behavior, change everything for the baby when I needed you to make changes for me. I wanted you to pick me. I needed to feel that from you, and I have. I have in so many ways." A tear fell, and he frowned, swiping it away.

"I'm so sorry I kept it from you. I shouldn't have." I hiccuped. "I had a plan to tell you tomorrow. I bought a little onesie, and I was gonna surprise you."

He smiled, and his gaze melted. "I'm not upset with you. Not at all."

"But why?" I sniffed as another wave of tears fell. "I made this choice to hide it from you, and I feel so selfish."

"You're not selfish." He leaned forward and gently pressed his lips against mine, the softness of the kiss almost breaking me. "We're working on us, and it had to be a shock to find out. I wish I had been with you, but I'm here now. I'm not going anywhere."

A ball of emotion formed in my throat, and I closed my eyes as more tears fell. He pulled me into a hug and rubbed my head in soft circles.

"Sleep, baby. I need you to rest. We can talk tomorrow. I'll be here when you wake up, okay?" he said, either ten minutes or two hours later. I wasn't sure.

I was exhausted, and the comfort of Connor's presence had lulled me into sleep fast. With a smile on my face and the first sense of real calm, I slept.

CHAPTER TWENTY-SIX

CONNOR

The relief of seeing Laney okay dulled the shock of learning she was pregnant—something she chose not to tell me. An older version of me, even from a few weeks ago, would've been angry. How could she keep a secret that important from me? I wouldn't have understood why she didn't tell me immediately.

But I saw her now. I saw what hurt her, what worried her, and how we could be better as a couple. I knew we'd have to talk it out, but the relief about her health outweighed every other feeling.

Her doctor still needed to clear her before we headed home, but she already seemed better this morning. Color had returned to her face, and the first thing she did was smile at me.

"Hi."

"Hi," I repeated, leaning forward and intertwining our fingers. Her ring finger lay bare, and I ran my thumb over it. Someday, she'd wear my ring again.

"You look like you feel better."

"I do." She yawned and did the little wiggle stretch she always did. I loved that combination.

"You look tired."

"I feel perfect." I meant it too. "The nurse came in a little bit ago and told me we'll get to leave soon. I figured, if you're up for it, we could stop at the café for soup and tea first?"

"Oh, the cute shop near Main Street?"

I nodded. "We can enjoy something warm and talk."

Her eyes clouded over as she swallowed. "We have a lot to discuss."

"Sure, but none of it changes a thing about us." I squeezed her fingers, waiting for her to meet my gaze. When she did, I spoke slower.

"We can talk about where we're gonna raise our family, what job you want to do. I can update you on the board meeting, and you can show me photos of the event. We can chat about all of that, but nothing changes how I feel about you, us, and our future."

I had no idea what my future career was anymore, but for the first time in my entire adult life, I didn't give a shit. The board meeting taught me that I really didn't want that stress and negativity in my life. It wasn't worth it. I missed an emergency call from my wife because of political bullshit, and I was done.

While Laney rested, I looked into the town more and its struggling businesses. I didn't have a full concept yet, but I used my notes app to create a proposal. If they wanted someone to get this place back on the map, I could be that guy. It was wild how life worked out. A month ago, you couldn't have paid me to leave my job. It defined me.

Now though? Maybe everything needed to break for us to rebuild and be stronger. It sucked, but I only felt hope at this moment. We'd be fine either way.

Her bottom lip trembled as she closed her eyes. "You should be mad at me."

"Baby, I missed your calls. I wasn't with you when I should've been. I missed the signs of how sick you felt. You should be mad at me."

"No, you were fighting at the board meeting, trying to change things at your job because I needed it. That's on me."

"You're wrong. I was promoting Petra and standing up for myself, for me, not just you." I laughed and set my hand over her heart. "We're financially okay, so no matter what happens after last night's meeting, we'll be safe. I promise you. I'll take care of you and our baby."

"I know you will." She sighed and leaned her face closer to me. Her lips were cracked, and her eyes had a darker hue to them, but she was still beautiful.

"Hey," she whispered.

"Hmm?" I fought a grin. The entire car ride here, I had thought the worst. Would I ever see her cute dimple again? Hear her sigh? Watch her eyes light up from happiness? It almost didn't seem fair that I had gotten another chance with her.

"Can we get the soup to go? I just want to be alone with you."

The knot in my chest loosened the final knot. "Of course."

The next hour flew by, with us chatting about what we should buy everyone for Christmas. It was in three days—somehow the month had gone fast and slow at the same time.

I knew that Laney was thoughtful with gifts, where I took the most convenient route. I didn't love that about myself.

"What if we only purchased gifts at the rest of the festival?" I suggested as I led us outside.

"What do you mean?" She gripped my arm as we walked outside in the cold. Petra had arranged a car for us and got a ride home with Matt. Despite the fact that Petra's presence in my life once hurt Laney, she had been helpful and supportive the last week. My chest ached with the thought of the board meeting and the way Dennis had spoken about her, but the vote was in. She'd be our new COO. That was worth the fight because she deserved it.

Me? I couldn't be sure. I'd stormed out. Almost blackmailed a board member. Cut off my dad. And missed calls from my wife before she passed out. If it weren't for learning I was gonna be a dad, yesterday could have been the worst day of my life.

"You spend so much time thinking of gifts to buy, and since I don't want you to carry that burden alone anymore, we can walk the festival tonight and pick out gifts."

"Oh. The photos. I need to call Becky."

"I'm sure your mom took care of it already, but I'm happy to be your assistant and take all the photos you need."

She smiled as I opened the passenger door for her. "Connor, I can buckle myself."

"Of course you can." I leaned in, kissed her neck, and buckled her in anyway. "Humor me. I spent forty minutes yesterday losing my fucking mind, so yeah, if I want to buckle my wife in and ensure she's safe, I'm going to."

"Oh lord," she said, but humor was in her tone.

We drove to the café and ordered two homemade chicken noodle soups to go with two hot chocolates before driving back to her parents' house. I parked in the driveway and ordered her to stay put.

"I'm opening your door for you."

"That's silly."

"I don't care. Now, stay."

Her eyes lit up, and she giggled. "Kinda hot when you're bossy."

Shit. The rasp in her words had my blood going south, but it was not the time. She was healing. Pregnant. Oh God. Could I sleep with my wife? Would that be weird?

I froze halfway to her side when her door opened, snapping me into gear. "What did I say, lady?"

"You took too long." She shut the door with her hip as she smiled at me. "Why do you look stressed?"

"We need to call your doctor." I grabbed the food, and instead of walking into her parents' house she marched next door.

"What are you doing?"

"I want to be alone with you." She pursed her lips. "And that means not being at my parents'."

"Laney. They'll want to see you."

"They will later. I want my husband right now, okay? Just you." She walked up and stood on her tiptoes, kissing me softly with her pillow lips.

I melted. I was Frosty on a beach. There was so much sweetness and love and tenderness in her gesture that my heart clenched.

"I love hearing you call me your husband."

"I know." She winked. "Now come on, hubs."

"That was too far." I laughed. "I'm not a hubs."

"You're my hubs."

Rolling my eyes, I let us into the house and prepared to get our food set up by the fire. We could talk through everything, fully, while Laney ate. But as I set the food down, she took my hand.

"Come." She tugged me.

"What? You need to eat, baby."

"I can eat later. I want to feel you against me."

"Honey," I groaned. "I don't... You can't... Can you eat first?"

"I ate breakfast at the hospital." She pulled me into the bedroom—because let's be real—I'd go wherever she wanted.

"I want to feel your skin on me."

My dick hardened as she tossed her jacket and sweater onto the floor, leaving her in a red lacy bra. Her nipples hardened and poked through, but not for long. She undid the back and tossed the fabric with the others.

"Laney."

"Please, Connor." She pouted. That fucking bottom lip stuck out as she slid her jeans and panties off too.

"I need this. I want to feel close to you."

"You're not feeling well." I tried to stay strong. I really did. But she crawled across the bed, naked and perfect, and tugged at my waistline. Her fingers dipped into my pants as she untucked my shirt. The slight touch of her cold hands had me sucking in a breath.

"I feel great. I'm hydrated. Happy. Home, since I'm with you." She stood, the apex of her thighs almost in my face as she pulled my shirt off. I wanted to be strong, but my wife was sexy as fuck, and her pussy was right there. "I researched and we're totally safe to still have sex."

I cupped her ass and brought my nose to her thighs, nipping her skin as she groaned loudly.

"Fuck, you're perfect."

She giggled and squirmed against me.

"Naked, Connor. I want you naked."

I teased her folds with my tongue, swirling her swollen bud a few times before gently sucking it.

"If you didn't just get out of the hospital, I'd have you straddle my face while I got you off with my tongue."

"I'm not fragile, you know."

"Mm-hmm." I sucked her again, and she let out the sexiest throaty moan.

"Let me treat you like you are."

I carefully set her on the bed, taking my time studying my favorite parts about her. The dusting of freckles on her nose. The mole under her eye. Her full lips and sexy neck.

I cupped her face and kissed her slowly.

"I love you, so much, Laney. And I'm gonna show you every day. You and our baby. I know why you didn't tell me right away, and it's okay. I hope you know I'll pick you always."

"Connor." Her eyes welled, and she tried to still me. "I'm so, so—"

"No apologizing." I kissed her neck and her clavicle, her beaded nipples my next target. I bit one, playing with the other with my fingers as I teased her.

"The only words you can say are *more, yes please,* and *okay, Connor.*" I sucked her other breast before dragging my tongue up and down her stomach.

"Your skin tastes so good. This feel okay?"

She nodded, her eyes bright and filled with lust as she watched me. "Can I say how hot you are?"

"Yes. Definitely." I winked at her before pushing one leg up and kissing it from her ankle to her inner thigh. "You are stunning. Perfect. Mine."

She shuddered. "Closer. I want you pressed against me."

I spread her open with my fingers and licked her hard before meeting her gaze. She bucked and sweat coated her skin as I touched her the way I knew she liked. The tremble of her thighs, the heat of her skin. My wife was divine. "Perfect."

"Make love to me, Connor."

"I am, baby. I always am." I crawled up her again, kissing every part of her as I brought my mouth to hers. "I. Love. You."

She sniffed as I shifted behind her, placed her back to my chest and pressed my cock to her. I cupped her lower stomach as I thrusted into her, bare. There was no room between us as I slowly fucked her.

"Yes, Connor, this was what I wanted. I can feel your heartbeat against me."

I kissed her jaw, and under her ear, and held her tighter against me. She rocked slowly against my cock, and we lay side by side, my gentle thrusts unhurried. The subtle scent of her vanilla shampoo combined with sweat, and it was intoxicating.

"You're fucking beautiful," I whispered, running my free hand down her body. Her smooth skin was so damn soft as I tugged her nipples. She mewed, and I sucked the spot where her shoulder met her neck.

"God, you feel so good. I love this, you, us," she whispered.

I found her clit and matched the rhythm to my thrusts, and Laney's entire body shook.

"You're close," I whispered. "Fall apart on me. I got you."

She cried out, her throaty moans filling the guest room as I held her through the orgasm. Her legs trembled and her pussy tightened as she came, and I focused on breathing. I didn't want this to end. I never once stopped my pace and continued touching and kissing her everywhere.

She sniffed, the watery sound making me pause.

"What's wrong? Are you hurting?"

"No, no. Don't you dare stop." She reached behind and gripped my thigh. "I just love this, and you, and I'm overwhelmed."

I smiled against her skin.

"You feel how good we are together. How we're meant to be together." I went back to slowly grinding into her, gripping her waist to change the angle slightly, and her breathing picked up. This wouldn't last long. She felt too good.

"I need you to come again, baby. Touch yourself for me."

She did what I asked, the wet sound of me going in and out of her joining our heavy breathing. She bucked a few times, her moans growing. I took over for her, desperate to bring her to the edge.

"Fuck, look at you," I gasped right as she cried out my name.

Her legs straightened, her eyes slammed closed, and her hands gripped the sheets around us as her orgasm ripped through her. I couldn't take it. I came too, holding on to my wife as wave after wave of pleasure hit me. I saw stars behind my eyes, and my ears roared so fiercely that I couldn't hear a thing after.

I gave myself two seconds to take in every feeling, catch my breath, before sliding out and cupping my wife's face.

"Are you okay? Do you hurt?"

Laney beamed at me. Her cheeks were red, and her pulse raced at the bottom of her neck, but her eyes gave her away. They were so clear, so beautiful.

"That was incredible."

I kissed her forehead. "Now that you're satisfied, wife, may I ask you to eat some damn soup?"

She snorted and tickled my sides.

"Don't ruin my post-sex vibe, Connor. I was dehydrated, not losing a limb."

"Don't care." I slid off the bed, helping her up with me. I grabbed one of my sweatshirts, slid it over her head, and rolled up the sleeves on her wrist.

"So cute," I teased, admiring the way my clothes hung on her. "You should only wear my clothes at home."

"I'm sure we could arrange it." She wiggled her brows as she looked me up and down.

"Have I told you I love your calves?"

"It's been a while." I smiled.

"Enough." I slid on some sweatpants and a long-sleeved shirt. "Soup and talking time."

"Old you would've been just fine cuddling naked and watching a show. This version of you really likes talking, huh?"

"I know you're teasing, but yes, I do. I'm not letting anything come between us, not even your distractions." I swatted her butt, and she yelped.

"Go turn the fire on, hon. I'll be right there."

We split, with one of us going into the living room and the other the kitchen, where I was preparing the food when my phone pinged with a message.

I expected it to be her parents, Petra, or our friends. Not Ryan... and just like that, my stomach dropped.

CHAPTER TWENTY-SEVEN

LANEY

I watched the fake flames flicker as heat surrounded me. Connor's scent cloaked me, and I trembled as I thought about our connection. I had to give us credit. I felt empowered to speak my feelings now. I wasn't worried or scared of our conversation. Sure, there were some nerves, but Connor opening up had changed our relationship.

I wanted to know about the board meeting. He hadn't mentioned anything. My hair was a mess, so I redid it in a messy bun as Connor walked into the living room with two bowls on a tray. I was about to flirt with him, but there was tension all around his eyes.

"Hey, what's wrong?"

His gaze met mine as he sat down, setting the tray between us.

"Ryan left a message."

Ah.

"You're worried about it."

"He asked me to call him back." Connor nudged my knee,

his pointed stare urging me to eat. "Laney, I will feed you if I have to."

"That might be fun."

He snorted, his lips quirking up on one side. I wanted to lighten the mood, but the tension in his shoulders was too noticeable.

Instead of fighting him, I took a few bites. He nodded in approval before he stared at the fire.

"All my life, I was told I had to fight to be good enough. My dad raised me without real love. It was all drive and competition to be the best. Being the CEO of a startup tech company was all I knew how to be. Then I met you, and you clashed with my plans a little. I had this beautiful soul loving me and wanting to be in my life. It was a gift. You are a gift."

My chest ached for him. The pain, the stress poured out of him. But he needed to do this. I rubbed his knee, drawing small circles on it as he took a deep breath and continued.

"My dad always liked having control over me. I used to think it was to help me succeed, but now... I don't even understand his motivations. When he told me to let you go, it broke something in me. Then he threatened me about Dennis and my position." Connor shook his head, his voice quieter now. "This isn't the life I want."

"Do you think Dennis has something on him?" I asked gently.

"I don't know," Connor admitted. "Or maybe it's just the way they all play the game. Dennis told me he'd only give the COO role to his nephew. It's all politics, and I'm tired of it. I thought this was my dream career, but... maybe it's not. I've been holding on to it so tightly, I didn't stop to ask if it was worth it."

"You're great at your job," I offered carefully. "You love leading, creating, negotiating. That's who you are."

"I do love those things," he said, his gaze meeting mine. "But not with all the strings attached. I've been so scared of losing their approval—or my position—that I forgot what really matters. Cutting ties with my dad doesn't hurt as much as I thought it would. Honestly, I feel relieved. But walking away from this company? That's harder."

I reached for his hand, squeezing it gently. "You're allowed to choose something new. Something better for you."

He smiled faintly, as if seeing the possibility for the first time. "Maybe I already have."

"What do you want, Connor? No filters, no second-guessing—what do you want? Six months from now, how do you want your life to look?"

His gaze moved from the fire to me, a soft, gentle expression on his face.

"I want you happy and looking at me like you are now. I want to see our child grow inside you, be there for every appointment, and laugh and cry with you as you waddle."

"I will not waddle!" I teased.

"Being here has reset my priorities. Cherrywood has magic to it." He flashed a nervous smile, his shoulders tensing. "You love it here."

I nodded. "Can I share something with you?"

"I'd be disappointed if you didn't. Honesty, forever, even if it's hard to hear." His voice quieted, but the intensity in his eyes stayed firm. "I want to know all of you—your thoughts, your dreams, your fears. I'll carry them with you, no matter what."

I took a deep breath, finding strength in his words. "I want to stay here. Full time. I've hinted at it before, but I need you to know—I don't just like Cherrywood; I feel like I belong here. It's not just the familiarity or my parents being nearby. It's everything. The small-town life, the friends I've reconnected with, the quiet moments. I'm not lonely here like I was in the city. I don't just want this to be a retreat. I want it to be home."

His gaze locked onto mine, unyielding and steady. "Keep going," he said, his voice low but encouraging.

"I also don't love the idea of you working an hour away all the time," I confessed, softer now. "If we lived here, you'd miss so much—coming home late, leaving early. It'd be just me again. And I want more for us, especially now."

His jaw tightened for a moment, then relaxed. "I've thought about this too," he admitted, a small smile tugging at his lips. "I even talked to Alex, our finance guy, a while back to see if we could afford to keep the condo and buy a house here. Turns out, we can. I was going to surprise you with the idea."

My eyes widened. "Two places? Really?"

"Yeah." He leaned back, running a hand over his jaw, a mix of hope and hesitation flickering across his face. "But after everything—the hospital, the baby—it's clearer to me now. A place in Cherrywood isn't just a second home. It's *our* home. And if that means finding a remote job or even something here, then that's what I'll do. I'm not going to miss a single moment of this life with you."

Tears stung my eyes, but they were from relief, not sadness. "You'd do that?"

He reached across the table, taking my hand in his. "Baby, I will do that. You're my future—this life we're building is my future. And I'll do whatever it takes to make it ours."

"Can you call Ryan back?" I whispered, my voice steady but full of hope. Connor needed clarity, and I believed this call would bring it. "You deserve to know the full story. Even if that's not what you want anymore, you need to know."

Connor hesitated, his brow furrowed. "You think I should hear him out?"

"I think you owe it to yourself—and us—to get the truth." I leaned forward, placing a hand on his knee. "And whatever happens, we'll figure it out."

He studied me for a moment, then nodded. "Alright."

He picked up his phone and called Ryan. I stayed close, offering silent support as the line connected.

"Connor, thanks for calling me back," Ryan said, his tone earnest. "I wanted to update you personally."

"I'm listening," Connor replied, his tone guarded.

"First off, I'm relieved Laney is doing better. We were all worried," Ryan began.

"She's fine, thanks," Connor said curtly. "Now tell me what's going on."

"We had an emergency board meeting this morning," Ryan continued. "Jen told us everything—how Dennis orchestrated the breach. It was a calculated move to undermine you and secure the chief operating officer position for his nephew. He thought if the company looked unstable, we'd turn to him for leadership."

Connor stiffened, his jaw tightening. "And my dad? Was he involved?"

"No," Ryan said firmly. "That's actually something I wanted to clear up. Your father wasn't part of this, Connor. In fact, he came to us last week to express concerns about Dennis's behavior. He was advocating for you."

Connor froze, his wide eyes meeting mine. "What?"

"Your dad's been in your corner this whole time," Ryan said. "I know your relationship has been strained, but he had your back. Dennis, on the other hand, has been removed from the board and is under investigation. He won't interfere with the company—or you—again."

The weight of Ryan's words settled over us. Connor's hand gripped the armrest, his knuckles white. He let out a slow breath before speaking. "I appreciate the clarification. I have conditions if I'm staying."

"Name them," Ryan replied without hesitation.

Connor leaned forward, his tone measured but resolute. "I'll stay for six months, working remotely most of the time. I'll help transition Petra into her leadership role."

There was a brief pause before Ryan responded, "Done. We should've given you that flexibility from the start. Thank you for staying on."

Connor's jaw tightened as he considered Ryan's words. "I'm agreeing to six months, Ryan. That's it. After that, I make no promises. I need to prioritize my family and where my life is headed."

"I understand," Ryan said quickly, his tone conciliatory. "You've more than earned the right to dictate your terms. We'll take it one step at a time."

Connor nodded, but his expression remained distant. His mind was clearly elsewhere. "I'll touch base after the holidays. I want these next few weeks to be about my wife and our plans. No interruptions."

"Absolutely," Ryan assured him. "Take all the time you need. Merry Christmas to you and Laney."

"Merry Christmas," Connor replied curtly before ending the call.

He set the phone down and exhaled, his shoulders sagging. I moved closer, resting my hand on his knee. "Six months?" I asked gently.

"That's all I can give them," he said, his voice low but firm. "I don't know what happens after that. Maybe I'll stay as a consultant, maybe I won't." He ran a hand over his face, sighing before meeting my gaze. His voice was quiet, almost disbelieving. "I was wrong about him. My dad wasn't working against me."

I reached for his hand, squeezing it gently. I could hardly believe it myself. "That's a lot to take in."

"It is," Connor admitted, his voice thick with emotion. "I've spent so much time assuming he was trying to control me, that he didn't even believe in me. But all this time, he secretly had my back. I don't get it."

I smiled softly, rubbing my thumb across his knuckles. "Maybe this is a chance to start fresh."

While I didn't love how his father treated us, with his grandchild on the way, maybe it was time to bridge the divide.

"Maybe," he said slowly, though his focus began to shift. He stood up, the tension in his body easing as he paced the living room. "But my future isn't with the company long term. It's here, in Cherrywood. I've been thinking…this town needs leadership. The businesses here are struggling, and I think I can bring everyone together."

I felt my chest swell with pride. "You want to help save the town?"

Connor's eyes were bright with determination as he spoke, and I couldn't help but smile at his enthusiasm. But I wanted to understand more—what this meant for him, for us, and for the town.

"Okay," I said slowly, shifting to face him. "But what about the six months with the company? How does that fit into your plans?"

He ran a hand through his hair, exhaling deeply. "That's the thing. It doesn't, not really. The six months are about making sure the company transitions smoothly, helping Petra find her footing, and tying up loose ends. I could stay on as a consultant for a short time, but after that? I'm done. My heart's not in it anymore."

I nodded, processing his words. "And what if you can't get the businesses here on board? What if Cherrywood doesn't respond the way you hope?"

Connor tilted his head, his expression thoughtful. "That's a risk I'm willing to take. But I don't think it'll come to that. This town is full of people who care deeply about it. They just need someone to rally them, to show them what's possible. I think I can do that."

"Are you sure you want this?" I asked softly. "This is a huge change."

He smiled. "I do. It's the first thing in a long time that feels... right. Like the work matters."

I bit my lip, a new question forming in my mind. "Do you think this is enough for you? You've always thrived in high-pressure roles, leading big teams, managing massive projects.

Will Cherrywood be challenging enough? What if you hate it and resent me for doing this?"

Connor laughed lightly, shaking his head. "You'd be surprised how challenging small-town politics and business coalitions can be. But honestly, it's not about the size of the challenge—it's about the impact. I want to see tangible results. I want to look around and know I made a difference. That's what's been missing for me. And, baby, I'd never resent you or our family." Connor's expression relaxed as he reached for my hand. "I'm choosing *us*, Laney. I'm choosing a life where I'm home more, where I'm not constantly tied to my phone or traveling for work. It means I'm building something that lets us both thrive—in Cherrywood, with the community, with our family."

A warmth spread through me at his words, but I still had one more question. "How do you even start something like this? Do you already have people in mind?"

He nodded, a spark of excitement returning. "Your dad for one. And Sean from the chamber of commerce. I'll need their advice and connections to get this off the ground. And I'll talk to local business owners—hear their concerns, figure out what they need most. It's going to take time, but I'm ready for that. I can work on this while I finish up the six months. That gives me half a year to get everything rolling."

I smiled, leaning forward to kiss his cheek. "You're amazing, you know that?"

He grinned, brushing a strand of hair behind my ear. His expression was pure joy, and my heart skipped a beat. He kissed my forehead and then stood. "Let's go talk to your parents. If I'm going to get this started, I'll need all the allies I can get."

I took his hand, my heart full as I followed him out the

door. Soon, we were seated around my parents' dining room table. My mom poured coffee for everyone while my dad sat back, arms crossed, his expression skeptical but attentive. Connor had spread out a few papers he'd brought, his excitement bubbling just beneath the surface.

"Alright, let's hear it," my dad said, leaning forward slightly. "Why did you gather us all today when I could be watching football?"

Connor cleared his throat. "Cherrywood needs a revival. This town has everything it needs to succeed—charm, history, a close-knit community—but the businesses here are struggling because there's no support system. I want to create one."

My dad's brows rose, and he shared a look with my mom. "Go on."

"We form a Cherrywood Business Alliance within the chamber of commerce," Connor explained, gesturing to his notes. "A coalition where local businesses can share resources, collaborate on marketing, and support each other. Cherrywood already has a strong foundation with the winter festival, but we can build on that and expand opportunities for small businesses year-round. Here's what I'm thinking."

He held up a finger. "First, we create seasonal pop-up events that tie into what local businesses already offer. For example, a spring garden market where nurseries, florists, and craft shops can showcase their products. We could do a fall food and music festival, bringing in foot traffic during slower months."

My mom tilted her head, intrigued. "And how do you convince business owners to get on board?"

Connor smiled, prepared for the question. "We start with

a trial run. No big investments upfront—maybe we secure a small grant or a sponsor to cover the costs. Once they see the results, they'll be more willing to commit. It's about building trust and showing them what's possible."

My dad scratched his chin, nodding slowly. "That's not a bad start. But what about long-term support? How do you keep it going?"

Connor's enthusiasm grew as he flipped to another page. "We hold monthly meetings to address challenges and brainstorm solutions. We organize workshops on things like social media marketing and e-commerce to help businesses grow. And eventually, we create an online marketplace for Cherrywood businesses to sell their products year-round."

My mom's eyes lit up. "That could be huge, especially for the artisans in town. They've been struggling to reach customers outside Cherrywood."

"Exactly," Connor said. "And the best part? It creates a sense of unity. When businesses work together, the whole town benefits."

My dad leaned forward, resting his elbows on the table. "You've thought this through."

"I have," Connor admitted. "I believe in what this could be."

My dad exchanged a glance with my mom before nodding. "You know, I've got a couple of buddies who've been struggling to keep their shops open. This could be exactly what they need. Sean from the chamber of commerce—he's been trying to rally support for something like this for years."

"I'd love to talk to him," Connor said. "The more people we get on board, the stronger this could be."

My mom smiled, her eyes shining as she stared at the notepad with Connor's scribbles. "This could really work, Connor. I think you're on to something."

My dad slapped the table lightly, a smile breaking across his face as he winked at me. "I agree. Let's make some calls. Sean's going to want to hear this."

As my dad grabbed his phone and started dialing, Connor turned to me, his eyes bright with hope. I hadn't seen him this happy in years, and I took his hand and intertwined our fingers. "This is happening, huh?"

"Yes, hon." He kissed the back of my hand. "If we want our baby to have the childhood you did, then we need to get this town back on track. I can't think of a better honor or role than this one."

I beamed at him, pride billowing in my chest. "You're sure. I can tell."

"This," he said, staring at our joined hands and motioning to my parents, "is what I was missing. And now I have it."

CHAPTER TWENTY-EIGHT

CONNOR

The Snowflake Festival was in full swing on Christmas Day. We woke up at Laney's parents' house, surrounded by presents. None of them were for us though. All of them were for our unborn child. It was too early to tell the gender, but the local doctor was able to fit Laney in on Christmas Eve and confirm that the baby was healthy and strong. Laney was nine weeks along—so we weren't going to share our news with anyone outside of her parents and Sophia, and that was fine with me.

Oh. And Petra, who sat at Laney's parents' kitchen table in an uncharacteristic ugly sweater.

"Small-town life suits you," I said, holding up a mug of coffee. "You might not be all robot."

"If I think too hard about what I'm doing here, I freak out. But I slept in flannel pajamas. A guy in glasses took me to dinner and bought me a present after knowing me for two weeks. My life is a weird Hallmark movie. It's giving me hives."

I chuckled as I poured Laney a cup of coffee. She was allowed two hundred milligrams of caffeine a day, and she assured me she'd use every one.

"I have conflicted feelings about Matt, but he seems like a solid guy."

"He's annoyingly wonderful."

"Who is?" Lancy walked into the kitchen wearing ripped jeans, a worn hoodie, and the biggest smile.

It was her joy that had attracted me to her, but now it held me captive. Hot coffee spilled on my hand as I realized I had forgotten to stop pouring. "Shit!"

"Hon." Laney grabbed a towel and wiped my hand. "Careful."

"He was staring at you," Petra chimed in.

I narrowed my gaze at her, but she smiled. Laney blushed as she brought my hand to her mouth and kissed the back.

"You look beautiful."

"You saw me ten minutes ago."

"Doesn't matter." I kissed her forehead. "You feeling okay? Need toast? Pancakes?"

"Nah, I'm okay. My dad will cook his buffet lunch in a few hours. I call dibs on all the potatoes."

"You can eat every one, Laney," her mom said as she walked in, also smiling, and waved at Petra. "Matt is quite smitten with you. I ran into him at the bakery this morning, and he asked if you were celebrating with us."

"Jesus, this guy."

"He is wonderful," Laney said, wiggling her brows. "He's like a happy, loyal puppy."

I grunted. I knew my wife didn't have feelings for the guy, but I resented that he had been there for her that night. I'd never be able to thank him for that, nor forgive myself.

Laney slid her arm around my middle and leaned her head on me.

"No grumbles, my sexy Grinch. Matt is harmless."

"He is harmless." Her mom bustled around the kitchen wearing a bright red sweater. "Okay, the plan is to head to the town center in an hour for photos and the gift exchange. Then half the town will stop in at the shop for the potluck."

"You have that many strangers come and eat your food?" Petra's eyebrows rose.

"They aren't strangers. I know everyone here," my mother-in-law boasted proudly. "It's a tradition. Everyone chips in for the food, and we hang out there for hours. Kids play, someone dresses as Santa. It's amazing."

"It really is. This place celebrates Christmas together, not in their houses alone. Too bad there isn't snow for a snowball fight." Laney sipped her coffee, her hazel eyes glowing. "That's always fun."

"Not sure you can this year, anyway." I bumped my hip against hers. "Gotta protect my baby."

She rolled her eyes.

"This is gonna be a long nine months."

"I know. I'm already stressing."

I got the women to laugh, like I meant to, and rubbed my hand down Laney's spine.

"Can I steal you away for twenty minutes?" I whispered into her ear.

Goose bumps spilled down her neck. I'd never tire of her body's reaction to me.

"Of course." She smiled up at me, mischief on her face. "For something naughty?"

"No. For something nice." I chuckled again. I'd laughed more the last week than I had in the last year.

She winked and moved to help her mom pull some pots and pans from the dishwasher. Laney's dad had instructed them to bring ten sheet pans to the hardware store when they were ready.

"How can I help today?" Petra asked, setting her mug on the counter with a hesitant smile.

"Oh, hon, we always need servers. Want to help at the store?"

"Serving food?"

"Yeah. Just plop some potatoes or eggs on people's plates. Super easy. We need adults manning the food though, 'cause the youths go wild."

"Yeah, I can do that." She nodded. "Thank you for letting me crash your morning. It was so kind of you." She said the words to Laney's mom, but her gaze was on my wife. "Unexpectedly kind."

"Nonsense. The more the merrier. Laney, I'm gonna load the car. You stop helping."

"I am totally capable of lifting a pan, Mom. My goodness." Laney rolled her eyes but plopped down onto the stool instead of lifting the dishes. My wife was stubborn and hated being helpless, but it was nice to see everyone cater to her. "This is ridiculous."

"It's us loving you," I said.

"Love me less."

"Not possible."

She scoffed, but I noticed the twinkle in her eye. While her mom and Petra loaded the car, I went over the plan in my head. I couldn't fuck this up. I'd been worrying, trying to get all the details perfect, to the point that Laney noticed I had seemed tired this morning.

It wasn't every day that I was going to propose again to my wife.

Everyone prepared for the lunch, and Petra offered to drive Laney's mom there, which was appreciated because I wanted time alone with my wife. They walked out, and when the door shut, I wiped my palms on my pants. They were sweatier than they should be.

"This might be my favorite Christmas ever." Laney twirled in the living room with her eyes closed, her hand reaching out to me. "Kiss me, Connor."

I tugged her to me, taking my time studying all her features. Her inky eyelashes, the freckles, the perfect cheekbones and full lips.

"Gladly, wife."

Her arms came around my neck as I kissed her, slowly. She tasted like coffee and smelled like heaven. Her body pressed against mine, her heat surrounding me, and I gripped her lower back, pulling her closer to me. She moaned, the little sound my favorite thing in the world.

"I love you," she whispered, her lips brushing mine. "Merry Christmas, Connor."

"Merry Christmas, baby." I cupped her face with both hands, my heart beating so fast it physically hurt. "Can we go for a walk?"

She scrunched her nose. "Right now?"

I nodded, unable to talk without giving away my nerves. I kissed her nose before pulling her coat off the hanger and helping her into it.

"We'll only be outside ten minutes."

"Hmm, this is weird, but you seem tense, so I'm game."

"I'm not tense."

"Only a tense person would say that," she retorted.

I pinched her side, my worry lessening with her joke.

"You dork."

"Maybe, but I'm your dork."

She put a knit cap on and pulled gloves out of her pockets, slipping them on. "Where to, boss?"

It took me thirty seconds to put on my coat and gloves. Then we were out the door.

"We're walking around the block. I need fresh air."

"Okie dokie. The cool air feels good in my lungs. Less nauseous when I'm cold."

My muscles clenched. "Stomach still upsetting you?"

"The medicine helped, yes, but the gross feeling is still there. Not as bad, but when the heat is up and there are people everywhere, I feel uncomfortably hot."

"Let me know if you're feeling that at all today, and we can sneak away."

"Sure will." She intertwined her arm with mine, closing her eyes as she took a deep breath.

I swear to God, a snowflake landed on her face. Then another one did.

"It's snowing."

"No way!" She screeched and stuck her tongue out. "This is perfect. White Christmases here are a dream. Oh, Connor, this is such a good sign."

My throat tightened as we neared the house for sale. This was the first surprise for us.

She laughed as the snow picked up, and she grinned at me. "Why are you staring at me like that?"

"Because I'm obsessed with you." I shrugged. The statement was true. "And, well, I have a surprise for you."

"Ooh, is this a gift?" Her eyes sparked with hope.

"It's a promise to you." I jutted my chin toward the house behind her. She glanced at it, her brows furrowing.

"I spoke to a Realtor earlier this week and asked for a major favor. It's Daniel, by the way. A former teacher of yours. He gave me this."

She glanced at me again. "A key?"

"I refused to buy the house without you seeing it because I'm not making decisions without us both being all in. Even if it's a surprise, we both will talk everything out, and it took every urge in me to not buy this."

"Connor." She sucked in a breath.

"We can tour the house right now, and if you love it, he's expecting my call tomorrow. It can be ours."

"It's a short walk to my parents." Her eyes watered, and her lip trembled. "It's five minutes to Main Street."

"It has four bedrooms and a basement. A large backyard too. Perfect for a family."

She rubbed her lips together, her tears spilling over her cheeks. "Are you for real?"

This was it. I took a breath and got down on one knee. Laney covered her mouth with her gloved hands, her eyes widening as I pulled out a ring from my pocket. It was her old ring, but I had work done on it. Rubies now surrounded the diamond.

"Rubies are the second strongest gem besides diamonds, and I wanted to ask you, again, to be my wife. I will never make you feel second. I'm going to protect you, your heart, your love as long as you let me. I love you so much and chose you. I will always choose you. Now, tomorrow, forever. Will you please stay my wife?"

Her face crumbled in a soft cry as she fell to her knees and threw her arms around my neck, quietly crying into my shoulder.

"Connor, this is...are you...of course I'm staying your wife! That wasn't in question."

"But it was, baby. For a little bit, and that's too much for me. We love the winter. We both love cold nights and the holidays, but for different reasons. This is me vowing to you that our life is better than anything I could dream up. You, our baby," I put my hand on her stomach, "are my future. My everything. I want our kid growing up with your parents showering them with love. I want you happy when I have to work. I want you comfortable and safe. Our future is here, in Cherrywood. It's where I got a second chance with you."

"Oh my God." She cried against me, her fingers digging hard into my back as she nodded. "Yes, yes, I love you so much, oh my God."

I laughed as my own eyes prickled.

"Also," I said, my voice returning to normal, "I'm fucking sick of seeing your ring finger bare."

"There he is." She snorted and lifted her tearstained face. "My possessive husband."

"I'm always in there." I kissed her. "But I needed to do this right."

"You did so well, it's not even funny. I want the ring, please." She held her hand between us, and I slipped it back on her finger.

The pain from seeing it left behind on the table at our old place disappeared. The agony of her leaving was gone. We were stronger. Better. Realigned in our priorities. I kissed her wrist and squeezed it six times.

"I love you so fucking much."

"Is that our new thing?" She grinned, staring at her ring. "Six squeezes now?"

"Yes, because it's true." I pushed up to one knee, helping her stand. "Want to look at our future house?"

"What if we don't like it?"

"Baby." I took her hand and laughed. "I guarantee we're going to like it. Now, let's go see all the new places I get to defile you on."

She tossed her head back and laughed, the sound echoing through the quiet, perfect neighborhood.

"Do they have cameras in there? Could...we?"

"You're perfect. Jesus." I groaned, tugging her with me toward the door. I unlocked it, pushing it open and smiling at her.

"After you, wife. Let's see what our new home looks like."

"Oh my God, Connor!"

CHAPTER TWENTY-NINE

LANEY

One year later...

Christmas music echoed off the walls of our home. The speakers my dad installed were just a hair too loud this early on Christmas morning. Not that I was complaining. Everyone we loved was here, at our new home in Cherrywood, celebrating our son's first Christmas.

"Is he done eating yet?" My mom poked her head into the nursery, her smile hopeful. "I'm having Sam withdrawals."

"Five more minutes, Mom."

"Do you need anything? Coffee? Food?"

I shook my head as gratitude washed over me. Connor was there every step, but a newborn was exhausting in a way I wasn't mentally prepared for. That's where my parents were incredible. It was strange that I loved Sam so much I couldn't breathe sometimes, but there were moments when I was so tired, so out of it, that the thought of trying to cook or make food was too much.

Connor spent every minute making sure I was healing and okay. And on the days or hours he had to work, my parents stepped right in. I was never alone, and I had never felt so loved.

I kissed my son's head, inhaling the sweet baby scent. He was four months now, and I couldn't believe how fast, and slow, it went. I loved this kid so damn much that it overwhelmed me. My eyes prickled, and I admired him as I nursed him. It was wild to think that this time last year, I had tried to leave Connor.

The nursery door opened again, and my husband walked in with a mug of coffee.

"Hi, is he eating? Are you hurting at all?"

He set the mug on the side table next to the rocker and leaned down to kiss me.

"Christmas cookies for breakfast?" I teased, tasting the sweetness from the frosting on his lips.

He laughed.

"Your dad. He instills terrible habits. I tried to eat a banana, but no, he insisted on the cookies."

"Eh, it's Christmas." I shrugged right as Sam passed out. "Oh, our boy is milk drunk."

Connor's face lit up as he stared at our son. "I'd be milk drunk too if I fed from your boobs."

"They're going to go back to normal at some point, you know." My face heated as I clipped my bra back together and burped Sam on my shoulder. Connor's latest obsession was my breasts. They'd grown in size—almost doubled from the pregnancy and nursing—and he legit couldn't get enough.

When they weren't too sore from nursing, we had fun, but it was still weird adjusting to a post-birth body.

"That's fine, hon, but I love your body. I love how you carried our perfect fucking son." He reached over and squeezed my wrist six times. His eyes warmed as he knelt down next to me, one hand landing on my knee, the other on Sam's back.

"Baby." He chuckled softly. "Here. Give him to me."

"My mom wants a turn."

"She can wait." He carefully lifted Sam from my chest and cradled him against his. "Hi, big guy. You eat enough from your momma? You're absolutely perfect." He patted Sam's butt, and within seconds, Sam was asleep again.

My eyes watered, staring at Connor and Sam. I was so happy.

"Are you crying?" he asked, his eyes widening. "What do you need?"

The entire postpartum experience was wild with emotions, but Connor was incredible. There was no other word for it. He held me when I cried for no reason, ensured I ate, scheduled visitors when he had to leave, and wouldn't let me clean the house or do anything but heal and love on Sam.

He encouraged us to go for walks in the crisp air and refused to let me clean a single piece of the pumping equipment. When I think about how dedicated and loving he is, my heart skips a beat.

"I'm fine. Just, so, so happy." I swiped my fingers under my eyes, hoping I wouldn't smear my mascara. I had put some on today with everyone coming over. And when I said everyone, I meant everyone.

My parents. Our neighbors who also had a young child. Petra. Matt. Some high school friends. Sophia and her situationship. The family across the street whose family lived in another country. We couldn't have them celebrate alone. Everyone came here, to our house, to celebrate.

"You deserve it, Laney." My husband's voice was deep and serious. "You deserve all the happiness, so don't question it."

"I like your bossy tone. Haven't heard it in a while. Missed that in the bedroom."

"Because you're healing," he replied with a tone of no shit. "Trust me. Part of me wishes everyone left so I could take my time with you today, unwrapping your clothes."

My skin heated. "Yes. Let's do that. Kick everyone out."

He barked out a laugh and shook his head. "You're cute. As much as I want to, we have Christmas to celebrate, and the man of the hour is hiding in here."

"It's my turn. No, you wait." My mom's voice carried through the hallway, and soon enough, she was there. "Hi, oh, Connor, give him to me. Don't let Suzie hold him."

Suzie was my mom's neighbor. She had made us about ten casseroles after I gave birth and declared herself a mix of grandmother and godmother.

"Here he is." Connor passed him off to my mom, who immediately kissed him a thousand times.

"I'm going to sit in the recliner, but you two take a minute alone. I'll hold the boy."

I frowned, her comment a little weird, but then Connor wiped his hands on his jeans—a clear sign of nerves.

"Is there a reason we need a moment alone?" I asked.

"I mean, I could do wicked things within five minutes if you dared me." He flashed a smile before his face returned to normal. "But no, I asked your mom for a few minutes with you."

He pulled me out of the rocker and ran his hands over my shoulders and arms, squeezing my hands at the end.

"God, you're beautiful. And strong. And incredible. Seeing you become a mom has been one of my favorite things ever, Laney. I'm in awe of you."

"Are you trying to make me cry?" Tears definitely fell now. "I'm an emotional mess today."

"That's okay." He cupped my face, wiping my tears before he kissed me. "I love you, our life, our boy, all of it."

"I do too." I wrapped my arms around him in a tight hug, the ache in my chest lessening. It was weird how I loved him even more than I had last year.

People told me that our marriage would change after having a child, but we went through the hard part before learning we were even pregnant. Connor recently wrapped up his time in the city. He remained on as a consultant for an entire year, helping them transition to a new CEO. They paid him well and kept the option open for more work in the future if needed. That spun an idea for Connor to start a consulting business—entirely remote. When he wasn't doing that, he helped our town. While the salary wasn't what we were used to, he was adjusting to his new role as director of economic growth. The chamber created the role and the alliance, and appointed him after he convinced them of the growth plan.

He was home by five every night. He never missed a meal. We had laughed, and cried, and celebrated more in the last year than we had in our entire relationship.

Petra left the company despite her promotion and split her time between Connor's office and the high school. And yes, she and Matt were officially together now. So much had changed in twelve months.

I didn't feel like I was in second place anymore. Slowly, and very intentionally, I trusted him that things would be different. Connor had come to every doctor's appointment and stayed home if I had a rough day—and there were a few. Pregnancy was not easy for me.

Our condo in the city still held so many good memories, and we'd spent a few nights with Sam there already, but Cherrywood was home for us. We just put it on the market and were going to use some of those funds to invest in Cherrywood.

This house, this town, this village of people loving us. It was more than I had ever hoped for.

"I want to tell you about your gift." He kissed my forehead before smiling again. Sometimes Connor just stared at me and smiled a soft, gentle smile, and it made my insides turn to squish. I hoped he never stopped that.

"My gift? I thought we agreed no gifts, Connor." I hadn't gotten him anything. "We talked about this!"

"Yeah, that's on me."

"You don't look that apologetic."

"'Cause I'm not." He winked and took a breath. "I hired a photographer for the whole day. You might know him."

"Is it Newt?" I asked, breathless. I still owned my own photography business, but I had taken half a year off for maternity leave. I'd go back on my own terms.

He nodded. "I want a new tradition to document our holidays with our family. We spent too many holidays alone, without the smells of food and noise of laughter. While I know you take great photos, today isn't about you working. I want to capture the moments when you smile at Sam, or your mom hogging him, or your dad singing at the top of his lungs as he cooks. I want all of it. I want to show Sam these photos and remind him of the people who love him."

Damn. I cried again.

"Happy tears, right?" he asked.

I nodded before a sob burst out.

"I love it. I love it so much I'm crying!"

"Oh, baby." He pulled me into a hug and rubbed my back. "You're pretty even when you're snotting all over me."

"Not helping!"

His deep rumble of a laugh vibrated against my face. I snuggled in closer, breathing in his cologne and having a sense of calm wash over me. He waited me out, patient as ever. He never rushed me.

"Okay," I said, sniffing and glancing up at him. "That is the best idea I've ever heard, but now I need to redo this eye makeup situation because I'm a raccoon."

"But a gorgeous, big-boobed raccoon."

"Connor." I pinched his side, making him laugh even more. He countered the attack, and then we ended up laughing and tickling and falling to the ground with me on top of him. He stared at me with those gorgeous, deep gray eyes, and I swooned. I was so lucky.

"I can't believe you're mine, you know?"

He scoffed.

"That's my line, Laney."

"Okay, how about...I can't believe we found each other and

built this life together? I wouldn't change a thing, you know." I chewed on my lip. "I love our story and how we got here."

"I do too." He sat up, me in his lap, his arms around me. "Makes me feel like I want to do a vow renewal with you. What do you think? Next year, at our eleventh wedding anniversary? We have a renewal in our backyard. Sam would be walking by then. Maybe you're knocked up again. I want to tell you and promise you again that I'll love you and choose you forever."

I nodded before I had time to think.

"Yes, I'd love that."

"It's a date. Don't make any plans next December, baby—we have some vows to renew."

And with that, we went back out to the living room where music played, people ate, Sam was cuddled against his grandma, and there was so much joy and happiness everywhere.

I grabbed Connor's hand and smiled. "Merry Christmas, Connor."

"You too, baby. Thanks for giving me the best gift ever."

"What's that?"

"Our family."

We shared a smile, and the day passed in a blur. Hours went by, and everyone left for their own places.

The snow fell softly outside, blanketing Cherrywood in a peaceful hush. Inside, the warm glow of twinkling lights wrapped around our Christmas tree while the fire crackled. Connor was sprawled on the couch with Sam in his arms, their matching dark hair a stark contrast to the red blanket draped over them. Sam's tiny hand grasped Connor's finger, and my heart melted at the sight.

"You know," I said, settling into the chair across from them, "today became my favorite Christmas."

Connor looked up, his eyes softening as they met mine. "Mine too."

Just as I was about to say more, there was a knock at the door. Connor rolled his eyes. "Ten bucks that's your dad who forgot something."

"Hey! Our family is quirky but forgetful." I stood and ruffled Connor's hair. "And I decline that bet because I'm not getting into your and my dad's little gambling wars." I twisted the handle just as he said, "You're afraid to lose!"

I froze. Connors's dad stood there, bundled against the cold with a slightly awkward smile on his face. He held a bag stuffed with brightly wrapped presents in one hand and a bottle of wine in the other.

"Mr. Reynolds," I greeted him, my voice cracking. "Uh, come in, it's cold." I stepped aside, my stomach bottoming out at this sudden appearance.

Connor and his dad had exchanged a few emails and a few texts on and off about his grandson. There were no phone calls or apologies. This was beyond a surprise.

"Thanks, Laney," he said, stepping inside and stamping snow off his boots. His eyes darted toward the living room, where Connor had risen from the couch, Sam still in his arms.

"Dad?" Connor's voice was cautious, his brow furrowed. "Why are you here?"

"I know I wasn't invited," his dad began, setting the presents and wine on the side table. "But I...I wanted to stop by. Thought it was time I made more of an effort."

Connor's grip on Sam tightened, but he didn't say anything.

I stepped closer to his dad, offering him a reassuring smile. "Can I take your coat?"

"Sure," he said, handing it to me as his gaze flicked back to Connor and Sam. "You've got quite the setup here. Cozy."

Connor nodded, his expression guarded. I could read him like a book, and he was torn between throwing his dad out or hearing what he had to say. "Yeah. It's home."

While my husband might not have shared it out loud, I knew the loss of their relationship bothered him. He was right to walk away, but cutting off the one parent you had was a special form of torture.

His dad took a hesitant step forward, his focus entirely on Sam now. "Is this...?"

"Sam," I supplied gently. "Your grandson."

His dad's face relaxed, and for a moment, he looked younger—less like the stern businessman I'd always known and more like someone caught in a memory. "Can...can I hold him?"

Connor hesitated, his jaw working as he processed the moment. Finally, he nodded, gently transferring Sam into his dad's waiting arms.

As soon as Sam settled against his chest, Connor's dad let out a shaky breath. "He's perfect," he whispered, his voice breaking. "Absolutely perfect."

He cradled Sam close, tears filling his eyes as he gazed down. "I should've been here sooner. I should've done more, for both of you and for him."

Connor's walls visibly crumbed as he watched his dad hold Sam. He cleared his throat and reached for me. I fit into the spot right under his arm, wrapping my arm around his waist.

The room fell silent except for the sound of the fire and Sam's soft cooing as his grandpa rubbed his back. Finally, his dad turned to Connor. "You've built something incredible here, son. You and Laney." His gaze moved to me, a beaming grin on his face. "I'm proud of you. Always have been—I just didn't know how to say it."

Connor nodded. "Thank you."

His dad had a tremble to his lips. "We have a lot to work through, and I know you shouldn't forgive me. I've been a horrible father. I want to try though." He kissed Sam's head and sniffed. "Is that... something we can do?"

I nodded and stood back as Connor placed a hand on his dad's shoulder. My heart swelled as Connor said, "Yeah, I think I'd like that. If you want to stay in town for a while, there's a house for rent next to Laney's parents that I think you'd like..."

My own eyes welled up as three generations of Reynolds boys stood together. There were still wounds to heal, but this moment was a start. And sometimes, that's all you need.

After all, Cherrywood had some magic to it.

ACKNOWLEDGMENTS

Writing a book is never a solo endeavor—it's a journey shaped by the support, encouragement, and hard work of countless others. As I sit down to write this, I'm overwhelmed with emotion because this book marks the final installment of my first trade publishing deal. This has truly been a dream come true. As a kid, I fantasized about seeing my books in stores and connecting with readers, and I've lived that dream. I did it. I am so incredibly proud of myself and endlessly grateful to everyone who helped make this happen.

First and foremost, to my husband—you've been my biggest cheerleader from day one. You let me vent, cry, and celebrate, always offering unwavering support and love. You've never doubted me for a second, and I cherish our conversations about the joys and challenges of art. These nearly fifteen years together have been the greatest adventure, and I can't wait for the next fifteen! (Well, more than fifteen but that sounded better.)

To my family, both my side and my husband's, thank you for

being part of this journey. Your love, excitement, and constant encouragement mean the world to me. Thank you for sending photos of my books, shouting about them to anyone who would listen, and being my biggest champions. Mom, Dad, CB, Kacie, Kathy, Greg, Leah, Ruth, Aunt Amy, Emma, Jake (and Katie!), and Siarah—I love you all to the moon and back.

I owe so much gratitude to my first agent, Cathie, and my current agent, Jessica. This business can be grueling, but having strong, badass women in my corner has been a gift.

To the incredible team at Forever—Dana, Estelle, Alex, and the entire cover team—you've made this journey unforgettable. Thank you for your hard work and vision.

Haley, Mikaela, Rachel Rumble, Megan, and Rachel Reiss, thank you for being my rocks. I adore each of you and am endlessly grateful to have you in my life.

This past year has been a whirlwind of unforgettable moments—from Book Bonanza to events at Changing Hands and The Poisoned Pen. Meeting the most incredible readers and authors has been a privilege, and I've never taken a single second of it for granted.

To my Chicago gals—Rachel, Tiffany, and Kelly—thank you for being such strong, inspiring women. To Julie and her amazing crew of decades, thank you for letting me join your meetups and experience the magic of your friendship. To the Phoenix book club, thank you for welcoming me and sharing your beautiful discussions about *Christmas Sweater Weather*. These are once-in-a-lifetime memories I'll always hold close.

To my work family, you've been so supportive and excited for me—thank you for letting me share this part of my life with you. Rachel, Tom, Phillip, Sarah Pearson, Joe, Delsey,

ACKNOWLEDGMENTS

Brandon, Luke, Mike, Alex I, Alex M, Gabby, Nichole, Martha, and Drew—you've all been amazing. Also, there are so many of you now. This is definitely not a secret anymore, haha.

And finally, to you, dear reader. Thank you for picking up my book and giving my stories a home in your heart. I love writing romances because they celebrate happiness, love, growth, and all the little joys life has to offer. I hope my stories give you a moment to escape and remind you of the beauty in life. You have my deepest gratitude.

ABOUT THE AUTHOR

Jaqueline Snowe lives in Arizona, where the "dry heat" really isn't that bad. She prefers drinking coffee all hours of the day and snacking on anything that has peanut butter or chocolate. She is the mother to two fur-babies who don't realize they aren't humans and a mom to the sweetest son and daughter. She is an avid reader and writer of romances and tends to write about athletes. Her husband works for an MLB team (not a player, lol) so she knows more about baseball than any human ever should.

RAISING READERS
Books Build Bright Futures

Thank you for reading this book and for being a reader of books in general. As an author, I am so grateful to share being part of a community of readers with you, and I hope you will join me in passing our love of books on to the next generation of readers.

Did you know that reading for enjoyment is the single biggest predictor of a child's future happiness and success?

More than family circumstances, parents' educational background, or income, reading impacts a child's future academic performance, emotional well-being, communication skills, economic security, ambition, and happiness.

Studies show that kids reading for enjoyment in the US is in rapid decline:

- In 2012, 53% of 9-year-olds read almost every day. Just 10 years later, in 2022, the number had fallen to 39%.
- In 2012, 27% of 13-year-olds read for fun daily. By 2023, that number was just 14%.

Together, we can commit to **Raising Readers** and change this trend. How?

- Read to children in your life daily.
- Model reading as a fun activity.
- Reduce screen time.
- Start a family, school, or community book club.
- Visit bookstores and libraries regularly.
- Listen to audiobooks.
- Read the book before you see the movie.
- Encourage your child to read aloud to a pet or stuffed animal.
- Give books as gifts.
- Donate books to families and communities in need.

Books build bright futures, and **Raising Readers** is our shared responsibility.

For more information, visit **JoinRaisingReaders.com**

Sources: National Endowment for the Arts, National Assessment of Educational Progress, WorldBookDay.org, Nielsen BookData's 2023 "Understanding the Children's Book Consumer"